Crown of Hearts

Crown of Hearts

E.V. Rivers

To Mom and Dad,
Thank you for giving me the first pieces of my heart.

Prologue

It has been 17 years since Queen Alice took the throne. While overall Wonderland is stable, many of its parts still suffer on the borderlines. The relations between various kingdoms have eroded. The Red and White Kingdoms are constantly at war with each other. The Diamond Kingdom, known for trading, now doesn't trade. The Club Kingdom, known for parties, has been silent.

The Heart Kingdom alone continues to grow and prosper under Queen Alice. Then again, that's not surprising given its capital, Atria, is where all the nobles have converged.

And last, the Spade Kingdom, in all its intricacy, has disappeared. No one knows where it sits; no one can enter.

And this
is where
Lucina's
story
begins...

Chapter One

hat backward corner of the Underland did this thing fall out of?

Illuminated by the first light of dawn, the intruder has me questioning my sanity. The trespasser is a six-foot moving wooden mannequin. It's one of those mannequins that artists use, the ones that are put together with glue and screws. It's in my father's room, going through his underwear drawer.

I'm mildly amused, mainly disturbed by what it's doing. I'm not sure if it's a he or a she because it has no face, but it's wearing black clothes. Like it matters, it's still a pervert.

I can take it out, I think.

We run a smithy, making the best weapons in the area.

I've been trained in all forms of combat since I could first stand, by the best fighter around—my dad. I never understood his incessant need to wake me up at the crack of dawn or in the middle of the night or even when I'm in the process of forging a weapon. He'd take me out and force me to fight until my body was drained.

So as far as fighting skills, I don't doubt mine.

But why is someone looking in my house at my dad's stuff? Could it be a disgruntled customer?

I don't know all our customers, since Dad sells a lot of his work abroad. He went to pick up some supplies but I don't know where. Maybe this thing is from the Red Kingdom. The Red and White Kingdoms are constantly bickering about something. And the Red Kingdom did employ Dad last year for a substantial number of weapons. Maybe him training the White Soldiers has angered them. But if so, why is this thing going through Dad's drawers?

Either way, this idiot picked the wrong home to invade. I'm a light sleeper so I wake up to any sound and a door creaking open will do it. Which is why I'm now crouched in the shadows of the landing, wearing my pajamas and dressing gown.

Stifling back yawns, I allow the induced adrenaline running through me to shake off the bouts of sleep and grogginess.

As the thing moves around, the morning sun reveals it has a red heart decorating one side of the black collar of its blazer. The number eight embellishes the other side.

Hearts with a number mean one thing—Queen Alice's Heart Pack. Her most esteemed soldiers. Only problem is, they're meant to be in the capital, Atria, carrying out Queen Alice's orders at the Heart Castle. They're definitely not meant to be invading people's homes.

Strangely, it's breaking the law by breaching my property. It's also odd that this soldier would come here to this little village off the Glass Coast in the middle of nowhere, where nothing happens. Has Dad angered Queen Alice somehow?

It doesn't matter who it is, I'm going to take it down. Dad always told me not to trust anybody, not even those who uphold the law, as the world is corrupt.

Should I get a weapon from the smithy, downstairs? If I do, I might alert the intruder to my presence.

The thing opens the wardrobe. And as far as I can tell, its head is angled that way. Great opportunity to attack.

I sprint across the floor, keeping my tread light. My arm stretches out and my fist slams into the thing's back, sending it stumbling forward, headfirst into the wardrobe. Before it can recover, I kick it. It catches my leg and flips me, causing my body to fall back.

Stupid move.

I use the momentum, place my forearms on the carpet, move my body into a forearm stand and kick it as hard as possible, connecting with its head. I hear the crack of wood splintering and I curse as I feel a sharp cut on my right foot. It burns. A note for next time—never fight with bare feet. I went in too strong, forgetting this thing is made out of wood. So, I adjust my weight, and change my next move. I wrap my feet around its head and pull it forward, grateful my nightgown provides cushioning to my arms from the carpet burns.

The thing crashes with such great force, the ground reverberates.

As I get up, I'm shocked by a blow to the back of my head. In that moment, a dizzy disorientation takes over. Thankfully, it settles quickly, and I roll away.

"*Look after number one.*" My father's voice echoes in my ears as if he's right beside me. Those words have been drilled into me for as long as I can remember and the closer the wooden thing gets to me, the more my muscles tighten.

I roll toward it and it jumps over me. I kick out, causing it to trip over. Hopefully, that will give me enough time to get up and smash it into pieces. When I'm up, I'm met by a flurry of punches, which I avoid and block.

We continue to jab, punch and kick, but I need to end this quickly. If Dad were here, he'd be angry at how long I've let it go on.

I kick the thing swiftly in the knee, and back away. It launches a pathetic kick that I manage to duck and sweep around it, ramming my elbow into its side. Ouch! Pain bites my arm and I grab it. I dance back as it grabs its side. It reveals a small knife in its hand and it cuts through my robe and nightdress like butter. Blood gushes from my arm.

During this, a mouth appears on the soldier and there is a black void inside. "You have attacked a member of the Pack and have violated the queen's rules. You will suffer the consequences." Its voice is male, monotonous and not heavily modulated like a robot.

It slashes on instinct and only meets air as I maneuver out of the way.

"No, *you'll* suffer for breaking into my property." I

smack it hard in the face, avoiding its slashes.

My knuckles crunch. I'm going to feel that later. Like Dad taught me, *"Fight in the moment, deal with the pain later."*

The sun's morning light glares into my eyes and an idea pops into my head. I grab its shoulders and push it into the window with all my strength. Shards of glass fly through and land on the floor. The light from the sun reflects off them.

It springs back as if nothing has happened. There's blood on its face, the blood from my feet. Stupid walking tree. At least now the thing is damaged with chips and splinters, not that it seems affected.

It may have a weapon, but I'm not defenseless. I know I can beat it. I simply need to change my strategy. Wood burns in fire. I have a forge downstairs in the smithy. All I need to do is shove this thing in it.

In a smooth, fluid move, its arms strike forward with its knife. I grab them with both hands, its knife nixes my left hand and I fall backward like I'm doing a backward roll. I plant a foot low on its waist and apply strong pressure, rolling onto my back and flipping it over. It crashes against the wall. I rush outside the bedroom into the landing with more blood spilling out.

I must say it's got some stamina on it, as it's already following me, which is exactly what I want. This fight will be over soon, I hope.

I don't make it to the stairs as I'm bombarded with kicks, jabs, and punches. At least there's no knife anymore, but the thing is like a machine. I pick off every strike, countering where I can, drawing it closer to the stairs. There, I'll throw it down and the fight will be almost over.

As I back toward the stair post, I seize the opportunity.

I lunge forward but something tugs at me, limiting my movements. I turn and find that my robe's belt is stuck on the stair's post. The walking tree lands a fist to my gut, followed by another, and another. My feet slip, already slick from the blood oozing out, and I fall backward.

Everything slows down. I lift my arms and cover my head and try to make myself into a ball so there's less damage. My body rolls and jerks as I take bumps down the stairs, eventually hitting the ground with a loud thud.

The stupid walking tree lets out a strange sound and the creepy void that is its mouth turns into a smile.

It was my own ego that created the opportunity for it to take me down. My fault for putting on a robe.

I'm a skilled fighter, I know it. Fighting is my life, it's what I was born to do, it's what gives me my independence. And no block of wood is going to beat me. All I need to do is get up, damn it.

Get up!

My heart buzzes in my chest. The thing starts to come down the stairs and I try to get up. A low humming thrums in my ears. I think I've hit my head too hard. The room darkens. Is this death? I can't die, my dad needs me. There's so much I need to do. No, I can't go down this easy.

A gust of wind rushes against my cheeks and playing cards come flying out of nowhere, filling the room. I try with all my might to keep my eyes open. It's a basic rule, never close your eyes.

"Ace!" The thing's voice cracks as it cries out. Its words take a while to enter my brain, as if through a fog. "Stop with these dramatics."

The raging wind soothes to a breeze, then disappears.

I open my eyes and search the smithy. Nothing is out of place. Well, except the paperwork, but neither Dad nor I are too worried about that.

I have to get up. Take the opportunity to regain my footing.

There's a creak and I glance up to find a young man above me. The last wisps of wind ruffle his honey-blond hair, making him appear birdlike. He stares at us with an air of authority, as if he's looking at maggots squirming around in the dirt.

He holds out a playing card.

"Ace, what are you doing here?" The walking tree asks.

That's Ace? That puny boy? He doesn't seem like he could be the highest ranked of all the queen's soldiers. I can take him down, too—once I get up.

"Queen Alice requires your attendance at the Heart Castle," Ace says in a cold, flat voice.

I'm not sure if he's talking to me. I don't think so.

The thing tries to get up. "I have this situation under control–"

Ace snaps his fingers. Magic thrums in the air like a note played on a harp. A blue playing card appears and covers the void—the thing's mouth. It tries to speak, but its voice is muffled.

"You always talk too much and act so brash." Ace gives a quick wave with his hand. "Toodle-do, now. Queen

Alice gives her best regards."

It disappears into thin air. I search the room, but the thing is gone. There's nothing left of it except a small playing card on the stair where it last stood. The playing card is the eight of hearts.

Ace's steely-blue eyes study my face, a wrinkle of uncertainty appearing between his brows. "I'm so sorry, Lucina Cordula, for the way Eight treated you today. Please rest assured that most of us who serve Queen Alice are not all alike."

"Where has… it gone?" I ask. "What's going on? Why was it here?"

And how does Ace know my name?

He offers out his hand and I whack it away. I roll to my right, grab the bottom stair and pull myself up with the post. My body aches all over.

"Queen Alice is looking forward to meeting you," he says.

The queen wants to see me? Why me?

"That thing started it, breaking into my house."

Ace stares at me, unblinking, and I stare back, because there's something strange about him.

"Don't worry about that. It's been dealt with," Ace says with an edge, and then his voice softens. "Are you all right?"

"I'm fine, I've been through much worse." I stare at the trail of blood I've created. "It's not as bad as it looks. I could have taken it out."

"Good, because I…we don't have the time." He steps in front of me. "Queen Alice requires your presence."

"What would Her Majesty want with me?"

"Don't be modest." His eyes shift to stare at the weapons displayed on the wall around us. "Queen Alice admires all, especially someone like you with such a fine lineage."

"Lineage?" I draw back, confused and slightly disgusted.

I'm nothing fancy; not a duchess, nor an inventor, nor a designer. There's nothing special about me. And my dad is no duke. If anything, he's the opposite—a pirate. Or, more to the point, a black-market salesman.

Then again, I don't know much about my dad's past. Unless this is about my mom, and I know virtually nothing about her. She died giving birth to me. It's a painful subject for my dad, which is frustrating because maybe if I knew something about her, I could figure myself out, and feel less empty inside.

"Queen Alice will explain everything." Ace glances down at his wrist and taps his watch. "We really don't have the time. We must leave now."

"I've got clients. I'm not just going to up and leave to meet the queen. Also, what about my dad? He's out on a work trip and when he comes back and finds I'm not here, he'll go nuts."

"You're right," Ace says, and a card appears in his hand. He flicks it on the cash register. "He'll catch up soon enough."

"Wait..."

It's too late. A breeze picks up. It gathers and gets stronger with each second, bitter and cold. And with it comes the tantalizing scent of... roses.

Chapter Two

he world is a blur and the wind swirls around me. It rages against my face and whips my hair all over the place. I wrap an arm over my eyes. My stomach rolls and waves of nausea hit me over and over.

It feels like an eternity has passed. I'm silently screaming for this to stop. I want to hurl. It reminds me of the feeling I get when I've ate a growing mushroom, followed immediately by a shrinking cake. Moments pass, and the violent winds around me come to an abrupt halt. My knees give in and I fall forward on my hands, landing on something that thankfully cushions my fall.

I open my eyes slowly; all that I can see in front of me is lush green.

"Are you okay?" I catch someone say.

It's too late. Saliva coats my mouth, and bile rises in my throat. Streams of last night's dinner spurt out of my mouth on what I now realize is grass. My hands tremble as everything comes out. Tears spill from my eyes, and I wipe them back with my sleeve.

I'm about to wipe my mouth when I catch a white handkerchief in front of me. I take the handkerchief, wipe my mouth and crawl away from my vomit.

A hand reaches out and I realize it's Ace hovering over me.

"Sorry about that," he says. "It always happens to newbies."

I ignore his hand and get back up by myself. I manage, if barely, on wobbly legs and with blood still dripping from my foot.

With a large sigh, I take in my surroundings. Greenery everywhere, far too many sculpted bushes shaped like rabbits, gryphons, dodos, caterpillars, butterflies and other animals. There are different variations of trees all neatly aligned and bearing many fruits. And, finally, bushes full of roses of the deepest red.

The pounding sound of the soldiers' boots marching in unison grabs my attention. Human-sized cards march the stone paths—card soldiers, the queen's guard. They're the ones who protect the castle and the capital.

"You're late," someone screeches, and a trumpet blares out.

A White Rabbit beastian emerges. He's wearing a tartan jacket, a yellow waistcoat, and a pocket watch. My whole village is full of beastians—humanized animals, so that's not very odd.

But this White Rabbit holds a trumpet in his hand, waving it around like a baton. It's so odd, I can't stop staring.

He weaves through the soldiers who move in such perfect unison, even their weapons clank simultaneously. The ones at the end of their rows are holding halberds covered with crimson, velvet flags. The flags are embroidered with a gold heart in the center and adorned with gold tassels.

There's an enormous castle in front of me. It has many pointed towers gilded in gold, reminding me of a crown. The walls are made of white stone and have gold roofs that glisten in the sun. However, it's the large stained-glass window in the middle of the building that captures my attention. There's a bright red heart with a bejeweled ruby crown wrapped around it.

No, no, no. It's not possible.

I can't be at the Heart Castle. It's a three-day journey by steam train. How did I get here so fast? It's not possible. This must be a dream. Or maybe a nightmare.

The White Rabbit rushes over, jumping up and down on his little hind legs. He waves his pocket watch in his hand and he's screaming. "You're late!"

"He's so annoying." Ace plucks out a card from the inside pocket of his jacket and flings it. It's a direct hit and the pocket watch flies apart, its pieces scattering onto the ground.

The White Rabbit gazes down at the watch, and his shoulders drop. He glances up, and his pink eyes grow wide. He charges over to Ace on his hind legs at an incredible speed.

"How dare you?" The White Rabbit points to his pocket watch on the ground. "How will I know if I'm late?"

"Does it matter? You always think you're late, even when you're early," Ace retorts. "Besides, don't you have hundreds of the same pocket watch model at home?"

The White Rabbit jumps up, grabs Ace by the collar, pulls him down and thrusts his face into Ace's. "Why do you always do that and why didn't you teleport inside the castle?"

"Why do you always have to bring up the time?" Ace grits his teeth, grabs the rabbit's head and turns it to face my vomit.

Seeing it makes me want to throw up again.

The White Rabbit jumps down and wrinkles his nose. He flicks his gaze toward me and gasps. His lips part and his pupils grow large. He raises his hands toward me.

"What in the Underland?" I finally find my voice. "Take me back home."

"Queen Alice wants to talk to you," Ace reminds me.

"You already said." I let out a low growl of annoyance. It's not like I can say no to the queen. "Okay, hurry up. It better not take too long."

"Yes, yes," the White Rabbit says, his hands still up in the air.

Ace crouches down and smacks his hands away. There's an edge to his voice. "Why are you here?"

The White Rabbit blinks, shakes his head and turns his attention to Ace. "The queen! She's been asking for you. You know how antsy she gets when she doesn't get her way."

"Well, then, let's get going. It's not like we have time to waste," Ace says and starts walking. "Come, Lucina, you really don't want to keep Queen Alice waiting."

"Oh, my, your foot," the White Rabbit gasps. "That needs tending, too."

"It's fine." I snort, giving him a lethal stare.

"Okay, if you say so. Come, come." The White Rabbit comes up behind me and pushes on my calves, forcing me to move. Then he runs over to Ace and whispers something in his ear.

Ace whacks him away. "Not now."

What am I doing here? I take long, hard, deep breaths, having no choice but to follow them.

My footsteps echo as I tread along the black-and-white tiles of the throne room. In the middle of the room is a large crystal chandelier, almost touching the floor. Gold candelabras decorate the walls with little ruby hearts. Heart motifs adorn different colored tapestries, and red dominates the room.

The throne at the far end is carved out of the finest metals, crested with rubies, white diamonds and black diamonds. The metal framing the throne bends and twists into intricate patterns that hold up a giant heart cushion.

Where's the queen? A pitter-patter of footsteps answers my silent question.

"Don't turn," the White Rabbit whispers next to me. "Keep your eyes forward."

I do as he says.

She comes into my periphery, a petite, beautiful, young woman in a long, shiny, pale blue dress that hugs her hour-glass figure. Long, wavy blonde hair cascades around her shoulders, appearing smooth and silky, almost as if it were gold fabric. She has light-blue eyes, delicate ears that frame a button nose and long, silver fingernails. She seems the complete opposite to me, with my blue hair and brown eyes, blunt fingernails, bloodied pajamas and nightgown.

The soft jingle of bells pricks at my ears. I search the room, but I can't find the source of the noise. The bells continue to tinker.

The queen takes a seat on her throne and places a hand over her mouth to stifle a yawn. Her sapphire eyes become hard. "Where have you been, Ace? I've been searching for you for over a week. I even had the White Rabbit send soldiers out to find you."

Ace bows. "Queen Alice, I told you I was leaving to obtain the asset."

"What are you talking about?"

Ach shifts on his feet, clearly uncomfortable. "My queen, I was tasked with—"

The cute blonde woman morphs in front of my eyes. She goes from angel-like monarch to snarling monster, her features tense up and her cheeks color in anger. "Enough! What have you found?"

Ace gestures with his hands over to me. Her expression doesn't change in the least.

"Who is this peasant?" the queen demands. "Why are they so scruffy and what are they wearing? It's the ugliest thing I've seen! And is that blood on the carpet?"

The stupid cloth they gave me to wrap around my foot isn't working.

"The maids will deal—" the White Rabbit starts.

"This is the Knave's daughter," Ace interrupts.

I presume he's referring to the Knave of Hearts, the most notorious warrior in the whole of Wonderland. He's famous for bringing the Broken Hearts War to an end.

What that has to do with me, I haven't the faintest idea. If he thinks that legendary hero is my father, then they've got the wrong person. I don't know the Knave.

The snarling expression falters, and Queen Alice glances at me quickly. It lasts only a moment before she turns her attention back to Ace, beckoning him over with her silver manicured nails. Whispers ensue between the two of them.

Moments pass, and the stinging in my foot gets worse.

The White Rabbit, who's been eerily quiet, gives me a gentle smile. "I'll tend to your foot after."

"My foot's fine," I lie. "So, can you explain why that wooden thing was going through my dad's drawers?"

"It was on a mission," the White Rabbit answers.

"What mission?"

"The Pack are the queen's elite fighting units. They're a special team that serve as bodyguards to the queen as well as carrying out counterterrorism missions, direct action missions, and special recon."

"I know what the Pack are," I hiss. "I'm asking why that thing was in my house?"

"They'll tell you soon enough," the White Rabbit says.

My gaze turns to the duo, noticing Ace's steely blue eyes are glowing.

Who is he? How can someone acquire so much magic? I thought only the Queen of Hearts had such power.

Before I can think it over some more, the whispering stops and the queen nods. Ace stands tall next to her.

She taps her chin with her index finger. "Oh, I see. Lucina... We've been searching for you for a very, very long time." The queen's frown disappears, her eyes brighten, and her smile widens. Her voice is sugary at first, and then it drops. "Well, your father."

I shake my head. "I think you've got the wrong person."

The queen wiggles her nose and snaps her head over to Ace. He doesn't flinch.

"She is the Knave's daughter," Ace says, his voice hard.

"I don't know the Knave," I blurt out.

"Ace informed me about your sheltered life." Alice tilts her head and smiles. "No, Lucina, I think you misunderstand."

"What are you talking about?"

The White Rabbit elbows my calf. "Manners?"

I sigh. "What are you talking about, Your Majesty?"

"Oh, my." The White Rabbit wipes his forehead with a handkerchief.

The queen stands and gestures for me to come closer. I don't want to get any closer, yet somehow my feet glide on their own, the blood trailing behind me. The sparkle of magic hits my ears and continues until the queen is only a foot away from me. I hate being close to anyone, especially someone who smells like cheap, rose-scented baby powder.

"Lucina, Jack Cordula or, as he is known here, Jack Goldenheart, is the Knave."

"No, you've still got the wrong person."

"*No*, we don't," Ace says. "I can prove it."

A scroll magically appears in his hand. He unrolls it,

revealing a younger version of my father, except with both eyes intact.

I frown, confusion swirling in my head, probably from being smacked. Yet the more I stare at the picture, the more I see my father. From the frown to the square jaw to the broad shoulders and the thick thighs. The only difference now is he has more age lines on his face, his black hair is salted with gray, and he wears a horrendous beard he refuses to shave.

The scroll disappears and Ace returns to the queen's side.

My mind is a tornado of thoughts. The more I think, the more I conclude it's most likely true. Dad's fighting knowledge is incomparable and he's so jaded about the world, which is probably down to being instrumental in the war. Also, what better career for him than being a blacksmith? Dad always says, "*War is inevitable bloodshed and someone will profit from it. Might as well be me.*"

"Don't fret, child," Alice interrupts my thoughts. "He disappeared soon after the Broken Hearts War."

I don't say anything because I don't understand why she thinks I'm fretting.

"Turns out his poor little heart couldn't handle all the bloodshed." The queen's voice softens momentarily and then she glances up, her eyes sharp. "But it had to be done. Ace, show her the contract I have with the Knave."

Ace steps forward and another scroll appears. This time, it unfolds all on its own.

I start reading it and within moments realize it's a long and detailed contract.

Jack Goldenheart is hereby required to come to the aid

of Queen Alice (further detailed in clause 2.3.2) at any such a time she requests his assistance. Any other duties he is currently undertaking must be ceased upon Queen Alice's request. In the receipt of these services, Jack Goldenheart will receive compensation in the form of...

The contract disappears before I can finish reading it.

Why would Dad sign a contract with the queen? What could he gain? Money? He loves money, but we've never had enough to spend. At least, not that I'm aware of. Everything he makes on the side goes into running the smithy.

"Quiet one, isn't she?" Alice says to Ace. "Just like her father."

Ace nods, his face unflinching, his gaze still cutting. "It's also a lot to process, Queen Alice."

"True, true," the queen says and takes a seat on her throne. "Come, child, you need not worry. Your father did what was right for Wonderland. Now we need his strength again."

"Right?" I drawl.

"We need your father's help in a new war," Queen Alice says.

I stare into the queen's big blue eyes. "What war?"

"The war with the Kingdom of Diamonds," the White Rabbit says.

"As I was saying, the Diamond Kingdom is getting..." Alice pauses and thinks deeply, "... out of hand. I can't let them get away with their crimes any longer."

"What crimes?" I narrow my eyes.

The queen turns to Ace and raises an eyebrow. He expresses no emotion, instead he shifts his eyes to the right.

The Queen bites her lip. "I suppose I can't hide it forever; more and more people are finding out." She drums her elegantly manicured fingers on her armchair. "Wonderland's magic is depleting."

Twisted shock rises in me. It's not possible. Magic is the lifeblood of Wonderland. It has been in abundance for as long as Wonderland has been alive.

"Your expression truly is cool and collected, just like your father's," the queen says and scrunches her face. "But I know what you're thinking. How did it happen? The Diamond Kingdom, that's how it happened."

"And how did they do that?" I blurt out.

She closes hers eyes momentarily and opens them. "They have been abusing magic, depleting it, believing it is rightly theirs. If we don't put a stop to them, Wonderland will cease to exist."

"So, what has this got to do with me?" I ask.

Queen Alice's eyes grow glassier with every second. "I cannot let my people down. The last thing I want is an all-out war with my kingdoms."

"Can you imagine?" The White Rabbit says. "The Red and White Kingdoms would destroy each other. The Club Kingdom would have a field day imposing their tricky ways and, well, the Spade Kingdom…"

"I must intervene," Queen Alice talks over the White Rabbit. "And I need your father. He is the greatest warrior in Wonderland and with him by my side, the war will be over quickly."

She has no idea that he's probably funded this upcoming war by selling them weapons. My father is on no one's side. All I know now is that he works for profit and doesn't shy away from taking the odd mercenary job.

Not like I can tell any of this to the queen. It would be akin to admitting he's breaking the law and being the reason he's imprisoned. However, the quicker I answer her—with anything—the quicker I can get home.

"I don't know where my dad is, he could be gone for..."

Ace interrupts. "I left him a message for when he returns."

Something occurs to me about his strange power. The one that had me throwing up. My stomach is still nauseous from the trip. "Why don't you just teleport to him?"

"It doesn't work like that," Ace snaps.

"I'm sorry, child," Alice interjects. "He's just... moody."

"I can only go to places the other members of the Heart Pack and I have visited," Ace adds, averting his eyes.

"Oh. Well, I can't help you there. He didn't give me details for his latest trip. He just comes and goes as he pleases."

"And he leaves you all alone?" The White Rabbit gasps.

"Yes. I'm seventeen, not seven."

"Quite right, child," the queen says.

With each passing moment, I'm more and more aware she makes no sense. She berates him for thinking I'm a child and yet she calls me one. Has she looked in a mirror? She must be about my age, maybe a few years older.

"If you want, I can go find him?" I chime in, saying anything to get out of here.

"No," Queen Alice states and swishes her hand in front of my face. "You will remain here."

My mouth opens and closes. "Huh?"

Alice speaks up. "It's best you remain here. You're not safe out there. With war looming nearby, and everyone knowing the Knave's loyalty to me, he has become a target. By association, that makes you a target, as well. I will protect you, for your father's sake. The Knave will immediately come here once he picks up Ace's calling card. In the meantime, we will take good care of you. You're an honored guest."

"I'm okay. I can take care of myself…" Words fail me, yet again. What am I going to do here? What about the smithy?

"Yes, your bloodied foot tells me that," the queen retorts and turns her attention over to the White Rabbit. She points a finger and circles it over me. "Do something about this. Make her presentable."

"Yes, Your Majesty," the White Rabbit says and bows.

"Good, good. Lucina, I will talk to you later at dinner. The White Rabbit will deal with you." Alice dismisses me with a flick of her hand.

I stand, baffled that I've been insulted and forced into doing something in the same sentence.

"Come," the White Rabbit says, and ushers me out of the room. "Let me take to you to your sleeping quarters."

As I leave, I watch several faceless figures dressed in red, black and white enter. The other members of the Pack. My anger flares, recalling the fight from earlier today.

The White Rabbit gestures for me to move and so I begrudgingly follow him. But not before taking a quick peek back. And as the door closes, I find Ace staring at me. A slow smile spreads upon his lips.

Chapter Three

Blood and dirt swirls down the drain. I place my hands against the walls of the shower, letting the water cleanse me. My bruises find relief in the warmth of the water but my cut stings.

I tilt my head to view the gash on my arm. My wound throbs, along with my ego and my head. Today, I've lost a fight against a chunk of wood, I've found out my dad is the Knave of Hearts and that he's also got a contract with Queen Alice.

What stings more, besides the cuts on my body, is my dad never told me about his life as the Knave. What was he afraid of?

I fiddle with the pendant around my neck, the one with

a picture of my mom and my dad. I never take it off as it's the only thing that has any sentimental value to me.

I always thought there were no secrets between Dad and me, only between us and everyone else. If anything, I was always under the impression that it was us against the world. We even write in a secret language to each other. All his letters are coded, as are mine. Though there's nothing much to be said in those letters, usually just orders for weapons or to check up on me.

Turns out he hid a lot from me. What else is he not telling me?

I press my forehead against the white marble tiles as the warm water cascades down my body. I know my dad; he wouldn't hide something without a reason. I have so many theories running through my head; he was embarrassed of the Knave title, he did it to protect me or he wanted a quiet life. None of them make any sense.

I pick up a bottle of shampoo from the shower tray and open it. The smell of lavender, petitgrain and ylang-ylang hits my nose. It's a delicate and sweet fragrance, the opposite of me. I lather the shampoo into my hair whilst trying to think of possible reasons Dad would hide such a major thing from me.

According to the history books, Wonderland went into disarray due to the previous monarchs' reign, but Dad would scoff at those books. Tell me not believe any of it. He never gave me his reasons for dismissing them, and I never asked because I hated seeing him all surly and angry.

So, why would he help Alice? Profit, perhaps. Nothing else really comes to mind.

In the end, maybe I simply don't know him as well as I thought I did.

"This room is disgusting." I glance around from my chair as I take in the daintiest room I've ever known.

The bedroom is so pink. It's decorated with sleek, cherry wood nightstands, rose gold vases filled with an assortment of pink flowers, light pink crystal lamps, and an ornate, hand-carved settee upholstered in a dark pink muslin. Dad would laugh his boots off if he saw this place.

I catch my reflection in the rose, gold-bordered oval mirror and I'm horrified by the bruises on my neck and face. I got too smug and didn't take my outfit into consideration. I should've beat that thing.

"The queen chose it especially for you." The White Rabbit wipes my foot with a moist tissue. With his free paw, he gestures to the bedroom.

"What am I, five?"

My eyes drift from the pattern of golden rays on the floor up to the large bay windows letting them in. Each window panel is different in size and has white panes that create motifs—some are hearts, others are roses.

An overpowering earthy smell drifts into my nose. I glance at my foot again, and the cream the White Rabbit is lathering on it. I think it's aloe vera. He then places a green-brown ointment onto my skin.

Ouch!

I bite back a curse as the cream stings my wound. And

I thought the shower I had was bad, though my back appreciated the heat. He picks up a roll of bandages and wraps it around my foot.

Thinking that we've finished, I start to get up, but he pushes me back down and gestures to the bruises on my knees, arms and face.

"Just give me the ointment, I can do this myself," I say. I hate it when people invade my personal space.

"You need another ointment for bruises."

"Fine, just give it me." I rub my forehead, and an idea strikes me. If he's around court all the time, maybe he knows more than I originally gave him credit. Maybe I could even get some answers. "Do you know my dad?"

"Yes." He goes over to a metal box.

"What was he like, when he lived here?"

The White Rabbit opens the box and pulls out a tube. "Quiet."

"That's it?"

His whiskers twitch. "He was a very private man."

"But why did he make a contract with Alice? What could he gain from it?"

"With the Knave, you never knew what he was thinking." The White Rabbit gives me a tube and looks to his upper right. "Money, I suppose, and to bring stability to Wonderland."

I pull up the sleeves of my dressing gown and rub the ointment in.

"Right, we need to get you in a dress," the White Rabbit says.

"I'm not wearing a dress."

The White Rabbit chuckles. "You sound like my youngest daughter, Bunny. She hated dresses, too, when she was your age."

I grunt. "Sounds like she's smart."

"Yes, she is." He lifts his chin with pride. "Her children, my grandchildren, apparently take after her. I wish I could see them."

"Then go to them," I say, wishing he'd go right this minute.

I continue to rub the ointment on. It smells like pine and sage, which is a much better odor than the stuff on my foot.

His eyes grow bigger and he whispers, "Maybe one day."

"Why can't you meet up with them now?"

He rubs his paws awkwardly, as if struggling with the answer. Before he can say more, there's a knock on the door.

"Come in," the White Rabbit calls out.

A maid pops her head through, then fully opens the door. Her eyes widen for a second, and she flashes a smile. "I have the dresses."

"I'm not wearing a dress," I reiterate, staring at the nauseating outfits she holds up. Disgustingly bright colors with too many frills.

The maid smiles. "You must wear one for breakfast, it's only proper."

"I don't do proper," I grumble. "Give me some pants, a shirt, a tunic or anything I can walk around in properly."

"You can walk in these properly," she says.

I tilt my head. "Get me some pants."

Her head turns to the White Rabbit. He pauses for a

moment and then nods. The maid leaves the room with those hideous clothes.

The White Rabbit clears his throat. "I only suggested dresses so you could fit in at breakfast with the others."

"Others?"

"Yes, the other nobility."

"That's great." Sarcasm drips from my mouth.

I hate socializing. I'm the worst when it comes to interacting with normal society, forget noble society. Everyone in school was frightened of me because I liked knives and when I have to interact with clients, I tend to give only one-word answers.

"I'm sure you'll get on with everyone," he says. "Everything will be fine; everyone will adore you."

Strangely, I don't think so.

I follow the maid through endless hallways into what appears to be a very large greenhouse. As I go through the glass tunnel, I can hear peculiar music blasting out in the room ahead. Green foliage covers it, from trees to vines and moss to plants. Flowers are in every nook and cranny; bluebells, lilies, petunias, periwinkles and, of course, roses.

The urge to rush out of the room grows stronger, especially when I notice how well dressed everyone is. The White Rabbit did warn me. Still, I prefer comfort over substance.

All the women are in beautiful dresses in every color of the rainbow. Some dresses are full of tulle, others are decorated with jewels, furs and feathers. All the ladies are wearing intricate hats with a range of decorations from feathers, jewels, nettings and flowers. It's as if they are having a competition to find out who can be the tallest. Their hats remind me of a cake tower ready to topple over.

The men are wearing traditional suits, also ranging in colors. They appear ridiculous to me with their overly lavish cravats and top hats that rival the women's absurd ones.

There's a variety of citizens from humans to beastians—animals that behave and act like humans, such as the White Rabbit and even the illusive duezans. I've never seen a duezan this close up. They're humans with a few animal features, usually ears and a tail. I catch a glimpse of a fox, a cat and a fish duezan.

At the end of the tunnel, I glance back at the exit to find the maid staring at me. She smiles and gently urges me on with a tilt of her head. Hesitantly, I step forward.

My mouth drops. This is not how I have my breakfast. There's a pig with an apple in its mouth on an open fire rotisserie, spinning around. There are twelve giant story cakes, an ice cream cart, a fudge stand, a large frier where nobles dip foods in candy, pickles, corn and butter. Some of the nobles are bobbing for candied apples in the fountain.

The tables are ridiculous. On them lie teacups, saucers, and small serving plates patterned with butterflies. They're in all shades—baby blues, pinks and greens, all with gold-rimmed edges. An enormous teapot matches the set on the side.

There are several layered tiers of plates with an assortment of treats that reach up to the ceiling. On it are sandwiches, quiches, scones, fruit pies, chocolate tortes and muffins, desserts, puddings and so much more.

Nausea hits me like a hammer. There is no way I can eat all of this. I'll throw it all up and I really don't want to throw up anymore in this place.

However, the ridiculousness continues as there is a Ferris Wheel inside the greenhouse and everyone in the carriages is sitting upside down. The women's bloomers are on full display. Some nobles are swinging on the chandeliers like trapeze artists.

I want to go home; this is too much for me.

"Oh, you poor dear." An older woman with a live peacock for a hat approaches me. "You're new here, aren't you?"

She's freaky. She's clearly old but fighting everything to appear young in the most disastrous way. She has long, curly auburn hair and the porcelain skin of her face is too tight. I don't even think her face can move. Her lips are very plump—dare I say, fattened—to look like a blue dolphin cichlid. She has very long thick eyelashes which are clearly false, and her body is very disproportionate, with a tiny waist and large breasts.

With a quick glance, I realize that everyone in the room has a similar tight face.

I can't say anything.

"I can tell," the older woman says, her face unmoving. "Where's your Face Fix?"

"My what?" I manage to utter.

She gestures to my face with her hand. "Everyone has them, darling. You can't be appearing in court with your natural face. It's barbaric."

What's barbaric is her face.

"If you want, I can spruce you up with some magic?" She wiggles her fingers at me.

"That's really okay," I say and walk off.

Dad hates magic and warned me against it. He might have lied about his real name, but that doesn't mean I'll stop listening to his advice.

"Well, at least let me fix your clothes," she calls after me. "Or at least your figure, yours is misshapen. You're a stick."

I pick up my pace. I don't want to turn into her.

As I walk further into the room, I see a bear beastian place his head in the candy floss machine. After a few moments pass, he takes his head out and the candy floss is piled up in a conical shape on top of his head.

There are a few nobles shooting paint at each other through guns. One noble is hugging and trying to kiss a large cactus plant and there's another whose tongue is stuck on an ice sculpture.

"Hello," a voice says, grabbing my attention. A young woman with blackish blue hair stands before me. She has wide brown eyes and plump red lips, and I don't think she's got a Face Fix. "You must be Lucina. I'm Edith, the Duchess' daughter."

"Hi," I mumble.

Someone clears their throat.

"This is my older brother, Daniel," Edith says. She gestures with her head to the man on her left and crosses her arms over her chest.

He's so tall that it hurts my neck to look up at him. I'm

surprised I didn't spot him earlier. It's hard not to. He has auburn hair, turquoise eyes and very prominent cheekbones, the complete opposite of Edith.

He tips his hat at me. "Lady Lucina? Oh, the Knave's daughter." His voice rises at my father's supposed title.

Lady what? I'm no lady. There is still a part of me in denial that my father is the Knave. I don't want him to be. I can't wait till he gets here so I can sort this all out with him. He's got a lot of explaining to do. The mere thought he knew these people baffles me.

Everyone's attention turns to me, and silence fills the room, with the exception of the music playing. Great. Exactly what I didn't want—attention.

I search around for an exit; a door, a window or any hole to get out of this room.

"Come, Lucina," Edith says, raising an eyebrow with her lips pursed. "Come sit with us."

Edith ushers me over to a table where a whole roster on individuals sit. The nobles return to whatever they were doing. However, I can still feel their eyes on me as I take a seat. The citizens at the table seem more natural than the others around, at least in terms of their appearance.

Not wanting to appear rude, I pick up a sandwich from a nearby cake stand and place it on the plate in front of me. Problem is, I don't want to eat in front of everybody. I don't eat in front of people in general and when I do, it's with Dad, and we sit in silence.

"Lady Lucina," a lady with a squirrel hat starts and bites her fat lip.

And they say I'm the one with fashion issues.

For the first time, it strikes me that everyone here talks in dulcet tones and they really pronounce their vowels, just like my dad. The signs he was from somewhere fancy were there—I just didn't know well enough to notice them.

"Yes," I say.

"You have such transparent skin and bright blue hair. People from the Spade Kingdom have blackish-navy hair. Am I right to assume you have Spade Kingdom blood?" she asks.

I'm a little taken aback since I didn't expect my appearance to give away my heritage.

I nod. "Yes, my mother."

"You're like me," Edith says with a tight smile. "My mother was from the Spade Kingdom, too."

I really want to ask her questions about the Spade Kingdom. I know nothing about my mother so even a few crumbs about her heritage would be enough for me.

In Wonderland, there are six kingdoms: The Heart Kingdom, the Club Kingdom, the Diamond Kingdom, the Spade Kingdom, the White Kingdom and the Red Kingdom. I'm definitely not home anymore, but I'm still within the Heart Kingdom.

"Your hair is a very different type of blue to other Spades I've seen," the lady with the squirrel hat says. "Normally they're like Edith here, with darkish blue and black hair, but yours is a royal blue. You rarely find anyone from the Spade Kingdom. There are enough Diamonds and Clubs around," the lady blabbers on. "We have more citizens from the White and Red kingdoms."

"Everyone knows why. The King of Spades cut off all

contact with the outside world when the former Queen of Hearts, his sister, died. After that, the Spade Kingdom disappeared off the map and no one has seen it since. Any Spades, who were on the outside, could not return to their home and were stuck wherever they happened to be," Edith says, her eyes downcast. "Like me."

"Oh, come on, Edith," Daniel says. "Mother and Father adopted you. And by the way, the Spade Kingdom is meant to be in complete shambles from what I've heard."

I'm not sure about that. One of the few things my dad told me about Mother was that her home was one of the most advanced of the kingdoms. Their buildings reached the skies, and their citizens were the most intelligent and tranquil.

"Have you been?" I ask, because it doesn't match up with what Dad said.

"No." Daniel laughs. "But that's what Queen Alice says."

"I can't remember the last time I saw the queen," a man says and smashes his teacup against the table. "She's probably too busy ruining and arranging people's marriages."

I jump in my chair. No one seems to react to his bizarre behavior and statement. Upon further inspection, I find many smashed plates of crockery on the floor and tables. Also, some nobles are drinking others' cups of tea. One of the sheep beastians on another table even has teacups lodged into her hair.

I'm not going to listen to any of them. They're all mad here.

"I heard the queen isn't the real queen, but she is in fact the queen," a female goat beastian says and takes a sip of Daniel's tea.

"Pardon?" I rub my forehead.

"It's obvious," Daniel laughs. "The queen is right."

"And wrong," the lady goat adds.

This is getting ridiculous. None of these people make any sense.

"The queen is always right." A lady with beehive auburn hair and a hat with silver deer antlers says. "I should know because I'm closest to the queen." She pulls a chair from a nearby table and sits down, heaving a great sigh.

Edith rolls her eyes. "Mother knows everything."

"Mother, this is the Knave's daughter." Daniel gestures with his hand.

The older woman's eyes widen, and she sits up on her chair. "I can see the Knave's features in you."

No one has ever said I look like my father. Clients at the smithy say I must take after my mother. My face is much softer than his, more heart-shaped—or so I've been told.

"Thanks," I reply the only way I can and take a bite of my sandwich.

"I knew your father," the older woman says. Like the rest of the people in the room, she has a very stretched smile. "Did he ever speak of me?"

"No," I reply.

She places her hand on her chest with wide eyes and disgust. "He never talked about moi!"

I don't understand her overreaction. Dad doesn't talk about anything. Getting information out of him is like trying to find a dodo.

"What about the former king and queen?"

I shake my head. "No."

"Not even the king. He was the king's best friend. He must have mentioned him," the Duchess prattles on.

"No." How many times do I have to tell her?

"Hello, I'm Hubert." A male giraffe beastian in a top hat greets me and comes over to the table. "Lady Lucina, did you know the past king?'

"Why would I know the past king?" I squint my eyes.

"Why wouldn't you not know him?" the giraffe replies.

The ridiculousness of this conversation becomes too much.

"No!" I shout, heat radiating from my face.

The women cover their mouths with their fans, and the men clear their throats.

What did I do? I haven't said anything stupid, yet somehow, I've drawn even more attention. I don't get it, since these people are doing far stupider things. It's like sparring with Dad with no weapons, being blindfolded and having my hands tied behind my back.

A part of me wants to cover my face with my hands and the other wants to flee. A cold sensation spreads across my chest and my heart beats slowly in my ears. It's the strangest feeling ever.

"Speaking of the queen, where is she?" Edith breaks the tension in the air and takes a sip of her tea.

Everyone's whispers change, reaching my ears in a cacophony of sound.

"Where is the queen?"

"Is this war necessary?"

"She shares nothing anymore."

The Duchess grimaces but quickly maintains her composure. "She's busy, dear."

"She's always busy," Edith says. "Who's she beheading now?"

"She hasn't turned up to an event in the last few months," the squirrel hat lady says. "I've almost forgotten her appearance."

The Duchess glares at Edith and speaks through gritted teeth. "These are trying times. She has a war to deal with and we have many spies in our midst. She is doing this for our safety."

"A war of convenience," Edith mutters and folds her arms.

What is Edith talking about? This war is to stop the misuse of magic. I've never used magic because Dad forbids it. Doesn't she want magic? Even if she doesn't have a Face Fix, she's done something strange to her features that requires magic, so obviously she uses it.

Is there a right way to have a war? For Dad, it's all about who he can exploit in those times, but these people seem to view it differently. I guess I've never thought about war from either viewpoint.

My chest warms up again, and life returns to my body. I spend the rest of the time in silence and continue to eat my overly buttered sandwich.

Chapter Four

here are acres of trimmed, checkered grass with some random trees placed here and there. Some of the trees have fruits on them. The one that has caught my eye is a pear tree. Its pears are all uniform, the same teardrop shape and green with a soft red blush on them.

I didn't eat much at lunch and I didn't like the idea of *sharing* my food. Also, the fatty foods were too much for me and all I really wanted was some fruits—and here they are, in trees. Just waiting to be plucked.

I want to climb up the tree and grab a pear but if I go up there, I know I'll just draw attention to myself again. And I've done enough of that already. Even though people have done far stupider things.

Even worse, I've been made to play this stupid game of croquet. None of it makes any sense to me. They're using hedgehogs as balls and flamingos as mallets. They've even made card soldiers stand on their hands and feet to make arches. These arches are what everyone has to get the balls—I mean hedgehogs—through.

To top things off, the citizens I'm playing with are very stupid. I mean, whenever I took part in games as a child with the other children in the village, we'd take turns. Right now, I'm surrounded by chaos. The nobles are all trying to play at once in the most impractical clothes.

Currently, there is one woman who's in a puffy lilac dress with layers upon layers of tulle. She grabs hold of her matching lilac flamingo and swings the mallet, only to hit the skirt of her dress, showing her undergarments to everyone else. Near her is the woman with a peacock hat and overly feathered dress. She is trying to get the flamingo close enough to her body to hit the hedgehog. She takes a swing and ends up chipping away at the grass.

She's not playing golf. All it needs is a soft swing.

"Watch it, you clumsy fool!" shouts one of the men, a rather large, chubby one next to me.

"Sorry," the other man says. His top hat has fallen in front of his eyes and he ends up hitting another man. "But if you weren't so big, you wouldn't have been in my way."

"How *very* dare you?" The larger man says.

"No, how dare *you* for being in my way!" The man with the top hat raises his voice.

It would have been taken more seriously if his hat hadn't fallen over his eyes. There is so much bickering, it's like being in a playpen at a nursery.

"Will you hit the ball already, Fredric?" A woman in a straight and loose dress with feathers says.

"I'm getting in the mind space, my dear," the man next to her replies with gritted teeth.

"Well, it's not getting you anyway!" She raises her voice.

"Oh, dear," Hubert, the giraffe beastian, says next to me. "They're fighting again."

"Maybe they should stay away from each other then," I say.

Hubert shakes his head. "They can't, they're married."

"Then they should consider a divorce."

"That has to go through the queen, and I doubt she would allow it."

I tilt my head. "Why would the queen involve herself in something so trivial?"

"She chooses who should marry whom in Wonderland, as well as who's allowed a divorce."

"That's absurd," I reply. "Everyone in my village got to choose who they married."

Hubert raises his flamingo. "Oh, villagers don't count. Only those the queen thinks are of some worth get arranged."

My head starts to throb. This is all too stupid. Everyone here is crazy. I'm not listening to anything they've got to say.

I walk away so I'm on the outskirts of the group. The hedgehog and flamingo that have been assigned to me follow me.

"You don't need to follow me," I tell them. "I have no intention of playing."

"Why not?" The red flamingo asks while the green hedgehog leans in.

"Hitting you doesn't seem right to me," I tell them.

The green hedgehog blinks several times. Her voice comes out like a tiny squeak. "But that is the way."

"Since when?" I ask.

The hedgehog and flamingo share a look. I'm not sure what to make of it.

"You okay, Lady Lucina?" Edith asks me. She's so elegant in a burgundy dress with lace from her neck right down to her waist. I could never pull off such a dress nor would I want to, in this heat.

"Just tired," I reply, blinking while taking in the chaos around me.

"Listen..." Edith rubs her palms together. "I know that conversation about the Spade Kingdom earlier must have been uncomfortable for you."

"Not really," I say.

"It's just, it's hard for me," Edith tells me with a pinched expression on her face. "I always wanted to know my parents since I never met them, so knowing anything about the Spade Kingdom is very important to me."

I don't really like talking about my feelings.

Edith chews on her lip and her forehead crinkles. "What was your mother like?"

I feel my eyebrows raise. "Why are you asking me that?"

"It's just, your mother was a Spade, like mine. So, I thought knowing about her would help me understand my own."

I let out a long sigh. "She died when I was a baby."

Edith makes a strange sound as if she's choking back a sob. "I'm so sorry for your loss."

I poke my tongue into my cheek. "I wish I'd known her."

"What about your dad?" Her eyes fill with tears, and she draws in deep, shaky breaths. "Didn't he talk about her?"

"No," I shake my head. "I think it's too sad for him to talk about."

Edith clears her throat. "Do you think he loved her?"

"Of course," I scoff.

A slow smile spreads across Edith's face. "I thought so."

"Come back here!" Daniel cries out.

The blue hedgehog he's been assigned keeps running away from him every time Daniel tries to hit him with his green flamingo. It's actually quite a funny sight, though I don't laugh out loud.

"So, what's the Knave like?" Edith asks.

I pick up the hedgehog and begin to stroke it. "Why would you want to know about my dad?"

She swallows tightly. "Everyone wants to know about the man who saved Wonderland."

I lift my head. "I wouldn't know that man. I only know the man who raised me."

"Scratch me," the flamingo asks.

I roll my eyes and rub the hedgehog with my thumb. With my free hand, I scratch the flamingo's neck as he leans in on my leg.

Edith lets a long, deep sigh. "What was he like?"

"Look, I don't know you," I tell her.

"I'm sorry." Edith's lower lips trembles. "I didn't mean to be nosy."

I don't like to upset people but she's really trying to get in my business, and that's putting me on edge.

Edith whispers, "You're lucky to know him."

This whole conversation is getting too awkward for me and I'm tired from this morning's activities. "I'm going back in the castle to get some rest. Tell the others whatever you want."

"Here, could you take my handkerchief with you? I dirtied it and need it for later," she says. "Just give it to one of the maids to wash up."

"Why don't you do it yourself?" I begin, but she's already opened my hand and placed the handkerchief in it.

She then gives me a strange glare. "Just do it, please," she pleads.

"Okay," I say and take it. I take a few steps back, completely puzzled by this conversation. I've been confused since I got here and all I want to do is go home.

"Remember, Lucina, not everything is as it seems." Her eyes are intense, lending weight to her words.

I pass some flowerbeds before coming over to a massive fountain. Two swans' heads make a heart shape in the middle. The fountain sprays water into the air.

As I stare at it, my gaze homes onto the heart gap made by the swans' heads. My skin starts to prickle and the tiny hairs on my arms go up. There is a crackle in the air. Magic.

Dad hates magic so we never use it at home, but some people in the village use it, very sparingly. It's how I learned to recognize it.

A rainbow shines in between the heart formed by the swans' heads and an ornate crown appears. It has rubies bejeweled all over and in the middle of it is a large red ruby in the shape of a heart.

I take a step closer and it disappears. I swing around, searching for a source, but I don't find anything out of the ordinary. Just a garden.

"*Lucina,*" A voice says. It's a male voice, an unfamiliar one.

"Who's there?" I call out.

"*Be careful.*"

"Excuse me?" I say.

There is no reply.

Was that a ghost? I shake it off. There are no such things as ghosts. And if it was a ghost, it wouldn't come out in the daytime. So, what was it?

Maybe I'm going crazy like everyone else here. The handkerchief in my hand starts to feel warm and I open my palm. A little piece of paper flutters down and I pick it up.

"*Find the crown.*"

I stare at the cursive handwriting, not understanding. Not at first. Everything's been so confusing since I got here, and this only adds to it.

Then it dawns on me—Edith. She must have spelled the handkerchief, hidden this message within it. But why?

I'll go mad in here. It doesn't help that this bedroom is reminding me of all the worst things about this place. My vision is already starting to turn pink. I'm afraid I'll turn into one of those girls who likes frilly dresses like my neighbor Nilly. The two of us were like oil and water.

A bit like me and Edith. I really didn't like the questions she was asking me. They were too personal. Anyway, I gave her stupid handkerchief to a maid. I couldn't see any dirt on it.

My brain can't even think. What am I doing here? Why did Edith give me a message about finding the crown? Maybe she's under a spell, or she's a spy. My best bet would be she's crazy.

I shake my head and open the bedroom door, popping my head through. No one's in sight and the hallways are dark, only illuminated by the dim candlelight.

Right now, my objective is to go to the bathroom. If I could hold it, I would. This place is a maze and I really don't want to get lost again. Also, it's full of crazies so I'm glad I have my trusty knife, just in case. Even though I stole it from the kitchen earlier. It's much better than nothing. Though I'd much rather prefer a sword.

I glance down the long hallway with its creepy portraits of citizens of Wonderland and its many doors. The tiny hairs on my body tingle, telling me to turn back. I have no idea what resides behind the doors and I don't care to find out unless it's the bathroom. No point opening a bunch of doors and disturbing everyone.

In the dark, anything and everything puts people on edge. According to Dad, it's the fear of the unknown. As a child, he'd make me camp out in the nearby pitch-black forest. *"Embrace the unknown, learn to expect the unexpected and then you can stare fear straight in its eyes and laugh."* That's Dad's theory.

Took me six months of camping in that forest for the fear to die and I'm grateful to my dad for his need to strengthen me.

I found a bathroom and I'm attempting to make my way back to my room. This place is crazy; it took me many lefts and rights, ups and downs to get there. Luckily, I have a good memory. Being stuck out in the forest forced the sense of direction right into me.

As I'm about to climb the stairs, a twinkling sound catches my ears. It reminds me of wind chimes. Is that magic?

"And cannot pleasures, while they last," a voice sings. Its timbre is low and calm, almost soothing.

I search the hallway.

"Be actual unless, when past, they leave us shuddering and aghast," the singing continues. "With anguish smarting..."

What in the Underland?

"Excuse me," I call out softly and climb the stairs where the voice is coming from. "Is someone there?"

"And cannot friends be firm and fast, and yet bear parting..." The voice stops.

"Hello?" I call out, my voice shaking ever so slightly.

The cold metal of the knife at my ankle under my nightdress reminds me of its presence. Dad always makes me carry a weapon. The longer I'm bathed in silence, the more I want to pull it out and thrust it everywhere and anywhere.

A soft gust of wind tickles my ears, and an upside down bright-white crescent moon shines through the windowsill on the stairs. A black silhouette appears and slowly becomes a plump, purple and blue-striped cat with long navy claws, turquoise eyes, and far too many teeth for me to count.

"What are you doing here?" I ask.

"What are *you* doing on my tier?" the cat repeats.

"I asked first."

"I asked because you asked and so you must answer last." The cat's white crescent moon smile widens.

This is exactly why Dad hates all animals. He thinks they are better off as pelts. I'm beginning to think he's right. Creatures never seem to make any sense.

"I needed to use the bathroom," I grumble and then I click my tongue. "Now, what are you doing here?"

"I have just one, but with eight to spare, I am usually friendly, but I sometimes act like I don't care. What am I?"

I hate riddles.

"I know you're a cat, but what is your name?"

"You're putting too much pressure on poor Cheshire," the cat says and slowly becomes a black silhouette yet again and disappears.

"Your name is Cheshire."

Magic fills the air; it sends goosebumps down my arms.

I search for Cheshire. "Where did you go?"

"Here, there, everywhere," he says, still nowhere to found. "I know who you are, little star. You're the one who snuck upon us without us knowing, and when all is revealed, Wonderland will be glowing."

"What?" My eyes dart everywhere, trying to find him. "What are you talking about?"

"You are it," it says.

"I don't know if that's a compliment or a criticism."

"You're lacking something that once has been." Cheshire reappears on the windowsill and shakes his head. "What is in you and is said to be broken without being touched, held or seen?"

"You're strange, you know that?" I cross my arms. "You make the accordion owl look good. Why can't you speak normally? And why aren't you answering any of my questions?"

Cheshire stares at me. "The time is nigh, and I must bid you bye-bye."

"Good, because you're annoying me." I flick my finger at his nose. "I have to go to sleep."

"The heart never forgets," Cheshire says.

His voice echoes around me, my heart beats slower and my eyes close on their own. Shreds of voices come out of the void in my mind. I know those words. I've heard them once before, I think, but when?

"Listen to your heart," Cheshire says. "Otherwise, you'll have regrets."

When I open my eyes again, the cat has disappeared.

I blink. Wonderland always had too much idiocy in it. Dad says there was a time without it, when eccentricity roamed but idiocy, never. I don't believe him, but I'm also too tired to care. There's been enough drama for me today.

Chapter Five

I yawn, massaging my neck in the process. Walking across the gardens, I'm trying not to close my eyes, but these people have no lives. They only do stupid things and talk nonsense or gossip about people I don't care about.

So far, I have learned that Henry is pining for Violet who is pining for Oscar who is pining for Clarissa who may be interested in Ace. But according to Edith, Ace is off-limits. No soldier of the queen can have any romantic relationships.

Edith knows everything and she loves to share it all. It's those type of people I'm wary of. She's far too interested in my life.

There have been some complaints about the queen and the war, along with theories on the queen's prolonged absences. How do they think it's not normal to be fighting the Diamond Kingdom? All I've been hearing this morning is everyone saying the Diamond Kingdom aren't the type of people to start a war over nothing. It leaves me even more confused. Are the Diamonds really abusing magic? If so, none of the nobles seem aware of it.

People in Wonderland have jobs, like running a store, selling goods, farming; providing services like law, teaching and so forth. Everyone contributes to society.

These nobles do nothing. How do they get their money? Every day, they do the same thing; have breakfast, go for a walk in the garden at eleven, have afternoon tea, play croquet at three and then they have supper at six.

I'm bored of this lifestyle after my second day. It's no wonder they're all mad and snobby! Give me some tools and let me work. I'd rather hear the smashing of metal than these people speak.

Then my interest piques when someone mentions the crown.

"I heard the Heart Crown rejected the queen," some man says.

"Don't be silly, she wouldn't be queen without it."

"You know what is strange? I haven't seen the Heart Crown in such a long time," one of the ladies says. "How long has it been?"

"You know, I was thinking the same thing," a man says.

"I haven't thought about it in such a long while," another lady says.

"What were we talking about again? Shoes—"

"Daniel was such a big baby," the Duchess chimes in as we stroll around the gardens.

Her words break the conversation I was overhearing, and I look in Daniel's direction. Right now, he's walking with Edith, I think. I can't be sure; everyone looks the same in their ridiculous outfits.

The gardens are huge, bigger than my village. We've strolled past the golf and croquet courses, through several orchards and over bridges with tiny fish in the ponds.

The only comfort I have is that I'm outside in the fresh air.

"Whatever," I mumble to the Duchess, not really caring what she is saying, like she doesn't care what I'm saying.

I catch sight of some large eagles hovering above. I wish I could call them over and ask them to pick me up and take me home.

"Queen Alice took care of him when she first arrived. He barely sat on her lap, but the queen was such a trooper. She took it upon herself to watch over him," the Duchess says and purses her lips. "Your father was a large man like my Daniel."

"Yes…" I say with hesitation. Dad's big, but he's pure muscle.

Daniel gazes back at us and smiles. Dad would break Daniel's hand with a handshake. Actually, I could, too. He's a man of very little muscle.

"I think Daniel has…" The Duchess trails off.

A heartbeat grabs my attention. It drums rhythmically

in my ears. I place a hand on my chest, but it's not mine. I stop walking and search the area.

There are a few trees with heart-shaped apples and rows upon rows of rose bushes. The hairs on my arms stand to attention as a militia of chills march down my spine. The beating gets louder and louder. As I step forward, the feelings grow stronger, almost overwhelming.

Everyone's ahead of me, laughing away about something. The Duchess has forgotten I'm there and continues to talk to an empty space. It pretty much sums up everyone here—stupid.

I find myself staring at a rose bush and at one rose in particular, one that sparkles under the sunlight as if it has jewels on it. Something feels strange about it, but it doesn't stop me from moving closer to it. The rose's petals unfold and its stem tilts backward, its leaves widen, and its tips becomes more pointed. I follow my gaze to the direction it points to and it's toward a hedge maze. One we have never entered or gone near.

In that moment, I come to conclusion that something or someone is watching me. My fingers trail over the knife hidden at my hip.

Dad taught me to be alert at all times, even in situations that appeared harmless. I stare at the rose, unsure whether it is my enemy.

The rose twists its petals and leans over to me, its leaves stretching, desperate to be touched. I stretch out my hand when a gust of wind surges around me, stinging my cheeks. I cross my arms under my cloak, but I can't stop shivering. Red rose petals fly around me.

The collective sigh of the ladies ahead catches my attention.

"Ace!" One of the ladies screams and waves at him frantically.

I find him standing ten feet away from me, on the grass, staring at me. His lips aren't smiling, but his eyes are. I avert my gaze and learn the group isn't as far ahead of me as I'd thought.

"Ace!" The Duchess squeals and runs over. "What are you doing here?"

Ace cocks his head over to her, scowls and narrows his eyes further. "Queen Alice wishes to talk to you."

The Duchess gasps. "Is everything all right?"

He sneers at her. "You know the protocol; no questions. Now get going."

The Duchess nods and starts walking toward the castle.

"She wants to see you fast," Ace adds to her retreating back. "You know how she hates waiting."

The Duchess' face pales, and she picks up her skirt and breaks out into a run. That's the first time I've seen her go quiet or run. I didn't think she'd be able to in that billowy dress of hers and with those high heels, too. Won't they get stuck in the grass?

My attention returns back to the rose, but it disappeared.

How can a flower just disappear? It didn't have legs. Unless it blew away with the wind. I look around at the other roses and they are still intact. That rose is nowhere in sight. On closer inspection, I find the other roses don't hold the same sheen or texture as that particular rose.

A breeze blows my hair into my face, distracting me.

"Hello, Lady Lucina."

A rush of cedar and sandalwood wafts through the air and Ace stands before me. He's standing too close, it's uncomfortable. I'm not used to men being so close to me. I've always kept them at a distance unless it's in a fight. The only man I've really been around is my dad.

"I'm no lady," I say and take a few steps back, brushing back my hair.

"Has your stay been pleasant so far?" His mouth curves into a smile.

I slip my hands into my pockets. His gaze is so direct and sharp, it makes me feel exposed. I turn my head. I'm angry with myself for acting so uncomfortable. I hate that I don't know how to talk to people. People coming into the smithy didn't count. Those conversations lasted a few moments, and were all work-related.

"It is what it is," I reply and take my hands out of my pockets and wrap my arms around myself.

My attention returns to the hedge maze. A twinkle of light catches my eyes and causes me to blink.

"Stay away from the maze," Ace warns. "It's not safe there."

"Why?" I force myself to look at him.

Ace heaves a great sigh. "As you know, magic is waning in Wonderland so it's not stable and that maze is full of magic—unpredictable magic."

"What do you mean by that?"

"Some parts of Wonderland are naturally more magical in nature and as Wonderland grows unstable, those places become unstable. They like to play tricks on you." His intense expression falters ever so slightly.

"What type of tricks?"

He scrunches his face and lowers his head. "Tricks that have caused us to lose soldiers."

"Then shouldn't it be cordoned off?"

"It keeps removing all our warnings," he says. "Don't fall into its trap. The last thing I need is the Knave coming after me. I may be magically inclined, but I don't think I can take on that brute strength."

Despite myself, I feel the ends of my lips tug. My dad could pull up a tree, roots and all. Ace would have no chance.

"A smile suits you," Ace says softly.

I snort. "Whatever."

Despite his words of warning, my gaze lingers back on the maze. It's not like I'll go there. I hate magic. People's reliance on it made them weak. My dad taught me that. Yet, the hedge's magic continues to ring in my ears, and I can't help feeling intrigued.

"What are you doing?'

I don't need to explain myself to him. I start searching the area for the others, but they've disappeared. It's not like I like them, but Ace's intensity is getting to me.

"Where have they gone?"

"To the castle for some afternoon tea." He smirks.

"Oh." The air around me grows thick and I feel unbearably hot from Ace's scrutiny. "I should really get going."

"Really?" He raises his eyebrows.

"What is that supposed to mean?"

He rolls his eyes. "You can't stand them."

"So, what if I don't? Will you allow me to go back home?"

"You know I can't do that."

"Then at least give me something better to do. Let me make weapons for the war or at least let me spar with the soldiers."

Truth be told, I really want to battle with those faceless freaks again. I know I can beat them, with the right clothes.

"Queen Alice would prefer you to stay safe."

I roll my eyes. Maybe it's for the best. I might destroy her soldiers and then she'd have no one on the battlefield against the Diamond Kingdom.

"You know, Lady Lucina, it's okay to act on your feelings. Sometimes those feelings are there for a reason. Like an instinct, telling you something. Maybe you should listen and act on them more."

"Are you trying to tell me something?" I purse my lips.

He doesn't reply, just stares at me as if he's trying to read my mind. His gaze does not waver, and his expression makes no sense. Part of him is staring at me with some sort of admiration and the other is etched in confusion.

"Lady Lucina!" someone calls out. It might be Edith; I can't be sure, they all sound the same.

The eye contact disappears. Ace throws his hands up in the air.

Edith runs over to me, twining her fingers though her blue-black hair. Her face is pinched, and she growls, "Lady Lucina, hurry, your food will get cold."

"I'm no lady," I bark. Also, I'm probably only going

to eat the sandwiches as everything else seems too heavy for me, so the sandwiches going cold doesn't bother me; they're meant to be cold. "I'll be there in a minute."

Ace grits his teeth and doesn't even bother to acknowledge Edith as she waves. Instead, he leans into me and whispers, "Remember, it's okay to listen to your instincts."

Edith looks at me like she's ready to break something.

A second later, Ace spins around and disappears. Rose petals fall from the sky. I cup my hands together and one of them lands on my palm. It's as smooth as silk.

I can't pay attention to any of the conversations around me. Not like I ever have, really. I can't stop thinking about the rose, the maze, the crown and Ace. His words have struck a chord inside me.

I don't do feelings and it's getting frustrating that people don't understand I like it like that. My dad taught me feelings make you do stupid things, and these nobles confirm everything he's said. "*Be rational, cautious, don't expose yourself,*" he'd say. Because feelings reveal weaknesses.

"Is it your birthday, Lucina?" Hubert, the giraffe beastian asks as I enter the greenhouse.

"No," I reply. I really need to stop being taken aback by these bizarre questions.

"Humpty!" Hubert cries out. "It's Lucina's Un-birthday."

A massive egg comes running over. It has large eyes and it's wearing a jester's outfit. In its hands, it holds a huge present wrapped in shiny blue paper and gold ribbons.

"Un-birthday?" I regret the words as soon as they come out of my lips.

Hubert clasps his hands together. "You've been missing out. It's a day you get presents when it isn't your birthday."

Humpty holds the present in front of me.

Everyone bursts out into song.

"Happy Un-Birthday to you
Happy Un-Birthday to you
Happy Un-Birthday dear Lucina,
Happy Un-Birthday to you.
From good friends and true,
From old friends and new,
May good luck go with you,
And happiness too.
How old are you now?
How old are you now?
How old, how old
How old are you now?"

A procession of cheers, claps and hoots follow.

"Open you present," Hubert asks.

"I prefer presents on my birthday," I lie. I just don't want to open whatever monstrosity lies inside. I'm sure it's going to be something terrible—or, worse, a pie to my face. And if that happens, I'm getting a sword and I will slash everyone.

"But your un-birthdays are more important than anyone else's." Hubert lowers his eyes.

Everything in my head tells me not to reply, but my curiosity gets the better of me. "Why is that?"

"Because you're the princess!" Humpty cries out.

Suddenly everyone is crying out, "Princess! Princess!"

Through gritted teeth, I manage to get out some very hoarse words. "I'm not a princess."

"Why, yes, you are." Hubert shines his pearly whites at me. "Princess Lucina of the Hearts."

There is no point reasoning with these lot. Next time I meet Ace, I'm going to demand I be in the barracks, unless all the soldiers are just as crazy as them.

I walk off while everyone sings happy un-birthday to someone else.

I really wish Dad was here. He'd know how to deal with these weirdos.

Thinking of him, I remember the pendant on my neck. I pull it out of my tunic and open it up. Inside is a photo of both my parents when they were younger. Just looking at them makes me feel better inside. Mom is beautiful with her barley curls and Dad is dashing with his hair slicked back.

"Is that them?" Edith startles me.

I close the pendant swiftly and place it back. "Yeah."

"Can I have a peek?"

"No," I scoff. She really doesn't understand personal boundaries.

Her eyes grow glassy for a moment and she purses her lips. "You were speaking to Ace for a long time."

"Not really." I take a seat at the table, hoping to get rid of Edith and her constant questions.

"He doesn't talk to anybody." Edith takes a seat nearby.

I ignore her and rub my head. It's going to be another bad day, I just know it.

Edith places her tea down and picks up a tea pot. "Well, Ace likes proper women, not ones wearing the same outfit every day, and a hideous one, too. Why can't you dress like a lady?"

What is up with her?

Edith's face scrunches tightly together.

"You're the Knave's daughter," Edith says, her nostrils flaring. "He's one of the richest men in Wonderland. Surely, you can go to a shop and pick something up. Or are you lazy, too?"

He's rich? He doesn't act like it. Where was that money when we needed it?

"I don't care," I tell her, trying to mask my irritation.

"You don't care about anything." Edith sports a puffy lip. "You don't know how lucky you are, and you just rub it in my face."

"What are you on about?"

"You're nothing like your father!" she shouts. "At least he cared about Wonderland and its people."

My skin grows hotter and my body tenses. I can hear my knuckles crack as my fingers tighten into my palms. She does not know my dad and she does not know me.

I jump to my feet. "You don't know my dad."

"No, Lady Lucina," Edith says and stares me straight in the eyes. "*You* don't know your father."

Everyone stops speaking. Their eyes and mouths are frozen wide open in an O.

Something twists in my heart at Edith's words—the

way they simply come out of her mouth without a single thought.

"I know my dad," I say as my fingernails cut the skin on my palms. "He's just different from the man you know."

"You have no idea." Edith's voice comes out as a strangled, desperate sound.

"What are you trying to say?" My hands slam against the table. "Stop speaking in riddles and tell me."

"You..." Edith opens her mouth and then closes and opens it again. "The queen..." She clasps her mouth and looks over to Daniel. "Why?"

"You can't interfere," Daniel says with an icy indifference.

Edith's confusion changes to hurt—then anger. "He betrayed the... queen."

Gasps echo around the room.

No one says anything. Anger rages against my chest. What does she mean? How did he betray the queen?

Dad helped Alice win the war; she owes him. She says she needs my dad for the war, unless she's lying and this is all but an elaborate ruse. It doesn't make any sense for Alice to lie. The queen even proved it to me with the signed scroll...

I hate that I'm questioning everything about my dad and the queen.

I take slow, deep breaths. I could snap Edith in half with my hands tied behind my back. I know I shouldn't, but I really want to. Except, I don't want to cause problems for the queen or for my dad.

What would Dad do? I think about the few arguments

we've had, and all he did was walk away.

That's a good idea.

I push the chair back. A woman shrieks.

Scalding heat lashes out at my arm and I let out a low yowl. I turn to see tea running down my shirt's sleeve. Seeing it almost makes the pain worse; I flinch back and grit my teeth together.

"I'm sorry," says the lady.

A mix of laughter and horror overtakes the room.

Typical rich people, finding others' suffering laughable. I won't give them the satisfaction of having a reaction. Besides, I'm a blacksmith, I've suffered far worse than this while working with metal. Curse words are on the tip of my tongue, but I push them back.

Daniel stands, his mouth agape. He picks up a napkin and starts to dab at my arm.

Some of the other gentry cackle around me, some have their eyes open wide and the others are confused.

"Just listen!" Edith shouts.

My head grows hotter with anger.

"You're so stupid," Edith continues her verbal assault. "You can't even see what's really going on."

I can see you're all just a bunch of idiots, I think, except I don't voice it.

"You have no idea what sacrifices have been made for you."

Rage rushes through my blood and I can't contain it anymore. Bells serenade my ears as I eye the knife on the table. Picking it up, I immediately pull it back with no hesitation and throw it. It slices through the air and hits my target, wedging itself perfectly on the sleeve of Edith's dress and the table.

Edith shrieks. "You're always taking everything from me!"

The room goes quiet.

This girl is truly deluded. First the strange message, then the questions, and now the snark. What have I done to her?

"I am my father's daughter," I say.

Daniel is still dabbing at my sleeve, biting his lip hard. I take the napkin from him and mouth a *thank you*. Head held high, I retreat, not looking back once.

Chapter Six

I stare at my oat-colored, long-sleeved shirt for what feels like the twentieth time. I did my best to wash it, but nothing gets the tea stains out. The shirt in my arms feels heavier. My bare feet pound the floor as I make my way across the hallway, up the stairs, across another hallway and down the stairs in hopes of getting back to my room.

A sound that reminds of fingers brushing over apothecary bottles catches my attention. A glint of something flickers on the periphery of my vision and the fresh scent of vanilla and saffron wafts in the air. The crescent moon appears, and it shines in the moonlight streaming in through the window. It twinkles like jewels under the light.

"Twinkle, twinkle little brat
I think you should kill that annoying rat!
Up above the world, you will fly,
Like a tea stain in the sky.
Twinkle, twinkle, little brat!
How I wonder where you're at!"

The voice belongs to that annoying cat. As expected, Cheshire appears on the windowsill, wide grin and all. His fluffy tail curls into his body.

"You?" I cry out.

"And you?" He says with a hearty laugh. "What are you doing out of the blue?"

I hold up my garment. "Trying to clean this."

"You didn't do a very good job, because there's still a big blob."

When I thought today couldn't get any worse, Cheshire rubs salt in my wounds.

"Thanks for cheering me up," I say.

Cheshire's body disappears and his eyes are all that remain. He rolls them. "You make your life ever so difficult for yourself with all your repelling. Why don't you try listening or at least looking and smelling? Maybe you'll finally see and when that happens, everyone will be free. Tweedledum and Tweedledee weren't this frustrating, I should mention. Yes, they're idiots, but at least they paid attention."

"What are you talking about?" I shout.

Cheshire reappears again, his smile gone. "You know what I'm talking about, but you refuse the call. What are you afraid of, beneath that wall?"

Quick, palpating thumps begin in my chest and my

head feels light. Something twists inside of me. It's buried so deep within and it's etching to claw its way out. I grit my teeth together, but a startled cry of pain escapes me.

"Ah, I see, the conflict of two kingdoms." Cheshire's blue irises shine brightly. "It beats, it pounds, it can't be found. Where did go? No one knows. It never forgets, but the feelings are a mess. While the other is good at chess, it needs its rest. If not, it goes insane, but when working it will reign. Both can be broken, and both can be repaired. Powerful on their own, but together nothing can compare."

I drop to my knees and my palms rub against the carpet, desperately trying to keep my body up. But it's as if gravity is working against me, pushing me down. My breath comes out hard and fast.

'My poor Lucina," Cheshire says and appears in front of me. "It's been too long, it seems I must right this wrong."

He places a paw on my hand. His fur is so soft and silky as well as dense in texture. Warmth seeps into my body from the tips of my toes and fingers to the crown of my head. The pain subsides and my breathing comes out normally once more.

I can't move nor speak. There are so many questions I want to ask.

"Don't worry, Lucina, you will be fixed soon enough." Cheshire stares at me with large solemn eyes. "You just have to listen for it. It's calling out for you. Don't be so tough."

I try to stretch out my hand. I need to know what he is talking about.

Cheshire disappears, and my eyes close.

The wind rushes against my face. I open my eyes and find that I'm on my back, my body's horizontal and my arms are dangling in front of me.

Am I flying? No, I'm free-falling slowly down a dark hole. It's the strangest yet most exhilarating experience I've ever had. It's like I'm a balloon but instead of going up, I'm going down. Light beams through and the first thing I notice is small playing cards floating around me. They slowly disappear and a teacup and teapot appear. Panic gushes over me at the thought of tea scalding me yet again, but like the playing cards, they vanish.

I finally comprehend that I'm falling down a well or some sort of tunnel. On the walls around me are the strangest objects—birdcages, a grandfather clock, a map of Wonderland, a silver-framed picture of a dodo, a caterpillar and a gryphon. Then there are golden-framed pictures of attractive people in crowns. As I pass them, I recognize they're all wearing the same crown. It's a tall, golden crown with several points, gilded in red rubies. A large red heart ruby lays in the middle of it, dangling with no support.

"I don't have the time," Ace's voice booms through.

"You mean *we* don't have the time," Cheshire says.

I search the tunnel but can't find them. Bells tinkle yet again, playing over and over. A bright spotlight beams onto me and I cover my eyes with my arms.

"Let me help her," Ace pleads.

"You can't," Cheshire says. "She has to find the path on her own."

"But she's not getting to it fast enough." Ace's voice sounds taut.

I move my arm from my face, expecting to find Ace and Cheshire, but instead the crown from the picture floats in front of me. It's even more beautiful in person and I'm fascinated by how the red heart in the middle of the ornate gold carving is managing to float there on its own. No strings are attached to it anywhere.

"*Come find me, Lucina,*" an unfamiliar voice says.

"Who are you?" I ask, reaching out to the crown. The tips of my fingers are so close.

"In the crown we must trust," Cheshire says.

Everything goes black.

Chapter Seven

When I open my eyes, I'm back in the pink bedroom. And all I can think is, *how did I get here?*

There is a dull ache in my body and when I sit up, it's like I'm carrying a bag of rocks on my back. All I know is I need to find Cheshire. He said some weird things about conflict, being overwhelmed, being in need of recharging and spoke a riddle that I can't seem to process.

I'm not used to riddles. Dad hates them. But Cheshire spoke to me with such familiarity... I think he knows my dad.

I remember the dream of the tunnel, the pictures, Ace and Cheshire talking to the crown. I need to find them—

Cheshire, Ace and the crown.

A knock on the door has me standing up.

The door opens. A card soldier appears. "Ace wants to talk to you."

The two card soldiers accompanying me keep ogling me whilst nudging each other. Yet somehow, they manage to march on in complete silence. Maybe they know about whole knife incident with Edith. I wouldn't be surprised, since any sort of news—good, bad and ridiculous—spreads around here like wildfire.

I really want to question them about their behavior, but before I can they come to an abrupt stop at an archway. The card soldiers leave with an awkward bow and scurry away.

My stomach churns. This is my chance to ask Ace about Cheshire and the crown.

Ace is outside, leaning against the curved wall of the heart-shaped entrance. His chin is tipped upward; soft golden rays enhance the luster of his short, ruffled honey-blond hair. His eyes are focused on something. He has no idea I'm here, which is odd; it's not like I'm being super quiet. As I come closer to him, the sweet ringing of magic is in the air. His blue eyes sparkle with an intense blue light, a starker shade than their regular hue.

I take another soft step toward him, intrigue running through my veins. Should he be using magic? What's he doing?

Ace turns his gaze toward me, and his eyes widen.

"Lucina." He gasps softly. He blinks, and his long lashes flutter. The light in his eyes disappears, and he shakes his head furiously like a wet dog trying to dry himself.

"You asked for me?"

"Yeah," he says and clears his throat. "I heard about what happened yesterday."

I cross my arms as heat rises to my face.

"You had someone insult your father and you had hot tea spilled over you," he says, his breathing heavy. He pushes himself off the wall. "You did what I would have done."

"Really?"

Ace's lips twist and he lets out a mocking laugh. "Those beings don't live in this world; it's like they live in dream."

"Speaking about dreams," I say. "I dreamt about you last night."

"Was it a romantic dream?" He quirks an eyebrow, his lips twitching into a sly smile.

"No." Flustered, I find myself turning away from him. "I had a dream where I heard you having a conversation with a cat—his name is Cheshire."

"Cheshire, a cat?"

"A blue cat with navy stripes that disappears and appears out of nowhere. He has a really wide smile."

When I face him again, he has a blank expression on his face. He scratches his cheek. "Never seen or heard of a cat like that."

"Oh." Disappointment crashes through me and I bite my lip. "Also, there was a crown, too."

"A crown? What type of crown?"

"A gold crown with spikes and rubies," I say. "And it also has a huge red ruby in the middle shaped like a heart and it's floating in between the gold framework. It's strange, because there's nothing holding it in place."

Ace narrows his eyes and his lips become a straight white line. "That sounds like the Heart Crown."

"The Heart Crown?" I whisper.

"You know, Queen's Alice's crown."

"But the crown I saw on her was full of diamonds," I say.

"That's not the Heart Crown." He pinches the bridge of his nose. "That's one of Her Majesty's many other crowns."

"Oh." My shoulders drop.

It finally occurs to me that the dream was just a dream. Maybe what happened with Cheshire earlier was a dream, too. It wouldn't surprise me if Cheshire is a figment of my imagination. Since everyone around here is mad, maybe it's starting to rub off on me.

Ace takes a step forward. I stand my ground, and we stare in each other's eyes. Not a flicker of movement.

After several painful seconds, he rolls his eyes and leans into my ear. "Sometimes destiny just needs a push."

"What?" Everyone here speaks in riddles and I give a light shove on his shoulder.

He walks toward a big silver gate decorated with roses. "Come on, then."

"Huh?"

"I didn't ask you to come here and dilly-dally. Queen Alice wants to meet you soon and you can't go dressed like that. Not with that stain on your sleeve."

"I'm not wearing a dress!"

They tried this morning to get me into a dress and there is no way I'm putting one on.

"You'd look nice in a frilly dress." He taunts me.

"Why don't you wear one, then?"

His eyes glint with mirth. "I don't have the bust for it."

"I'm not wearing a dress." I give him my death glare.

"Fine, but you will have to wear one for the ball tomorrow. It's not really that much different from a tunic, I guess."

"Ball?" I shake my head. "Like dancing and music and…"

"And dresses," he says in a mocking tone and continues to walk away from me.

"The only dresses I ever wore were when I was a child. Growing up, they became less practical. You know, with running the smithy and all and actually doing something."

"I get it," he says. "I hate wearing suits. This uniform is restricting. But the queen demands it."

"At least you can move in it."

"Come on, let's sort out your outfit."

I run over toward him and try to match his fast pace. "I'm not wearing a dress."

"You said that already."

The card soldiers are bowing as we make our way up the stone path.

"Why is she having a ball, anyway?" I demand. "She has a war to deal with, she shouldn't be thinking of such frivolous things."

"Well, you can tell her that over lunch," he says.

I stop in my tracks. Damn him, he knows I won't.

Ace points his fingers to the gate and flicks his hand. The gates open.

"Where are we going?" I ask.

He turns around. "To the maddest person in all of Wonderland."

I rush over to him. Curiosity gets the better of me. Why would he take me to meet a madman?

Ivy and ferns grow through the crevices of the old winding stone path. It all leads directly to a house shaped like a top hat. It's wide at the bottom, and then at the first floor, it narrows. It's about one hundred feet tall, a total of five stories high. The windows are all different shapes and sizes. The brick work makes no sense, but it's beautiful all the same time. A small rose garden is at the front; obviously loved, there are no weeds in sight.

"Is it safe to go in there?" I ask.

Ace crosses his arms. "I admit it's seen better days, but it's very stable. I can't say the same for a certain individual living there."

"Why don't we go to someone who's sane?"

"Sane is boring," Ace says and drops his hands to his sides. "Also, I think you'll like this person."

I doubt it. I'm thinking I'm more like my father than I'd like to admit. He hates people and I think I do, too.

Ace and I head up the porch, and Ace raps his knuckles

on the door. When there's no answer, he knocks louder.

"No one's home," I say, hoping to have an excuse to leave.

"They will come," he says.

The door creaks open.

A beautiful woman steps through the archway wearing a bright blue wrap dress. Her hair is in several plaits, all wrapped with different colored scarves. Her skin is the color of desert sand.

"Hello," she says, and her eyes widen in delight. "Ace, what are you doing here? Is everything all right? Is Rhyme…"

"Everything is fine," he tells her, fiddling with his collar. "Rhyme is… Rhyme."

Who's Rhyme? What a strange name…

The woman lowers her head, and her shoulders droop. "Oh, I was just expecting, no, hoping—"

"Sorry," Ace says and clears his throat. "But I'm here in need of a favor."

She presses her lips in a hard smile. "What type of favor?"

"I need an outfit for this young lady to meet the queen."

"I'm no lady," I mumble under my breath. When are these people going to get that?

The woman's face tightens. "You know he won't do anything for…"

"I know," Ace brushes her off. "But I need this for Lucina, the Knave's daughter."

The woman's mouth drops and then closes, and she repeats this process several times. Her eyebrows lift with surprise and tiny creases ring her eyes and mouth. Her hands move from her mouth to her apron. She stares at me as if a rabbit has sprouted from my head. Tears prick at the corners of her eyes.

"Come on, Candy," Ace says. "Don't dawdle."

She rubs her hands over her apron and nods. "I'll tell him, but you know him." She gestures with her hand and smiles at me. "Come through. I'm Cadence, but you can call me Candy."

The inside of the house is just as bizarre, but like the outside, it works. It's a nonsensical organized mess. Polished wood floors and a graceful banister that curves up toward a soaring second-floor gallery. Prints of different hats decorate the walls and lights shaped as dresses, top hats, and suits adorn every nook and cranny. Going farther in, I find the ceilings are covered with mirrors that change color as I walk.

The furniture doesn't match. I find tables and chairs on the ceilings, cabinets placed in the middle of the rooms. Candy guides us through the maze, going from one archway to another.

We pass a room filled with rolls and rolls of fabric, splayed around without a care. There are sketches that have been scribbled on and crumbled up papers around a large wooden workstation. Sequins, buttons and zippers are scattered all over.

If my workstation was a mess, I'd die.

Ace and I follow her into yet another room. It's equally messy, but this time there are mannequins, pins, needles, feathers, sewing machines and shiny fabrics. A top hat shaped archway is conjoined to another room where a man is mumbling to himself.

Candy stops. "You're a pretty girl."

That's the first compliment I've received since being here. Actually, I think it's the first compliment I've ever had. Dad doesn't believe in them. He says they are made to build you up and knock you down.

"Okay," I reply after a moment, not sure what to say.

"She needs an outfit for now and one for the ball," Ace says. "Where's Hatter?"

Candy gestures with her head to the archway. "He'll come out on his own. It's best not to push him. You know how overwhelmed he can get."

Ace picks up a bright orange fabric roll, sneers at it and puts it down. "Well, we're in a hurry. She needs to meet the queen soon. Great, now I sound like the White Rabbit."

Candy laughs. "He's bound to rub off on you. The two of you spend so much time together."

Ace jerks his head and winces. His eyes illuminate to that magical blue hue I saw earlier. He closes them and pinches the bridge of his nose.

"Go into the other room," Candy says, worry etched in the lines of her face. "You know you're welcome to."

"Thanks." Ace nods with his eyes still shut. He takes a few steps back, leans against a wall and bends over, as if he's in pain.

What's going on? Is he okay? I've never seen him like this.

"It sounds urgent," Candy says. "Go."

"Going," Ace says. He opens his eyes slowly and leaves the room.

Candy watches him go, whispering, "Poor thing."

"What was that about?" I ask.

"Nothing." She brushes it off with a smile, which is really odd. "It's a royal thing. He's being summoned."

Was that what happened earlier with Ace by the wall?

I want to run away, but I'm distracted by her circling me. She taps her finger on her chin. "Any color would suit you, but I think red would be the best."

"I like dark colors," I tell her.

Also, red stands out. It's the color that represents anger, passion, and love. It's an emotionally charged color. A color whose attributes I don't possess.

"Psh." A man enters the room. I presume he's the Hatter, judging by the enormous top hat on his head. He's wearing a red jacket, a white shirt with red bunnies on it and black trousers. "Red was all the rage before, until the actual rage..."

"Stop it, Mads," Candy says.

"Oh, my darling." He widens his bright green eyes. "I cannot live another day under these pretenses."

"Ignore him," Candy says tensely. "I think a nice black dress would suit you."

"What?" Hatter cries out. "No, no, no. We don't do this anymore, Candy."

Candy places her hand on her waist. "What do you think she's here for?"

"Perhaps she's an interior decorator." He shrugs.

Candy rolls her eyes. "Really, Mads. Really?"

Hatter breaks out into a large, wide grin. "There is very little that amuses me."

She places a hand on her hip. "You wouldn't let

anyone else decorate this house or anything else of yours. We both know you can't stand not being in creative control."

His eyebrows draw inwards. "We don't make dresses anymore. Tell her to leave."

"Okay," I say, a part of me feeling awkward for being part of the marital squabble and the other glad to be leaving.

"Mads," Candy says with an edge to her voice. She shakes her head at him, and he shrugs his shoulders back at her. Both her hands go to her hips and her body leans forward.

He blinks and his mouth twitches. Hatter scratches the back of his neck and fixates his eyes on the hare clock on his right, his chin high and spine straight. "Just playing with the bad hand they have dealt me."

Ace returns to the room. "Life is not a matter of holding good cards, but sometimes, playing a poor hand well. You know that better than anyone."

"Ace!" Hatter cries out. "Where's Rhyme? Is he okay? Has she hurt him?"

"He's fine." Ace grimaces.

"He's not fine," Hatter raises his voice further. "She's twisted him. Every time I get a glimpse of him, I can see him changing into something far darker."

"Everything will be okay." Ace winks.

"Both my children are out of my reach," Hatter spits out and mutters something inaudible.

Frustration spreads into my fingers, causing them to curl into my palms. I never know what these people are talking about it. I didn't mind it in the beginning, because

I didn't care. I thought Dad would be here soon.

There's a part of me that likes to think Dad would do anything to find me. A part of me likes to think he knows I'm here and the other is no longer convinced. Because if he knew, then why haven't I heard from him? He should at least send me a pigeon to tell me what's going on. I'm so alone here and I'm used to being alone. But because everyone here has connections and I have none, it only highlights my loneliness. The only connection I have are the memories of my father and the man he used to be.

"I need to you to do me this favor," Ace says.

"What? Making a dress for a girl?" Hatter scoffs.

"No. Preparing her." Ace's tone has a biting edge to it, one I haven't heard before.

"Why should I?"

"Because the hands are about to turn."

Hatter's mouth twists.

Ace smiles at Candy. "Have you introduced Lucina to Hatter?"

She shakes his head. Hatter squints.

"This is Lucina," Ace says. "The Knave's daughter."

Hatter steps back, a wobble in his step. "Jack's girl."

That's the first time anyone beside the queen has referred to him as Jack and not the Knave. It's strange to hear someone call him the name I've known him by.

Hatter's gaze lands on me and his eyes lose the defensiveness and soften. "Jack and I were very close."

"Really?" I can't imagine Dad being close to anyone. Then again, the Duchess said Dad was close to the former king, too.

Hatter pokes his mouth with his tongue and wrings his fingers. His gaze flickers from the window to me. "Yes. Friendly chap, then it all changed. Something clicked. He became so overly cautious, worried about everything, over prepared. It was quite extreme even and then toward the end, he was... demons..."

"We don't have time," Ace rudely interrupts. "The queen wants to meet her. I need her in an outfit pronto. Can you do that?"

"I can't." Hatter shakes his head and walks into the other room with a top hat shaped entrance. "Please, I don't want to suffer any more. Don't give me false hope."

Ace follows him. "But we have hope—"

Candy touches my shoulder. "Come on, I'll give you an old outfit."

Candy ushers me gently away as Ace trails behind Hatter into another room.

Chapter Eight

Some card guards escort me to the dining room. Same as the others, they give me the occasional glance over the shoulder.

I'm wearing a white pantsuit with an elegant off the shoulder lace top. It's pretty and adorned with intricate hand-sewn lace embroideries of scenes from the woodlands such as trees, birds and animals. It's long sleeved, but I feel exposed because of the lace. It's the most delicate I've ever been.

I step into the dining room with its hundreds of tables. Hesitant, I stand at the entrance and fiddle with my fingers. Where should I go?

Queen Alice walks over to me, away from the other gentry. Ace stands beside me, his face unreadable.

Alice's eyes widen. "You're wearing one of Hatter's designs. Very good choice."

I'm met with curious faces and a deep scowl from Edith. I ignore her and all the other glares.

"Come, Lucina," Alice says and glides away.

She turns and waves me over to a table far away from everyone. It's in a corner, sheltered by the tall plants with many leaves and even taller guards. No one else is at the table and I can feel everyone's eyes still on me as I take a seat in the booth. The queen sits down, and she scrunches her face tightly together.

She darts a look at Ace. "I didn't think Hatter designed any more clothes."

Ace bends over and murmurs into her ear. "He doesn't. It's one of his old creations. I arranged it since she didn't have time to pack."

"Oh good, good," the queen says and waves Ace off. "This will have to do for now."

I'm sure the queen is used to finer things, but this is the prettiest outfit I've ever worn. Anything the queen wears would look outstanding on her. Compared to her, I'm like a little girl dressing up. I miss my regular clothes, but at least I can move freely in this, though I wish I wasn't so exposed.

"How are you finding life here?" Alice asks.

"N-nice..." I stutter, staring down at the black-and-white checkered table. I think that's the closest I've gotten to omitting the truth.

"Really?" The queen's eyelashes flutter. "How so?"

"It's very luxurious."

"That's odd." The queen purses her lips. "The Knave lapped up the luxury, so I presumed you lived like that also."

"He did?" I gasp.

It nearly makes my heart stop dead with shock. Edith was telling the truth, then. But why would Dad get in a contract with her? What did he want? And why don't we have any of that money?

"Oh, my!" The queen gasps and places a finger on her chin. "Them two would make a lovely couple."

"What?"

I follow the queen's finger to a male wolf beastian and a female rabbit beastian who are eating canapés near the indoor fountain.

"Uh…" I hesitate.

"Don't you think those two would make the best couple?"

No! The wolf is five times the height of the rabbit and only a hundred years ago, wolf beastians used to eat rabbit beastians. That was until the king at the time banned anyone from eating a beastian or the beastians themselves from eating one another. Though, I've heard whispers the Club Kingdom has a black market which sells beastian meat…

Surely Alice isn't going to set them up? Then again, maybe she will. Maybe Hubert wasn't joking. How strange.

"Yes, they will do." Alice claps her hands and lifts her finger and curls it. "You! Get here."

A card soldier comes running to her.

She leans in and whispers something to him before turning her attention back to me. "What were we talking about?"

"My dad being rich." I shake off the stupid marriage thoughts. The queen said nothing about marriage.

"Ah, yes." The queen wiggles her eyebrows. "He came from luxury. He was an aristocrat; his father was the Baron of Galon. Your grandfather kept the family tradition of being an elite soldier in the Heart army. But your father outdid them all, he was First Knave—and most likely the last."

"Are my grandparents still alive?" I ask. Hope surges through me at the thought of family nearby.

The queen pauses and releases a deep sigh. "No. They died in the last war. One of the many casualties."

My head drops. There I was, hoping for a connection. I wish I hadn't bothered asking. I got my hopes up for nothing.

The queen places her elbow on the table. "What else is different about life here?"

I scratch the back of my neck, knowing I have to answer carefully. I can't tell her about all the stupid things that have been happening with me. She has more important things to deal with, such as war and a dumb ball.

"Everything all right, Lucina?" she says.

"Yes." I nod too quickly.

"You're a very quiet one." She presses her lips into a fine line, and her gaze darts around the room as if she wants something, until it finally snaps back to me. "What have they been saying about me?"

"Pardon?"

"I'm not stupid, Lucina." Her gaze doesn't waver. She sucks in a deep breath, and her long, manicured nails tap against the table. "I know these people. I don't trust any of them. I know they speak ill of me."

My heart speeds up. "They speak ill of everyone."

The queen's eyes narrow. "I knew it. Tell me what they're saying."

Why is she asking me? I've only been here for a while. She knows them better than me. What am I, her spy?

I pick up a nearby napkin and fumble with it. I bite my lips together. I don't want to answer this question. I don't want to get involved.

"The lady worries of discretion," Ace cuts in. His response strangely eases my tension.

"I'm not a lady." I scrunch my nose.

"Ah, of course." The queen looks over to Ace. She leans in and whispers, "Lucina, no one will know you have spoken to me. Please, I have many enemies. I really wish you will not be one of them."

"No..." I shake my head and Ace mouths, *Your Majesty.* "...Your Majesty." "Then tell me what they have said," she pleads, her face softening.

I look around carefully. Making sure not to make eye contact with anyone, I lean in and whisper. I tell the queen how everyone is questioning the war with the Diamond Kingdom. Tell her how everyone believes the Diamond Kingdom are not ones to fight without a necessary cause. That they believe magic is not depleting.

The queen listens on intently, nodding and shaking her head, her face twisting in thought. After the talk, she leans back. She clutches at the pearls around her neck and silence looms over us.

I should have kept my mouth shut. I turn to Ace, but his expression is a complete blank. When we're alone, he's more natural. I suppose that is the way of the soldier, forever a statue.

The queen's eyes are glassy when she finally speaks. "Who has said these things?"

"Mostly everyone." I don't want to get anyone in particular in trouble.

"I see." She crosses her arms and her lips become a thin white line.

The queen's irritation gives me something to focus on other than my own thoughts. Thinking about this whole crown thing, Edith, Hatter and my dad is exhausting.

"So, Lucina, how did you spend your time with your father?" Alice asks.

I'm a little taken aback by her change of topic. Why would she want to know? Unless Dad did betray her like Edith said and she's scoping me out for information.

"We just mainly sparred and made weapons."

She tilts her head over to Ace. "I thought you were joking."

"I never joke," Ace says.

"Of course, you don't," Queen Alice says with a sneer. "Lucina, please eat up. You're far too skinny. That father of yours has kept you away from food. He probably ate it all himself. He always had a sweet tooth."

She laughs, but Ace and I don't. She doesn't appear happy, and her laugh sounds fake.

"Please, indulge me, Lucy," Queen Alice goes on. "What has your father been doing these past years?"

Lucy. No one has every called me that. I hate it, but I can't say that to the queen. Lucina is the name my mother gave me and every time it's said, I feel some form of connection with her.

I shrug. "Just making weapons and raising me, I guess."

"The greatest warrior of Wonderland, reduced to being a babysitter. What about your mother? Where is she?"

"She died when I was a baby."

The queen shrieks. "Midori is dead!"

"You knew my mother?" I ask. Why didn't I ask about her earlier? How stupid of me.

The queen throws her head back and wails. The tears burst forth like water from a dam, spilling down her face. The Duchess comes running over.

"Your Majesty," the Duchess cries out, cradling the queen in her arms. She holds the queen in silence, rocking her slowly as the queen's tears soak into the Duchess's chest. More people gather around.

I glance around to find some looks of concern, but the rest are more of intrigue. The only face that hasn't changed is Ace's, who appears bored.

"Oh, Midori was the loveliest woman in Wonderland." The queen continues to sob and pushes the Duchess away. "No one could wash clothes like her."

I take a sip of the tea. I may be terrible with emotions, but my brain is smart enough to know not to do anything in this scenario. Those tears aren't over my mother. People who are truly crying over something upsetting usually take a minute to build up the tears. Also, she's doing nothing to hide her face. And why would she make a comment about my mother's washing? Surely if she knew her that well, she'd say something more meaningful.

"Oh, my poor Lucina, no wonder you're the way you are. Your hideous taste in fashion, your horrific skin, that... hair," she sobs. "All because you have no mother. You poor, poor child."

Really? Would having a mother have changed me so drastically?

I catch Ace rolling his eyes.

I want to ask Alice more about my mother, but more men and women rush over to deal with the grieving queen. I never grieved over my mother; I didn't know her, so what could I miss?

As the crowd around me gets bigger, I find myself shrinking away. I don't belong here.

"Will someone please go get Joker?" One man cries out. "The queen needs a good joke."

A joke. One joke will not solve this problem, this is more deep-rooted.

I take another sip of my tea. It tastes like cinnamon; strong and sweet, but woody at the same time. The more I drink, the more bitter it becomes.

"No, no," the queen exclaims and bats her hand. "Joker is off on an important errand. I'm fine, just let me be."

"But, Your Majesty—" someone says.

"Ace!" she shouts. "Sort them out."

Ace raises his voice. "Give the queen some room and get back to your seats."

The people don't move.

Ace grits his teeth as his hand comes down on the table with a crash. There's a dark timbre and a very full, round sound. A bright blue light flashes and I close my eyes. Wind storms the room and I struggle to keep my eyes open. The queen's hair is not moving, unlike my own, which is battering against my face. I lean forward, barely able to make out anything. It isn't until I squint that I can make out a thin blue shield surrounding the queen. Ace's eyes are glowing.

I tilt my head to shield my face from the tempest within the room. I catch a male noble skidding backward. He hits a plant pot and loses his balance, falling onto the floor on his knees. The Duchess's hoop skirt inflates like a balloon and her feet lift up; she goes flying backward and slams against the wall. Many other women in hoop skirts similarly fly full force into something or someone. Other nobles' wigs and hats fall victim to the pulverizing winds and circle the air as if they are in a tornado. Only the card guards remain still, silent and unmoving.

Finally, the wind starts to slow down. It moves from a hurricane, to a gust, to a breeze, and then the air becomes still.

Glancing around the room, I take in the carnage; it's like it's been ransacked by thieves. Tables have been flipped upside down and masses of nobles are pressed against the walls. Those who have clung onto sturdy objects have remained at their posts.

The queen stands. The tears and anger all gone, bizarrely.

"Come, Lucy, let's get out of here," she says staring at her nails.

What in the Underland was that? The queen's just as mad the people here.

I'm ready to protest, tell her that we need to make sure people are not hurt, until I catch sight of Ace and a few other card soldiers. They are all behind the queen with a single finger on their lips. What's going on?

"Mr. Rabbit," the queen calls out.

The White Rabbit rushes into the room, his trumpet in his hand. He's unaffected by the chaos that has occurred. "Yes, Your Majesty."

"Deal with all of this." The queen brushes a strand of her hair back and upturns her nose, staring at the nobles with disgust. She begins to walk away. "Come, Lucina."

My body remains frozen on the seat and my fingernails have indented into the booth's table. Ace grabs my shoulders and pulls me up. My hair falls in front of my face as he ushers me out the booth and pushes me forward. My legs wobble at first, but I manage to get my footing eventually.

Ace whispers a warning and urges me onward. "Don't keep her waiting."

I brush my hair back and there's the cry of the trumpet.

"Hear ye, hear ye, the queen has requested your obedience and you have not—" The White Rabbit starts.

Unfortunately, I am unable to catch his next words as I'm ushered out of the room and into the hallway.

Chapter Nine

I walk out of the dining room and the guards around me disperse. Ace is waiting for me beside the painting of a gray cat with a crown on it. He has something black in his hand.

Our eyes meet, and he doesn't appear so cold and brash anymore.

"Queen Alice wishes to show you something," he says with a glint in his eye. He holds up an eye mask. "But first I must blindfold you."

What in the Underland is going on? Have I done something?

Maybe Edith was right in that my father betrayed Alice and she's about to inflict her revenge upon me. I mean, she already let the nobles in the room have it, over nothing.

"What? Why?"

"It's the queen's request," he says. "She wants you to become one of the rare few people to see this."

"See what?" My thoughts go to the worst-case scenario—maybe she's going to execute me.

"You'll have to wait and see."

He moves closer to me and tremors run down my body.

"Is it really that important?"

"Let's just say it's life changing," Ace says with an amused smile as he eagerly lifts up the eye mask.

I knew it. I'm going to be killed.

Automatically, I search the hallways for exits. Damn, if only I had paid more attention to this place and stopped following the guards and maids so mindlessly. Running wouldn't be a great option. The puny golden-haired boy can appear anywhere. Then I have all the other guards to contend with. I'm a good fighter but no one's good enough to take out an entire army of soldiers.

"Why have you gone so pale?" Ace asks. "Also, are you trembling?"

I open my mouth, but only a strange grunt comes out instead of words.

"Lucina, are you scared?"

"No!" I laugh it off, still trying to figure out how to get out of here.

Ace's face softens and he leans in. "You have nothing to be scared of. Not with me by your side."

Who is this guy? As corny as his words sound to my ear, he seems genuine and an unexpected warmth floods through me. I stare at the picture of the little gray cat with the crown, anything to distract me from Ace. I betray myself and out of the corner of my eye I can see Ace watching me. His face is incredibly close to mine.

I turn to face him. "What are you looking at?"

He's unbelievably close and I can smell him; his scent is sweet, like jasmine. It makes me so self-conscious that I wish I had put on some perfume this morning. I hope I don't smell of sweat like I usually do. I can feel myself blushing.

"I'm trying to put the mask on."

"Oh," I say, noticing the disappointment in my voice. I clear my throat. "Where are we going?"

"I already told you, it's a surprise."

I bite my lip.

"It's a good surprise," he tries to reassure me.

"But if I'm blindfolded, how will I know where I'm going? I'll just bump into everything."

"I'll guide you." Ace takes my hand and lowers his lips to it. "I swear to protect you from all obstacles, stairs and corners."

I feel his smirk on my hand. He pulls away and I stare at the warm spot on my hand, stunned for a moment.

"Trust me," he whispers and places the mask over my eyes.

"You can take off the blindfold," the queen says.

I don't understand why the queen has me blindfolded in

the first place, but I'm glad when the blindfold comes undone. The heat of Ace's hand wrapped around mine was making me feel strange, a cross between giddiness and nausea.

I blink a few times as my eyes adjust to the light whilst brushing my hair back.

Lustrous gold braziers encircle twelve marble columns. They light up the entire throne hall and cover it in dancing shadows at the same time. The intricate golden patterns on the domed ceiling dance in the flickering light, while stone effigies glare down upon the checkered black-and-white tiled floor. Heart-shaped banners with gilded ornaments drape from the walls. Between each banner hang small gold chandeliers. Many of them have been lit and in turn illuminate the statues of previous kings and queens below them. Huge, stained-glass windows depicting important moments in Wonderland history are covered by draperies of the same crimson as the banners. The curtains are adorned with gold embroidery and fine patterns.

I dare to look at Ace, standing next to me. He stares outside of the plain windows. I follow his gaze to the fountain with the swans shaped like a heart; the same one where I saw the crown in the fountain and heard the voice.

"This is it, Lucy." Queen Alice glides down the scarlet rug that runs down the middle of the room. She stops at a glass box on a pedestal. Within it is a crown on a black velvet cushion. Alice places her long elegant fingers on the glass delicately. "Beautiful, isn't it?"

I suppose it's better than execution.

I nod, following her to the glass box with Ace beside me, until we're on the opposite side of the box, facing Alice.

The crown is pretty, but not as grand as I'd expected. It's smaller, golden, but with a few small rubies in it that lack luster. It's nothing like the one in my dream, instead more of a headband or tiara than an actual crown.

So, my dream meant nothing at all, just my mind playing tricks on me. There I was, thinking I had stepped into a big mystery only to find nothing. A mystery about a crown, now that is absurd.

Still, my gaze doesn't move from it.

"This is the Heart Crown and this crown, no, *my* crown, proves my legitimacy," the queen continues.

"*Lies,*" a voice says. It's the same male's voice from before, when I was at the fountain. It's smooth, with a sophisticated accent.

My body jolts. "Who said that?"

"The Book of Hearts," the queen replies. "Did you not go to school?"

"No, no, that's not what I mean—" I stutter.

"What she means, Your Majesty, is how dare anyone doubt your legitimacy to the crown?" Ace intervenes and steps forward in front of me.

"Quite right, Lucy," the queen smiles, her gaze unwavering from the crown.

"That's—" I start again.

"Amazing," Ace cuts me yet again. This time, he gives me an ominous glare.

Again, not what I was going to say, but Ace's gaze hardens, and it feels like he's going to set me on fire with his eyes. I remain quiet.

"So," the queen continues, "next time any of those buffoons try to question my reign, I want you to tell them you've seen the crown and you understand I am the one true heir."

"*She's lying,*" that smooth voice chips in.

It becomes clear to me that no one else can hear this voice, since there is no reaction from anyone—not the queen, nor Ace and not even the card guards. Also, none of the people in the room are talking, which means someone else is speaking, someone only I can hear.

I scrutinize the crown, taking in every single detail.

"*Come claim me,*" the voice says.

Is the crown talking to me?

"*Don't fight your destiny.*"

I'm going mad, just like everyone else. I need to go home, back to the tranquility and sanity of my village.

"*This is your home.*"

I take a step back.

The snap of fingers breaks me out of the trance. Ace is somehow in front of me; his short, honey-blond hair hangs around his ears and his ice blue eyes stare down at me with a mix of wonder and scrutiny.

"You there?" Ace asks.

I gape, my mouth fishing for words I can't find.

"So, Lucy, I would like you to shut all those non-believers up. Will you do that for me?" The queen raises her voice in question, still with her eyes on the crown.

"But why me... Your Majesty?" I say, still flustered from my growing state of madness.

"Because your father believed in me and your father was respected by all." The queen's sapphire blue eyes narrow on me.

"But I'm not my father."

The queen gives me a devious smile. "Lucina, after yesterday, it's clear that you're very much your father's daughter. I only wish I had been there to see Edith's face."

"You're not angry about that?" I ask.

"Of course not." The queen laughs. "If anything, you did me proud."

"Protect the people. Protect the innocent."

Okay, now I'm certain I'm going insane.

"Not everything is what it seems."

The number of times I've heard these words since I've come to this place is unnerving.

The queen twitches one of her eyes as she moves away from the glass. "Come, Lucina, that's enough dawdle for today. I have a meeting with the Pack to attend. The card soldiers will escort you back to the dining room or to wherever those buffoons have gone."

"Put me on."

My feet are still rooted to the ground.

Is the crown asking me to put it on? I can't ask the queen to let me put on the crown, because that's just weird. Also, I can't ask her to let me stay here, because again, that's strange. Maybe I can come back later.

The solution comes to me in a flash. "Your Majesty, I was wondering if I could return to my room. I'm feeling very tired."

"I suppose," the queen says, staring at her nails. "Mr. Rabbit!"

"He's predisposed, Your Majesty," Ace informs her.

The queen curls her lip. "What's he doing?"

"Sorting out the dining room, Queen Alice," Ace replies.

The queen crosses her arms and clenches her jaw. "Who's going to sort out my nails?"

There doesn't look seem to be anything wrong with her nails.

"I'll escort him to the meeting." Ace spins around and disappears. All that remains are a few rose petals where he'd stood.

"Let's get a move on." Queen Alice snaps her fingers and begins to walk with a sway in her step. She spins around suddenly and stares at the card guards. "And remember to blindfold Lucy."

"You have to come back."

"No offense, Lucy, but the crown needs to be protected," Queen Alice says. "I can't have it falling into the wrong hands. That would be a disaster to all."

"Wonderland is already a disaster. Don't leave. You have to put me on."

I look over from the queen to the crown. I need to come back and talk to this crown and the best way I can do that is by knowing the way here.

"Chop, chop, darlings." The queen claps her hands. "I have more important things to do with my time."

The blindfold covers me before I can protest. My shoulders drop.

"Come back."

There's nothing I can do but allow the soldiers to guide me back. I wish it was Ace and not them. But maybe I can learn the path while being blindfolded. I just need to know every turn and movement I make and reverse it. Dad did teach me how to go without my sense of sight in combat, and I'm sure this will be similar.

Don't worry, I'll be back, I tell myself.

"Come get me." The voice echoes over and over.

I've been scouring the hallways for the past three hours. I've had to wait until dark to make my move, but I'm sure I've been retracing my steps correctly. My biggest worry was the hallways would be full of card guards but so far, they've been empty. Still, I make sure to keep my footsteps light.

I swear I've been down this hallway already. But then, most of the hallways appear identical. They all have the same red plush carpets, magnolia walls with gold heart patterns and the occasional candelabra to light the way. The doors are a glossy black and the only way I'm able to differentiate places is by the paintings on the walls as well as on the staircases.

The last picture I saw was of an empty bottle with a label that says 'drink me' on it. I know I have passed that before because it's an odd painting.

And something even odder is happening here.

Magic, it's got to be.

But magic usually has a sound or at least a hum and I'm getting nothing. As much as I want to go back to my room, I keep hearing that voice telling me to come and the voice does not get louder or quieter wherever I go, so I don't even know if I'm close by.

I rub the temples of my head and take a deep breath. Cheshire crops up into my mind. Every time I come across him, he is always telling me to look and listen. And I am, but I can hear no magic or spot any change in my surroundings.

"Hurry, they don't have time."

It's frustrating because I want to ask who, but I know I will not get an answer. Still, I refuse to give up.

I end up walking for another fifteen minutes when I find a lone card soldier standing beside a painting. This one is floor-to-ceiling tall, which is odd since the other paintings are all square. I attempt to hide behind the bend where I came from, but it's disappeared and all that's left is a long hallway.

Magic is definitely at play here.

With no way other option, I go up to the soldier.

"Excuse me," I say.

The soldier doesn't reply; he's a three of clubs.

"Umm, I think I'm lost," I go on. I feel like covering my face in shame for saying that.

The soldier doesn't say anything, he remains perfectly still.

"Umm... hello?"

There's still no response.

My arms flail up. I want to flop down in the middle of the hallway and hug my knees and go to sleep.

"Wait."

His dark eyes move to the right, where the picture lays. I stare at the picture. It's of the Jabberwocky, the mystical beast. No one actually knows its appearance, but this creature in the picture is a large, winged chimera with the body of a dragon, a whiskered, fish-like head, insectile antennae and a pair of talon-like hands on both its arms and its wings.

"*Poor thing.*"

As I continue to stare at the picture, it starts to ripple like water. Slowly, the picture starts to dissolve, melting away. After a few moments, a hallway is revealed, similar to the one I'm standing in.

"That's odd." I place a finger to my lips.

The card soldier moves his arms slowly and points to the picture.

"What?"

Sweat drips down the soldier's temple, his cheeks are red, and his limbs are twitching. There's a slight movement on his lips and more sweat drips down from his forehead.

"Are you okay?" I search my pockets and pull out a handkerchief. The White Rabbit insisted I needed one, if I didn't want to wear dresses. I use it to wipe the sweat off the soldier's head. "I should get help."

"Go," he says, his voice cracking and hoarse. "Through."

"Go through," I repeat. Magic crackles through the air.

He struggles, his face twisting with effort and he finally gasps, "Painting."

I scrutinize the painting whilst wiping off more of his sweat. It seems with each word, he's in more pain. "You want me to go through the painting?"

He winces and blinks.

"I'll take that as a yes."

His lips move ever so slightly, and I think he's trying to smile. The smell of fresh lemons wafts in the air. Magic.

The soldier's trying to help me, but he's going against some form of magic.

"Okay," I nod. "You've helped me enough. Don't strain yourself anymore."

He blinks twice.

I place the handkerchief in his hand as I go and stand in front of the picture. I hold out my hand and move it forward. The picture goes all soft, like a gauze, then turns into some form of liquid, then finally turns into mist. The rest of my body moves through the picture; it's like walking through water.

When I emerge on the other side, I come into another hallway like the one I was in, but this time there's a card soldier every two doors apart. I continue to move. The card soldiers remain absolutely still and silent, like the previous one.

After a few moments, I come to a three-way junction and stop.

Which way now? I tap my foot on the carpet.

"This is a maze," I cry out, placing my hands over my face. The only thing I'm doing is managing to get lost to the point of no return.

Someone clears their throat and I search around. I find a soldier on the right moving his arm. His index finger opens from his palm and he points to the right.

I nod and follow his direction.

As I go on, I come across more soldiers who do the same, pointing out the path. I thank them as they help and go left, right, right and then straight forward to reach a grand set of large spiraling stairs that merge into one. When I get to the top of the stairs, I'm met by a large oval door and, beyond it, I find a dark room.

The moon shines in shafts of pure silver through the windows. Straight ahead, the light catches the crown. My hands tremble in excitement as I make my way over. My body grows cold, dizzy and disoriented. My heart raps against my ribcage. It beats in rhythm with my footsteps.

"*No!*" There's a scream. The word echoes into the dark like a howling wind. I jump as the word bounces off the pillars, the glass windows and the marble.

"What was that?" I whisper.

A breath like a bitter laugh causes me to jump. I swirl around and search desperately for the culprit.

"The heart never forgets."

I instantly recognize that voice. It's just stupid Cheshire.

"Where are you?" I snarl.

The large white smile takes shape, and Cheshire appears. He sits on the glass box containing the crown. I'm surprised there are no guards in the room or by the doors. Surely, there should be security on the crown. It's meant to possess the essence of the magic in Wonderland, or so my teachers said.

But there's no one. And more to the point, the crown is still a gold tiara with a few rubies on it. How can something so tiny possess the essence of Wonderland itself?

"You must listen, because you will embark on a mission," Cheshire says, causing me to jump.

I step over to him. "What do you want?"

"Happiness, so stop it with your cattiness."

"You seem thrilled," I say.

"Perceptions are never true, so have you figured out you?"

"What?"

Cheshire snickers. "Mother's wit and father's spirit."

"Do you know my parents?" I ask.

"Do you?"

"Now you're just speaking nonsense."

"I am not speaking nonsense. Have you ever perhaps thought it is you that's speaking nonsense?"

"I'm not speaking nonsense!" I shout but then the soft jingle of bells grabs my attention and I'm staring at the crown.

"Isn't the crown so pretty? I think it would suit your head so please indulge this poor kitty."

"The only thing I have is a headache," I say.

"Heavy is the head that wears the crown."

"That crown doesn't appear heavy."

"But the rightful one will turn it upside down."

Cheshire disappears.

"Hey, come back."

I wanted to question him about my dream. So, I search the room again. No sound, no freaky smile and no Cheshire. I tell myself I'm hallucinating. It's better that way. There's a click and the glass box opens.

"*Hurry up.*"

I can't believe I'm listening to the crazy voice in my head, or from the crown, or wherever it's from. I lean over to pick up the crown. My fingers brush the precious metal, and a flash of brilliant white light takes over.

"Please do not make me do this!"

That voice... I know it. It's so familiar... It belongs to my dad.

I grab my head. There's a methodical pounding in my

ears. The voices disappear. I wince, trying to open my eyes.

What was that? I reach for the crown once again.

As my eyes open, the crown has taken a different shape. The small tiara is gone. In its place is a tall gold crown with an abundance of rubies shaped like hearts and one large ruby heart sitting in the middle. The same crown I saw in my dream.

What does this mean? Do I have magic? Maybe I'm going mad like the people here? Or maybe I'm uncovering something.

How is this happening?

I reach for the crown and pick it up; it's glowing radiantly. There's a slight sting—a zap, like a static shock—and I let go. It falls onto the marble floor with a clatter, the cushion in tow.

"*What do I?*" a male voice says—another one I don't recognize. "*I can't do anything… Lucina.*"

I recoil my hand.

"*Lucina, Lucina,*" the words repeat softly. "*My sweet Lucina. Come to me.*"

Is the crown talking to me? No, it's a voice in my head.

"Hello," I say to it.

Silence bathes the room. My throat tightens as if someone is strangling me. The words in me fight to come out.

I wait patiently. I don't know how much time passes, but all I know is I must get out of here. I pick up the crown quickly and place it on the cushion as fast as I can. The heartbeats in my chest quicken.

"*Lucina,*" a voice whispers.

"No, no, no," I whimper. I'm losing it.

"Take the crown."

"You take the crown."

"Try it."

"No!" I shout.

"Put it on."

I can't. I place the cushion with the crown in the box, and I take a step back. The glass doesn't shut.

"Place it on your head. It is yours."

The voice grows more intense, more demanding. I can't take it anymore. I take the crown from the glass box again. Warmth spreads through my fingertips to the rest of my body as I touch it.

The voices increase in strength, in my head and my heart; they flow through my blood into every part of my body. So many voices at once, that I only catch snippets of conversations. Some voices are recognizable, whilst most I don't know. However, there's one male voice that dominates. It's modulated and husky, clear and direct.

As the crown gets closer to my head, it becomes more dominant.

The crown sits on my head and a bombardment of feelings and emotions overtake me. Images flood my mind until they stop on a single figure.

A handsome man in his early twenties. His hair is gold and coiffed to perfection. Lacquered and enameled by the sun, he radiates energy. His bright red eyes sparkle like rubies.

"Come on, Jack," the man says and laughs. He is riding a horse, and he bolts down a steep hill with jagged rocks, without hesitation or worry.

"Your Highness!" My father calls out. "Please be more careful."

My father comes into view. He's younger, his hair is jet black, his eyes are still dark brown, with no eye patch. His form is still broad, yet slender. My father chases after the other man on a horse, his face full of trepidation.

"Oh, Jack," the blond laughs. "You're such a dull boy."

"Why must you make me worry so? You're going to send me to an early grave," Dad says. "I wish you'd think about my heart and what you do to it."

The handsome man stops and pats his horse and glances back my father. "I wouldn't be the King of Hearts if I didn't know what was going on with my citizens' hearts."

"Your Highness." Dad blushes.

This can't be my dad, he doesn't blush or get flushed, this has to be some sort of hallucination.

The king smiles. "Race you back to the castle."

My heart beats frantically, and the image changes.

I gasp and coldness washes over me.

My teeth chatter and I fall onto my knees.

I feel a stab to my heart, sharp, piercing—a grave and mortal wound. What do I do? I've never felt this way before.

"Dad," I utter.

I bury my face in my hands, my throat constricts and there is nothing to relieve the pressure building inside me.

I've never yearned for my dad like I have now. To hold him like I have never done before. To know I'm not alone in this world, to feel safe.

"Lucina, don't worry. I'm here."

"Who are you?" I cry out with fury. "I'm going insane."

"This is all real and I'll always be here for you. I don't really have a name, but I suppose Wonder will do."

I feel the warmth of a presence around me as if it were a soft blanket that's been wrapped around me. It holds me tight, shields me with its protective barrier. In that moment, I know I'm not alone anymore.

"Wonder," I whisper.

"Lucina."

I know that voice. It's Ace. I've been caught.

I shake my head. A splutter of coughs follows. I have to hide it all, my mind yells at me. Hide these feelings, these strange feelings that threaten to consume me.

I push myself up onto my feet, composing myself on the outside while my insides still... feel...yearn for that warmth. I'm not sure what I'm feeling.

"What are you doing?" Ace asks quietly.

I catch his silhouette leaning against a wall. I can only hope the darkness of the room hides the crown atop my head.

"Nothing." I desperately try to cover the cracks in my voice.

"You're trying on new hats." I can hear the smile in his voice.

"I got lost." The lie spills out of me with no problem. A light sweat breaks onto my forehead. What's he going to do? Is he going to tell Alice? Will I get my head chopped off?

"And the crown just walked onto your head."

"I..." Nothing comes out. What do I say?

Ace walks over to me and sighs. "I've had a horrible night. Some guards distracted me, believing they saw the Jabberwocky."

"Jabberwocky," I stutter. Why is he talking about this when he should be reprimanding me for putting on the queen's crown?

"Had to calm them down, it was so annoying." He rolls his eyes.

"How did you manage that?" I try to keep my breath composed. Better to keep him focused on that then me.

"A little help from a caterpillar's vapor."

I swerve around. "Isn't that stuff dangerous?"

Dad taught me that. Told me never to listen to caterpillars, cats and anything that began with C-A-T. He doesn't like rabbits, either. Said they were annoying, but caterpillars, he loathed them. Saw them as weeds of society, only another thing to make Wonderland stupid.

"No," Ace shrugs. "It's a mild sedative. I mean, yeah, it makes you say strange things, but everyone here is strange."

That's an understatement.

"Why didn't you put the light on?" Ace snaps his fingers.

Light flashes on and I blink. My hands go straight for my eyes and I hiss.

Oh, no. How do I explain this? He'll know the crown has changed. He'll think I did something to it. I'm sweating so much that even wiping my palms down my pants doesn't do anything to help.

"I knew the crown would suit you," Ace says.

Seriously? What an odd thing to say. He's the queen's number one soldier. He should be yelling at me for trespassing or attempted robbery. I struggle to open my eyes. Ace's footsteps echo around me as he keeps moving.

"What are you doing?" I ask.

When my eyes finally adjust, I find Ace in front of me.

"I know it looks good on you, but you have to put it back."

I fight the flush moving up my cheeks.

"The crown won't let anyone put it on."

I stiffen and try to stand tall. "What—"

Ace takes the crown off my head and places it back in the glass container. And just like that, it's back to its original form.

What happened? It was different a second ago. Also, why isn't he questioning me about what I'm doing here?

"Well, you look like death. You really need some sleep," Ace says.

"What do you say about the crown?"

"It's very particular about who rules Wonderland."

"You're so weird."

"Why thank you, Your Majesty." He grins and bows.

I gently shove him. "Get up."

He smirks, gets up and offers me his hand. This strange feeling courses through me. As embarrassing as this has been, I take his hand. Anything to get me out of trouble.

"Come on, let's go." He escorts me back to my bedroom.

A part of me wants to ask him why I'm not being scolded for coming into the room and trying on the crown, but he doesn't say a word and neither do I. He's being so nonchalant about this whole situation, but I'm just glad he's not full-out interrogating me.

Especially since I have no plausible explanation for what just happened.

Back in my bedroom, I pace up and down, my body shivering and my blood pumping. What happened back there? I mean, the crown changed right in front of me while Ace didn't even react to me.

There's a tap on my window that makes me jump. It's a pigeon with a message attached to his leg. *Dad?*

I rush over to the window. As soon as the letter is in my clutches, I take a seat on the dresser chair. As expected, the letter is coded but it's very short. My heart flutters in happiness from the familiarity of the situation and it takes me a moment to decode it.

Dear Lucina,

Get out of the Heart Castle immediately. You're not safe there.

Dad

P.S. Burn this note.

What? If I'm not safe here, then why doesn't he come get me? Or at least give me instructions to get out.

I'm not going anywhere. There are too many secrets and I have to find out what's really going. Because I know he won't tell me anything. I mean, he doesn't even ask if I'm okay or say that he misses me. What sort of dad is he?

The more I stare at the note, the angrier I get. The heat from the rage continues to rise—it needs a release. I throw the letter pathetically in front of me and it taps the rosewood mirror.

But as I look at my reflection, I notice a change. My brown eyes shift and turn a bright red.

Chapter Ten

he queen lives on the outskirts of Atria, the capital city of the Heart Kingdom. When we want to go in the capital itself, we all have to take a carriage into the city.

I'm greeted by quaint colorful buildings, citizens shopping, and the soft hum of conversation. The excursion is exactly what I needed. I've had a poor night of sleep. My head's full of questions.

Why were the guards in pain when they tried to help me find the crown? And why did they help me if it hurt them? Why was Cheshire there? Why did the crown change shape and became the one in my dream? What was with Ace's underreaction to finding me with the crown? Why didn't he tell the queen?

Will he tell the queen? I don't think he will. He was actually really nice yesterday.

And to top it all off, why does my dad have to send me such a cryptic letter? Why can't he be more loving? I don't care about his warning. I need to find out the truth.

Aside from all that chaos in my head, it's good to be out in the fresh air. Exciting, even. But most importantly, my eyes are no longer red.

The ride to Atria was awkward. Hubert, the giraffe beastian, tried to start a conversation. He was only met with grunts from me as I was not in the mood to talk. He received hisses from Edith, the witch, and polite smiles from the other passengers.

Once we get in the capital, I'm met with a wide variety of shops; antique and art stalls, jewelry and accessory shops, luxury boutiques and souvenir shops. I search for the weapons shop, wanting to check out the competition.

Unfortunately, I soon find myself stuck in the Mock Turtle's clothing boutique. Sitting on a teal chaise longue, under bright spotlights that make me feel hot, I'm holding a glass of champagne I haven't yet drank.

I stare at my reflection in a nearby mirror—my eyes are brown. I keep checking. I'm not going mad; they were definitely red yesterday after the crown incident. But why?

A light blue dress flies past me. Some of the nobles are throwing clothes off the racks and onto their servants. I think they're having a competition to find out which one of their servants can hold the most the clothes.

Hubert saunters over to me. "What do you think, Lady Lucina?"

The sequined orange suit is hideous and does not go well with his complexion. I gulp. "It's very orange."

"Fantastic, isn't it?" He tips his extremely tall top hat. "What do you think of my top hat?"

What I really want to tell him is that he needs a smaller hat. He barely managed to get through the door to the boutique and he wants to add more to his height. I fake a smile. "It's orange."

"I knew I could count on you," Hubert says, admiring himself in the mirror. "I'm going to be super dapper at the ball tonight."

"Tonight?" I blurt out. "The ball's tonight? I thought it was next week."

"But next week is today." He grins. "What are you going to wear?"

Oh, no, I'm not going, but I'm not going to tell anyone that. I'm going to plan being ill and avoid it. Also, I'm not going to listen to anymore nonsense. I've had my fair share since being here.

I take a sip of champagne and grimace. It's so sour and salty.

"I think pink will suit you." Hubert blabbers on. "It's going to be amazing. It's been a while since we've had a ball."

Not being able to stand the taste of the champagne in my mouth anymore, I lean over the chaise longue to a plant pot nearby and spit it out.

"You're watering the plants," Hubert exclaims and takes my champagne, takes a swig of it and spits it out into the plant pot, too.

Nothing should surprise me anymore, but it does. I jump off the chaise longue and walk toward the door. I can't be in this store anymore. I only stayed for the Duchess and she hasn't come out of the changing room for over half an hour.

"Tell the Duchess I'm going to another store," I tell Hubert.

I'm already through the door before he can reply. It jingles as I walk out and into the bustling marketplace. A dolphin beastian holds up a catfish in front of me that smells like rotting fish. I can taste it in my mouth, and it makes me want to vomit.

"No, thank you," I say.

He still keeps it in front of me. I don't think he can hear me amongst all these voices, so I hold up my hand to say no. He takes my hand, turns it horizontal and places the fish in my hand. It's wet, slippery and its gills are so slimy. I shove it back in the dolphin beastian's hands.

"No, I don't want a fish!" I say louder. "I'm searching for the weapons shop."

"A fish can be a weapon," the dolphin beastian shouts back, and slaps a nearby woman, browsing a trinket stall, with the fish. She shrieks and slaps him around the face. I use this moment to make my escape and slide into the busy crowd.

I search amongst the winding streets of the city. They're filled with numerous fountains shaped like hearts; plazas, stone and brick bridges, and town squares complete the setup. The longer I search, the more certain I become that this place is a maze of insanity. I manage to find an apothecary, several inns, a cookware store and many clothing boutiques, but no weapons store.

The atmosphere is different from what I'm used to, but it's comforting being with the public; it feels less lonely.

Still, a part of me yearns to see my dad, especially after what happened yesterday with the crown—even if his message sucked. I want to know more about his relationship with the previous king. Why would he turn on his best friend?

Warmth spreads through me and a chime like a bell rings in my ears. Every cell in my body tingles. Magic pops up once again.

"I don't think I can afford that."

"I don't want to go to the stupid ball."

"I wonder if they'll like this gift."

Who's speaking?

I glance around and find myself stumbling to the side, away from the people. Voices. I think they're the voices of the people nearby. But how?

The ground trembles. I assume it's some guards marching nearby.

"Is the Diamond Kingdom really coming?"

'That queen is full of lies."

So many voices in my head... All are different, and none of them are Wonder, whose voice is soft and loving. Why am I hearing these new voices?

The cobblestone streets shake again, and a deafening pounding sound follows. Shrill screams echo in my ears and the continuous pounding of the ground grows stronger. I dare not move, not even blink an eye, hoping the pounding will stop and that it's just a one-off tremor.

"Run!" It's Wonder.

The pounding grows stronger. I'm not sure if the pounding is my heart or the ground. I run over to one of the plazas, away from other buildings, archways and fountains that may fall on me. My vision is blurry as the buildings around me shake. The shops are jumping up and down as if they're simply a pile of children's block toys ready to be dismantled, and the walls begin to creak under the pressure.

A card soldier, a five of diamonds, runs over to me and grabs my elbow. "We've got to get you to safety."

"What's going on?"

"We don't know," he says. "But Ace insisted on your safety."

The peal of the city's warning bells echoes through my ears.

"Danger!" Wonder shouts.

"No!" I shake his grip of my elbow. "We need to help the people."

A black-trimmed carriage shrieks to a halt in front of me and a soldier at the front cries out. "Lady Lucina, get in."

"Save the people."

Protect the innocent, just like my dad always said.

"No," I say.

"Please, if anything happens to you, Ace will have us," the five of diamonds pleads.

"We have to help everyone," I say.

"No, Lucina!" the five of diamonds yells.

I barely hear him through the hysterical screams and shouts of the other citizens.

I survey the area, but there's nothing except the trembling ground and decaying buildings. A tremendous roar fills the air, turning my warm blood to ice.

"*Pure...evil...*"

My stomach clenches, my heart races and my head searches for answers.

"Monster!" someone yells.

I follow the cries and turn around a corner to find a creature unlike any other.

The beast is enormous in size, larger than any creature I've ever seen.

He towers over us all like a tall building, about four hundred feet tall, his shadow blocking out the light as if it were an eclipse. He comes out from behind one of the tall buildings to reveal his hideous face; large, red, hellish eyes, and demonic black horns on his forehead. His snout looks similar to a giant bull's, with a huge gold ring gleaming in its nose.

The creature's body bulges in thick, tight muscles and translucent black diamond skin. White diamond patches cover its jaw, torso and the line of his back. Darkened spikes protrude from his back and tail. The ground trembles with every step he takes on his four legs. He glistens in the light and his scales reflect it onto buildings.

A string of curses unravels from my tongue, like yarn unfurling, as the creature advances.

"It's a Behemoth!" the five of diamonds inhales, trailing behind me and pushing me behind a cart.

"Good idea, seeking cover. Examine its weaknesses," I say.

"We're taking you to safety," the five of diamond says.

"We?"

"The driver, Nine, is coming."

I see nothing but panicked faces, screaming children and women. I have to help them. It's my duty as a warrior. This is what my dad trained me to be. This is where I excel. I can't do luncheons, or croquet, or even dresses, but I can sure as Underland fight.

"I need a sword," I say to him.

"Oh, no," he shakes his head. "I'm here to take you to back to the Heart Castle."

"I'm the Knave's daughter," I say with pride. "I may not know the man you all talk about, but one thing he taught me was to fight and I like to fight."

"I can't," he stutters. "Ace will…"

I unsheathe his sword. "Too bad."

He gasps. "How did you…"

"Five," I say. "Go and get everyone to safety."

"What are you going to do?"

"Fight that thing."

"Are you crazy?" He screams. "It's made out of diamonds, it's invulnerable."

Just feeling the metal handle of his sword has me breathing easier.

"Everything has a weakness," I say. "I just need to find it."

"How do you plan on doing that?"

"By getting up close to it."

"Oh, no, let Ace and the Pack deal with this, they will be here soon," the five of diamonds begs.

"Act like a soldier!" I bark. "We're not cowards."

"We also follow orders."

As if on cue, soldiers burst through the streets, pushing the civilians back and behind them.

The battle cry of the trumpet shrieks. Following the noise, I find the White Rabbit on top of a flat-roofed building. The soldiers stop and hold up their shields to form a tortoise shell. Their weapons clank in unison like a well-oiled machine.

It's a wondrous sound—the sound of battle.

"Hear ye, hear ye," the White Rabbit cries out, his voice hoarse. "The queen asks you to stand down, beast, and she shall grant mercy on you."

The beast snorts, tendrils of black smoke floods out of his nostrils and he laughs, his voice bitter. "Pitiful Hearts, you cannot defeat me."

"So, I take it you will not concede to the queen's wishes?" Even from this distance, I can see the White Rabbit's small frame trembling, his white fur on its ends.

My chest pounds hard with adrenaline, and my free hand lurches forward using the cart as leverage.

"*Danger!*"

The beast opens his mouth and a monstrous roar echoes across the city. A bright white light radiates from his mouth and he shoots an orb of energy toward the White Rabbit. There's a blinding flash, followed by the deafening crash of thunder.

When I open my eyes, a huge ball of fire erupts into the sky, and black smoke consumes the area. When the smoke subsides, a mass of orange light burns bright—fire. Waves of heat swarm the city.

The White Rabbit, is he...?

The dust clears and the White Rabbit is still standing, completely unscathed from the attack. The fire dances around him.

How is that possible?

My gaze doesn't flicker from the spot as I watch on. When I squint, I can make out a blue dome-shaped magical shield around him and the soldiers. I could never see magic like this before. I wonder what has changed.

The White Rabbit blows his trumpet, and the card guards march forward from all angles as the angry flames rise into the sky.

The Pack, the mannequin-like soldiers, appear. They surround the creature, some on the roofs, a few in buildings and some on the ground. Faceless, with unnatural limbs. They creep out of their positions, one by one, each in their own unique version of the heart uniform, their number highlighted. Queen Alice's Pack in all their glory.

The citizens cheer.

They shouldn't cheer yet. They should be getting to safety.

The Pack member Nine attacks first. With its bow and arrow, it shoots at the creature-like fireworks. Ten comes out with a staff and waves it around; moments later, it attacks, and smoke appears. The theatrics continue with each Pack member trying to outdo the other. The more it goes on, the less impressed I become.

Soldiers are meant for war, not cheap parlor tricks. It's just too many theatrics, not enough substance. I'm reminded of my father; he is always yelling at me if I do fancy moves. *"Extravagant moves get you killed, go for the jugular."* A real fight is over in minutes. One that lasts longer is not a fight but a show.

During their attacks, the Behemoth swats at the Pack with his paws, swipes at them with his tail. Their attacks do nothing. Diamond is the hardest substance; they need to attack him elsewhere, somewhere that he's vulnerable. I analyze the creature, ignoring the pleas of the five of diamonds—he's still trying to lead me away.

My thoughts are interrupted by a deafening roar.

A chant emerges. I struggle to catch it at first.

Soon, I am able to make it out— "Ace."

"Ace!" A woman shrieks; it's Edith.

"Get back inside," I yell at her. A part of me is angry with Edith from yesterday's events and the other is angry at her for standing outside like a dolt.

Edith doesn't listen and stands in the doorway of the boutique, gawking at the whole scene. Ace materializes on the city gate's arch and forces a smile on his face, but I can tell it's more for the crowd.

As I predicted, his smile vanishes, and he takes out a pack of cards from his pockets. He shuffles them with the same theatrics as the other Pack members. From his left hand to his right, behind his back and then he juggles them. The urge to roll my eyes at his act surges with his every movement. Then Ace flicks the cards out into the sky, and they burst into fireworks. The crowd cheers on.

Why isn't he attacking?

Some cards fall down from the sky like shooting stars. I narrow my eyes and the cards transform into swords as they come down. They bounce off the creature's armor, leaving not a single bit of damage behind.

This is ridiculous. They need to change their tactics.

The Behemoth continues to laugh.

Ace sneers and throws out cards viciously; they circle him. He holds a card in his hand and his mouth moves. He's chanting a spell. Why is chanting? He's never chanted before. His voice comes out monophonic in texture and has no precise rhythm.

The Behemoth opens his mouth again. Ace does not flinch. He throws the card into the air; several large bolts of purple lightning fall out of the sky and hit the ground. A purple rune that resembles a cross with a hat on it appears on the floor and glows. I cover my eyes; the light is blinding.

When the light disappears, I move my arm and find a red-and-black dragon in front of Ace and the archway. The dragon roars, blasting through the air. The wind generated is vicious, blowing some citizens back. Large charcoal tendrils stream out from his noise, and his eyes are blood red. The black dragon opens his mouth to let out a cobalt blue flame, and the Behemoth raises his paws up in defense. The dragon's fire does nothing.

The Behemoth's eyes widen momentarily. He leans back and lunges forward at the dragon, horns first. The dragon lifts his claws, seizing the horns. The Behemoth rages on, pushing all his weight onto the dragon. A sea of nearby buildings crumple into their foundations. The mighty dragon pushes back as the Behemoth's paws wrap around the dragon's torso. He's trying to spear the dragon into the ground. The dragon's tail flicks back, knocking over a few streetlights and damaging the bricks of a shop.

The other Pack members attack, but their attacks are inefficient. The Behemoth picks a member of the Pack and tosses it like a ball. Ouch. That's got to hurt, even for these lifeless things.

Ace holds out another card and a large crystal snowflake appears above the beasts. It breaks into pieces and falls down onto the Behemoth, but the sharp icicles still do not crack the surface.

"Hit the tail or his eyes. They're vulnerable!" My voice is drowned out by the noise of the fight.

The Behemoth swipes his claws into the dragon's sides, causing the dragon to lose his grip over his horns and smash into a pawn shop. The Behemoth's vicious jaws snap only inches away from the dragon's face.

The dragon retaliates by grabbing the Behemoth's face and slamming it into the building. Shards of glass and a mass of bricks fly everywhere. The beast screams, slashing his paws in a frenzied manner at the dragon. The spikes on the Behemoth's back crackle with energy, and an intense yellow light emerges around the Behemoth, causing the dragon to close his eyes. The beast pushes the dragon back and spins around, smacking his sharp tail into the already decimated buildings and the dragon. The dragon stumbles on his footing as the Pack continue on with their worthless onslaught.

It doesn't feel real. This is not a fight. Why don't they go for the obvious weakness?

"Then show them how to fight."

Panting sounds come from behind me. I turn to find a nine of spades. His face is flushed red and sweat drips down his card frame.

"Come, Lucina, let's go," the nine of spades says. "There's nothing we can do. Even the Pack are struggling."

"We should have taken those warnings more seriously," the five of diamonds says.

Warnings? What warnings?

No, I'll save my questions for later. I must help. So I run toward the monsters who are now near a plaza; the card soldiers are too slow to stop me. Dad would be disgusted at their lack of fitness. I rush forward, jumping, ducking and avoiding the scorching flames and debris. I'm glad Candy has a holster in the outfit, and I sheathe the five of diamond's sword into it.

The card soldiers call out for me. I ignore them, quickening my pace. The Pack member, Nine, is my target. Last I saw, it was shooting arrows out of a window on the west side of the Behemoth—a very stupid maneuver. It needs to be higher up for what I have planned.

The carnage continues to unfold. The Pack, the dragon and Ace continue their foolish efforts as I dart from building to building. I find the building Nine is in, a clothing shop, and rush in.

The shop's owner is huddled under the desk. He doesn't even ask me why I'm here, just continues to quiver.

I grab a ribbon from nearby and tie back my hair. I rush up the stairs. Dust falls on my head as the building quakes from the fighting outside. I search all the rooms until I find Nine in a room full of mannequins and fabric.

The mannequins could quite easily pass as its cousins. Nine has the window wide open and fires out arrows too slowly for my liking.

I charge into the room and push him. Nine falls forward and crashes against a wall.

"You're completely useless," I say and grab its bow and arrow, attaching it around myself.

"What are you doing?" Nine says, grabbing my ankle.

"Saving everyone." I kick it and it lets go.

I slip through the window without a care. My limbs automatically climb. My fingers take over, going up brick by brick. My chest tightens. Blood pounds in my ears. When I reach the top, I realize I need to get higher if I want to hit my target.

The next building is higher and requires more climbing. No problem.

I jump and catch the windowsill of an old sandstone building, shimmy my way up the drainpipe, jump and catch another windowsill and climb the bricks until I can pull myself onto the roof. Settling my elbows on the balustrade, I survey the scene.

The buildings tremble. I stare at the Behemoth. He's distracted by all the useless attacks, which is perfect. Size does not matter. I beat my dad often enough. The bigger the target, the harder it falls.

I draw an arrow from the quiver on my back and notch it. I zero in on the Behemoth's amber eyes and let the arrow fly. Holding my breath, I watch as the arrow careens across the battlefield; everything feels like it's in slow motion. The bowstring twangs as my arrow finds its mark.

The Behemoth screeches, ripping at my ears, but it doesn't stop the smile from curling onto my face. I replace the arrow automatically. Another sound. Another arrow hits as I continue firing, sometimes missing.

The Behemoth closes his eyes. The dragon moves forward and pounces on the Behemoth, pushing him back and toward me.

Stupid creature. He's not a hard one to figure out. My arrows fly fast and thick from my quiver now, finding his eyes every time. Even with closed eyes, it's going to hurt. The creature roars and swings around.

I throw the bow and quiver off me. I run up the sloped roof, unsheathe my sword and run down the other side. Drawing out my sword in front of me, I rush toward the beast, who is now only five or six feet away.

I fly through the air and my sword catches his tail. The one part of him that isn't diamond. My sword pierces into his flesh and the Behemoth's shrieks continue. The dragon continues to force the Behemoth back toward the building I jumped off.

My muscles tighten as I pull at the sword, but it's stuck. And I have to move, as the Behemoth's rear end is closing in on the shop. The sword will have to remain there, as I don't want to be squashed like a bug.

I climb up the creature's back, my fingers scratching against the jagged edges of the diamond armor. I drag myself up, rips appearing all over my white trousers.

The Behemoth crashes into the building, stretches his body up and roars.

I clench my hands hard into the diamond armor. Blood

flows out of them. Pain sears through me, almost causing me to lose my grip. Battle isn't just about physical strength, it's about mental strength. I manage to hold on as the Behemoth crashes into a building. Bricks cover his tail. He flicks them off.

I hold on tight, gritting my teeth. So glad Dad made me run those insane obstacle courses. I'd feel better with him here, though.

Was this what Dad was talking about in the letter? No, I refuse to believe my dad would sit back and let something horrible like this happen if he'd had knowledge of it.

And where is the queen? Isn't she the most powerful magic user? Why doesn't she do anything?

Seeing citizens running around gives me a boost in adrenaline. To save them, I need to get higher, so I climb. My arms burn the higher I climb. My bloodied palm prints stain the diamond skin and I stop when I reach the Behemoth's back. His neck has no grooves, making it slippery.

How am I supposed to climb that?

Damn, this is harder than I thought.

Through it all, the dragon still pushes at the Behemoth.

Yeah, that's it, stupid dragon, destroy more buildings and cause more casualties.

Blasts of pure energy hit the Behemoth's armor. With a quick glance around, I find the Pack are surrounding the beast, and still attacking uselessly. By the Underland, haven't these idiots figured out that the eyes are his weakness?

The Behemoth gets angrier and stands on his hind legs, almost causing me to fall. I hold on tight. He swipes the dragon with a paw. The dragon hisses. An extremely bright light emerges from the right. It's the Pack member with the staff, creating a large ball of energy above it, bigger than anything I've seen.

The Pack member raises its staff.

Oh, no.

It hurls the mass of energy toward the Behemoth.

Great. I have no choice.

I jump off the creature bending my knees, keeping my elbows close to my body, and tucking my chin in so it's close to my neck.

I keep my eyes fixed forward and my feet and knees together as I land. My jump is a success.

Can't say the same for the Pack member's attack. There's been no damage to the Behemoth, but instead a building has been decimated, and now there's smoke and fire everywhere.

"Finn!" It's a cry of pure anguish, coming from Ace.

He's standing on the bridge, his gaze transfixed on the burning building. His face is deathly pale, his eyes are wide and frozen over, like the surface of a pond. He's shaking and his hands clasp the bridge's railings.

The dragon and the Behemoth continue to fight, but Ace's gaze is unmoving. I get up and follow his gaze to the collapsed building, and it finally clicks.

The White Rabbit was on that building with all those soldiers.

No...

Even though Ace is so far away from me, I can see him up close as if I have tunnel vision. How am I able to do this? Is it magic?

I don't care, as his chest is moving up and down slowly. I swear I can hear his long-expelled breaths, each one coming out more ragged than the last. He continues to stare at the building the way my father looks at pictures of my mother. There's a tear in his eyes that refuses to fall.

"Danger."

A torso-sized ball of tarmac fires toward me. I roll out of the way, feeling it shudder as it hits the ground. I need to get back up on the Behemoth. I wipe my bloodied hands on the white pant suit. I give a quick glance over to the bridge—Ace is no longer there.

I take in several deep breaths and for the first time in a long time, I'm not sure what to do.

"There's always a way to win, Lucina," I hear my dad's voice. *"You just have to keep looking."*

The ground jerks beneath me and I do everything to maintain my balance.

Ace appears on top of the dragon. His nostrils are flaring, and he stands like a stone, his fists clenched at his sides.

"You took something precious from me, you took from Wonderland. You took from a family and for that you will pay and witness my wrath."

Ace's voice is so loud, so thunderous, that I can't recognize him. He's become a different person. His eyes have warped into full-blown hate.

Magic crackles in the air like lightning. The sky above us turns gray. A ripple of thunder crashes around me. The trees and buildings start to wither and flail, their groans of pain carried away by the wind.

"Go save him."

Ace unleashes a mix of spells—fire that burns furiously, earth that rises from the ground, ice in the form of large crystals hurtling at the monster, wind like a tornado, water as devasting as a tsunami, lightning thrashing from the sky and dark magic.

The dark magic is a large black void that's unknown to me but sends a shiver down my spine. The plethora of magic creates a tempest like no other. One that will destroy the city.

I don't know if the attacks are doing anything to the Behemoth, but if Ace continues like this, then there will be no city to save.

My heart pounds and a surge of energy comes over me and I blink. I have to climb the dragon. I'm already moving. The dragon's tail swishes back and forth. With little choice, I jump onto the base of the tail. Turns out the dragon is considerably easier to climb than the Behemoth, given he has grooves where my hands and feet can go.

I've been climbing since childhood and even with this blur of pain, I know I can continue up his back with ease. It still takes me several minutes to reach Ace.

Cold, vengeful winds blow at me, whipping the small, loose curls of my hair.

"Ace," I call out.

He does not reply. I edge closer.

"Ace," I shriek. "You're going to destroy this city."

Again, nothing. His shoulders droop and I have no choice; I rush forward and tackle him. We both land in a thud atop the dragon. I place my thighs around his and trap him under my weight.

"What are you doing?" Ace snaps at me.

I twist his head to the side. "Stopping you from destroying this city."

His hard eyes widen.

"Yeah, a thank you would do."

After the shroud of smoke settles, I find the Behemoth... And, no, his diamond armor hasn't been affected. I scan him again; he shakes his head and lets out a monstrous roar. At the back of his skull, I notice a crack, exposing some skin.

I need to strike it, but I don't have a weapon. All I have is a dagger, but that's not going to do anything. The Behemoth lunges at the dragon and the dragon blocks. They lock into an arm drag.

"You wouldn't happen to have a sword, would you?"

Ace looks at me as if I've slapped him.

"Do you have a sword?" I yell at him, grabbing him by the collar and shaking him. "Do you want more lives lost?"

Ace's eyes flash that brilliant blue I saw earlier. "In my pouch."

I stare at the pouch at his side. Is he deluded? A sword can't fit in that tiny little thing. I take the pouch from his side and give it to him.

"Can you get off me?" he asks.

The dragon's body continues to shake.

I roll off Ace, careful not to use too much momentum. Sweat courses down my back as I take a moment to breathe.

Ace gets up to his knees, opens the bag and dives his whole arm in. That shouldn't be possible, but it's happening right in front of my eyes.

After a few moments, he pulls a sword out. It has a gold handle and a gold heart embellished in the cross guard. It's beautifully crafted and I can hear its magic. It's not tingling or chiming; instead, it sings. I've never felt such warmth, such light, such happiness. This thing has an abundant source of magic.

Ace hands it me. "What are you going to do?"

I push myself onward, ignoring my trembling muscles. My target's almost within reach.

I blink the sweat from my eyes and take the sword. I have no idea how many lives have been taken, but I know there have been casualties. The vast amount of destruction tells me that. I won't let any more people die. I will put an end to this.

"When an opportunity comes, you have to take it," Dad says. So here is me doing that.

The Behemoth manages to lurch forward, pushing back the dragon, almost causing me to lose my balance. Ace grabs me by my hip.

"If I don't make it, hit his eyes," I tell him.

Ace's eyes widen. "What?"

I push his hand off me and swing the sword back. The dragon jolts forward again and, using the momentum, I sprint forward, jump off the top of the dragon's nose and lunge forward.

I have to make it.

A peal of bells hits my ears, and a peculiar force pushes me forward. I end up jumping farther than I'd expected and my sword plunges into the Behemoth's eye. I hold on for dear life.

The Behemoth roars, deep and sinister. I plunge my foot into his eyes and thrust the sword back in again. I move up his head. The creature tries to swat me, but his arms are blocked off and held back by Ace's mass of cards. I rush up the Behemoth's forehead and onto his back, where the exposed skin lays. I thrust my sword in and the Behemoth screams.

"Lucina! Hurry."

I ignore Ace and continue to pull the sword in and out. Blood spews all over me.

Never let your guard down, Dad says.

Blood covers everything. It's coated all my skin and clothes, but I don't stop until I find its brain, its weak point. Black blood oozes through its edges as I continue to stab the creature.

Almost there—I can feel it as I get closer to its brain.

The Behemoth jerks, screaming. I have found its weak point. With all my body, I thrust the sword all the way down until all that's left of the sword is the pommel.

The creature shrieks and my heart clenches. I took my first life.

This wasn't supposed to happen. This is not what we agreed. She lied. I was not meant to die.

That was the Behemoth's voice. Not mine or anyone else's.

Chapter Eleven

y knees cave in and fall into the broken and bloodied flesh of the monster. Both my hands hold the sword as the Behemoth arches back and flops onto the ground.

Sweet silence falls across the kingdom, a welcome to my ringing ears that took the full brunt of both monsters' cries. There's a bright light and the dragon disappears.

My breath comes out ragged as I pull the sword up. I manage to pull it halfway before my hands slip off it and onto my lap. A lone tear streaks down my bloodied face.

"Dad," I whisper, wrapping my hand momentarily around my locket. He would be so proud.

The sword glistens in the sun and, strangely, there's not

a speck of blood on it. My gaze focuses on the blade and I catch my reflection—my eyes are red again. I blink a few times to make sure I'm not hallucinating, since I'm not sure if the things I've seen are a figment of my imagination or reality.

A golden glow emanates from the sword. It moves from the top of the handle all the way down, till the light bathes the entire sword. My hand moves forward to grab it, but goes through the sword as if it were mist. The sword disappears, the light breaks up and golden glow flies appear, flying up into the sky.

"Lucina!"

I tilt my head at the familiar cry. Unfortunately, it's Edith, her hazel eyes wide. My hand goes to my head, sweeping my hair back. Blood oozes from my hand and into my scalp, and I regret the move immediately.

"Someone, get a medic," Edith shrieks.

She's standing next to the Behemoth's dead body, holding out her hands above her in an attempt to reach me. The creature is too large, even if it is lying down.

Edith tries to climb up the creature. Watching her makes me stifle back laughter. She isn't going to get anywhere in those heels.

"She's delirious!" Edith shouts out.

I swing my legs out from under me and turn my body to face Edith. Placing my hands by my sides, I slide forward and slip off the Behemoth, landing horribly on my feet. Edith rushes over and props me up before I can fall.

As much as I hate it, my body gives in to the fatigue and my hand grabs her shoulder for support. "Oops, I bloodied your dress."

"It's fine," she says with sharp tone. "We should all be thanking you."

"It's nothing." I push myself off her and take a step forward. I wobble, but that's to be expected.

Edith grabs me again, placing her arm around my shoulders. "For goodness' sake, let me help."

"This is nothing." I take a few steps with Edith until I can find my balance once again

"But there's so much blood. . ." She trails off, her eyes widening momentarily.

"Most of it is his." I try to reassure her.

Her lips press into a straight line. "I'm just glad you're safe."

I take in my surroundings. The city is in ruins; fires plague buildings, bricks are scrambled all over the floor and there's broken glass everywhere. Anger courses through my veins. I should have gotten in there faster and not dawdled by watching the pathetic attempts of the Pack.

A chill runs down my spine as magic trembles in the air.

"Ace," I whisper.

A blue light emits in the distance and Ace materializes. He's at the building where the White Rabbit... I can't even think it.

"Finn!" he cries out. Flicking his hand, he lifts piles of debris off the destroyed site and shoves them on a nearby road.

I rush to stand before Ace. Everything hurts, my hands sting, my thighs are burning, and my legs want to collapse onto the floor. But something tells me I need to be here.

Ace ignores me as he waves his hands frantically,

deposing the rubble. All I can do is stand and watch. Dead bodies of soldiers appear. When Ace finds them, he places them to the side carefully, folding their hands over their chests.

Edith comes and stands next to me. Like me, she doesn't utter a word, instead watches on solemnly.

Five minutes pass, and Ace lets out a disgruntled sound and rushes forward. He collapses onto his knees. I take a few tentative steps forward and there's—white fur.

I avert my gaze. This is Ace's moment.

The air is heavy with the smell of smoke. It hangs over the city, partially obscuring the midday sun. Some of the buildings are now skeletons, ghosts of what they were, and the skies are empty, with no birds flying or singing. Some citizens are trying to help each other, while others waddle through, aimlessly lost in confusion.

"Let someone tend to your wounds," Edith whispers.

"Give me a minute." I continue to stare at Ace.

Edith says nothing, she simply folds her arms and sighs. I suppose this is Edith's version of being nice. She's been, curt but nice. That saying that tragedy brings people together is true, but it's sad that it's what it takes to bind people together.

A member of the Pack comes over to Ace. I can't help but roll my eyes at it. I'm not sure if it's male or female. Pathetic beings. They did nothing in that battle.

How did I lose to one of them in the smithy? My own stupidity. I won't let that happen again.

"The queen wants you," the one with the axe says.

Ace doesn't move. His hand is now wrapped around

the White Rabbit's paw. His eyes are downcast.

"Ace," the axe Pack member repeats.

He places the White Rabbit's paw down softly and snaps his head toward the Pack member. "Shut up."

"But…"

"Tell Queen Alice I'll come in my own time!" he shouts and throws a card at mannequin.

The card lands on the Pack member's arm and explodes. Wood chips and pieces of clothes spread around the area, some drifting with the wind.

The Pack member grabs the empty space where its arm used to be. A small flame licks the wood. It waves its hand over the fire, trying its best to put out the flames. I'm still sore about the incident in the smithy, and I'm still in no mood to help. Even if it wasn't this particular thing I'd battled then.

Another Pack member comes along—the one with the mace—and places a wet cloth on the flames. "Control yourself, Ace."

"You're all disposable," Ace shouts as he gets up. Fires of fury and hatred smolder in his narrowed eyes. "Like any of you matter. Lifeless freaks."

"The queen requires your presence." The mace Pack member grabs the other one.

"And I said I'll come in my own time." Ace's voice is filled with venom. A strange laugh comes out of his mouth and he holds up a card. "Or do you want to burn, too?"

"Have it your way," the mace Pack member says and leaves, instructing the other member to follow. There is some hesitation on the axe's member part, but it follows.

Ace's gaze is transfixed on the White Rabbit, and his eyes soften.

"Come, let's go," Edith whispers.

I'm about to nod when Ace spins his body toward me, his eyes harden with accusation. He lifts his hand and points at me. "This is all your fault."

"What?" I gasp.

A cruel sneer forms on his smooth face and he leans forward. "If only you'd... open your senses, really look, hear, smell, taste, even feel. But no, you're too stupid to see it all. This would have never happened. Things would've been different."

"Why are you angry at me?"

He starts to laugh. With each new breath, his laugh becomes more twisted and darker. "If you'd only do what you were supposed to, you could bring him back."

"What are you talking about?" I ask.

"Let's go," Edith tugs at my arm. "He's grieving."

"Oh, Edith." Ace grits his teeth. "Stop protecting her. You, out of everyone, have the most reason to hate her."

What? Why? Does this mean he hates me, too?

Edith lowers her head. "You're not in the right state of mind. Come talk to us when you've gathered some form of sanity."

"No," he barks and takes a few steps forward, pointing at me again. "You know what, Lucina? You're exactly like those wooden soldiers. You're heartless."

Heartless? What's he on about?

"No, I'm not," I tell him. "I just saved everyone. If I let you continue with your manic actions, you would have blown up the whole city."

Ace claps his hands together and gives the most bitter laugh. "You still don't get it, do you? Wake up, Lucina. Seriously, we've practically shoved it in your face and you still don't get it."

"Ace!" Edith steps in front of me. "Leave it."

His lips tighten into a line. "How many more lives are we going to lose because…"

"I agree with you that she's an idiot. As much as I hate to admit it, she did a lot back there, she saved lives. So, I'll give her credit where it's due." Edith stares him down. "Back off."

Ace snorts and turns away from us, walking back to the White Rabbit's dead body.

How dare he? All I wanted to do was comfort him in his hour of need and he effectively punches me in the gut. My anger rises, hot and sharp.

"Lucina, we need someone to tend to your wounds now," Edith demands and taps my arm. "Come on."

"No," I shout. "You don't act or speak for me."

Edith's eyebrows come up for the briefest of moments, her twisted face conveying her disgust. "There's no winning with…"

"Shut up," I interject, but I don't care about her. I spin toward Ace, shocked that I liked him as a person. "And you, how dare you blame me for his death? I watched the fight. You were pathetic. It was so obvious what you should have done but, no, it's all theatrics here."

Ace draws in a staggered breath. "You're mad…"

I jump in again. "The only regret I have in that battle

is I should have gone in sooner. It would have saved you from having blood on your hands."

Edith gasps but I ignore her.

As he slowly takes in my words, Ace's expression falls into shock. His lips part and his eyebrows furrow. He's searching for the words, but they're lost to him. I can't stand the sight of him, so I do what my father does best, and walk away.

"Lucina, what are you doing?" Edith says. "This isn't the way to your room."

Because I'm not going back to my room. I'm going to talk to Alice and ask her what in the Underland is going on. That attack was too strange.

Edith tries to hold me back, but I push her off with ease, and draw closer to Queen Alice's throne room.

I'm sick of all of this. I want answers. My boots leave a dirty trail as I storm down the marble hallway. I draw closer to the room where I met the queen for the first time. My heart accelerates and thumps wildly against my chest.

As I come to the junction where the room is, I find everywhere is packed with card soldiers. Some are guarding the door, others are scrambling around; everyone's frantic. There's no need for this behavior now that the beast is gone.

"Off with their heads," the queen screeches from inside the room.

The card soldiers in the hallway all tremble.

"Not again," one of the soldier's whines.

"What's going on?" I rush over to a nearby guard.

"The queen has ordered the beheading of two nobles—Hubert and Humpty Dumpty," he tells me.

"Why?" Those two are the biggest idiots in the world. What could they have possibly done wrong?

"I don't know."

This is getting ridiculous. What is she doing?

The cogs start to turn in my head. Were all the nobles telling the truth?

"I need to see the queen," I demand.

"You can't," the soldier says. "She's busy."

"But..." My brain starts to stutter.

"Everyone, please make your way over to the royal balcony," someone shouts. "The queen has a very important message to give to all the residents."

What's going on?

"My citizens." Alice's voice booms over the crowd, a strident timbre in her voice.

There's a cacophony of applause and cheering, and palpable excitement buzzes through the charged air.

Barely an hour has passed since the battle. My argument with Ace loops through my head and my chest in unbearably tight. Queen Alice, on the other hand, was quick to call for a mandatory emergency meeting.

Which is why I'm here, and not in my bedroom, sleeping off the exhaustion of the fight. Like I can sleep, knowing that Alice wants to behead citizens. No, even worse—*has* beheaded citizens.

The nobles and I are on the castle balcony looking out onto the citizens. I'm seated on a chair in the back. Somehow, I'm stuck with Edith tending to my wounds. She won't leave my side. I really wish she would, because all I want to do is kick her.

Yet something about all of this seems off. The smiles are too wide, the clapping is too loud. Nothing feels genuine.

I shake my head. I'm thinking too much into this. What do I know of crowds? The biggest crowd I've ever been in, before today, was of twenty people, and that's the monthly village meeting Dad refuses to go to. Nothing of interest happens there. Not like this place.

My white clothes are covered in dried blood, dirt and have many cuts and holes in them. I smell like rotten eggs, but I can't shower because I'm forced to listen to this emergency meeting. I try to stifle a yawn.

Edith wipes my hands with a moist tissue, then places an aloe vera ointment onto my skin. I bite back a curse as the cream stings my wounds. She picks up a roll of bandages and wraps it around my left hand, then does the same with my right hand.

I get a bizarre sense of déjà-vu. I did this with the White Rabbit and remembering it gives me a strange pang in my heart.

"Today, we will celebrate." The queen's voice is loud and clear, as if she's standing right next to me. "The Diamonds have been relentless and brought this war to us. I refuse to back down and cower. We are the mighty Hearts of

Wonderland and we are what the land needs to function. The Diamonds are merciless, consumed by greed and power, and we shall not be intimidated by them. Thanks to the Pack of Hearts, we are safe, but for how long? How long can we stand back? Our home was destroyed today, and people have lost their lives, livelihoods and we have suffered many casualties. I will not stand for this. We have recently learned that some people from our Kingdom were working with the Diamond Kingdom to pull this monstrosity off..."

She continues to prattle on at the front the balcony. I don't believe her. If she's talking about Hubert and Humpty, then she's out of her mind.

I recall the Behemoth's words. *This wasn't supposed to happen. This is not what we agreed. She lied. I was not meant to die.*

It's all too convenient. Dad always taught me there's no such thing as coincidences, and something about this feels wrong. Especially after I learned from the card soldiers that Alice had the guards on full alert today.

If she'd known there was going to be an attack, then why didn't the soldiers get to the Behemoth before it entered the city? They could've hardly missed it.

As the queen blabbers on, her words sound too rehearsed.

Did she know something about this? Is she beheading people and using them as scapegoats? Everything about this has the makings of an authoritarian ruler, but it's like no one else seems to notice. Does Ace even realize what's happening?

No, he's distraught over the White Rabbit. Strangely, Alice doesn't seem to care. She hasn't even mentioned his death.

My heart sinks at the thought of Ace. Was I too harsh earlier?

Edith is still treating me. After the speech with the citizens, the nobles and us were forced into the hideous tea party room by the queen. The sight of the cakes makes me want to vomit.

As Edith treats my wounds, I can't help but hiss and scowl at her. The sounds I make remind me of my dad and the home sickness manifests. It also has me thinking of my dad's past, a rather unwelcome side effect.

Queen Alice stands from her table and slides into her authoritarian role with such ease. "My citizens, my role as your queen is to make you happy and with these troubling times ahead, I will not forsake you and let you give up. I will still hold the ball tonight, a grand one that transforms all the negatives to positives, and Wonderland will smile once more."

The people in the room go wild at Alice's speech. Their cheers and whoops resound thunderously in the glass room.

It's disgusting to witness. People have *died*. You mourn the dead, not party.

Alice doesn't care about her people. The White Rabbit was her most loyal follower and she's shown no compassion for him. His poor family, I wonder if they know.

None of this makes any sense. If Alice is so worried about war, she should have security set to the max, not hold a celebration and behead people without proof. She couldn't have gathered proof within an hour. But I can't really say anything against her, which is making my blood boil.

"You shouldn't have gone out there," Edith says softly.

"If I hadn't, you'd be dead," I say.

Edith lowers her head and laughs.

The muscle in my jaw twitches. "Why are you laughing?"

"You're so blunt," she says.

I can't stand not knowing. "What was Ace talking about earlier? About you hating me?"

"He's grieving over Finn, so ignore him. Finn would be devastated to see him like this."

"Finn?"

"The White Rabbit's real name." Edith rolls her eyes. "You didn't know his name?"

I don't reply.

Edith shakes her head. "Lucina, you don't make things easy, do you?"

"Huh?"

Edith scratches her nose. "Okay, let me put it like this. If someone killed your dad, how would you feel?"

"I'd kill them," I reply.

Edith slowly nods her head. "But how would you *feel*?"

How would I feel? Sad, of course. Dad is always there for me except for when he's on one of his trips. But when he's not around, I feel so alone. Because I know he'll be back, I'm okay with him being gone. But if he didn't come back…

My heart jolts, as if someone has stabbed in me in the chest. I'm finding it hard to breathe. I know Ace must be sad, but I never considered the full extent of what his loss would mean.

"Lucina." Queen Alice interrupts my thoughts and hovers over me.

"Your Majesty." I begin to stand.

"Sit down," she says. "You must rest. You were unbelievably brave today."

"It was nothing, Your Majesty."

"You outdid the Pack, and even Ace." The queen wrinkles her nose. "Wherever he is."

"It's what my father would have done." I grunt, and a thought crosses my mind. "Speaking of my father, I was thinking about my mother and I was wondering about the Kingdom of Spades."

"The Kingdom of Spades?" A slight frown appears on Alice's face.

"Yeah. What's it like?" I ask.

"You know, they... wear robes, carry swords... all that stuff," Alice trails off.

"But what's the actual city itself like?" I ask.

Alice's expression becomes eerily familiar, reminding me of someone else. Painful and sharp, it's wrought with pain. Alice bites her teeth together tightly, like the basket dog in the woods every time he sees Dad. Her nose upturns and then her red lips retract and turn into a smile.

"The Kingdom of Spades is off limits to everyone," she says. "Even me."

A single laugh explodes in the room. It grows and becomes louder and louder till it stops and ricochets into a crescendo of lone claps.

I turn to find Hatter. He walks in with a strange swagger I'm not accustomed to and a smile so unbearably wide. His claps become louder and slower until he comes to an abrupt stop in front of the queen.

"There's no place kept from the reigning Heart monarch," Hatter says, his eyes narrowing. "Because you're not the…"

"Quiet!" The queen bangs her fists against the table.

Hatter smirks. "Tell yourself what you have to. It's not like we…"

"What did I say?" The queen's shout reverberates against the room. "Shut up, you pathetic mad man."

"I'm mad in the fun way, unlike you, who is mad with anger," Hatter continues to speak.

"Where was this voice when I needed it?" The queen pokes a finger at Hatter's chest.

"What are you going to do?" Hatter says. "You can't do…"

Edith steps in between Hatter and the queen. "Hatter, I suggest you go get ready for the ball."

The queen sits back down and stares at her nails. "If I'm correct, you're meant to be working on my dress."

"That's sacrilegious." Hatter's voice raises to a strange, strangled pitch.

Edith gives Hatter a sharp look. "Please, just leave."

He only stares back at her, unflinching, until her eyes water with tears.

"For Finn," Edith whispers.

"For Finn." Hatter raises his eyebrows and pats Edith's hand and turns to the queen. "We all love a good party, but you know, Alice, I'm not going to just make a dress for you. I'm going to make one for our young heroine, too."

The queen's eyes widen, pupils dilated. "Oh, really? How nice."

"Isn't it, just." Hatter takes off his enormous hat and curtsies to the queen and then tilts his head my way. "It seems my wife has your measurements."

Before I can beg him not to make me a dress, he struts off.

I watch Hatter leave and find it odd. He is clicking his heels together every now and then. A strange cheer is in his step that wasn't there before. How odd?

Edith's gaze lowers to the floor and a ghost of a smile appears for a single moment. "I think you should go rest," she tells me.

"But I need to ask the queen…"

"She's busy," she cuts off. It's not like she is lying, as I find the queen surrounded by the gentry. "Go rest and get ready for the ball."

I can't be bothered to argue as fatigue takes its toll on me.

Chapter Twelve

I stare at my reflection and I can't help but wonder if my eyesight has been affected by the fight with the Behemoth. The girl staring back at me is not me. She's beautiful.

It's got to be the dress, I tell myself.

It's midnight blue, the color of the sky before the night fully captures it. The skirt is puffy and arranged in three tiers. Thousands of gold crystals shaped like butterflies are scattered around the skirt and farther up the bodice, the crystals disperse to nothing. The bodice has a sweetheart neckline conjoined with a gold necklace that holds it up. There are sleeves—more like gloves—up to my arms, puffy with holes that are shaped like hearts all the way down.

They cover my bandaged hands, still hurting from the fight.

I turn around and gape at my bare back, then face my reflection once more. Tiny gold droplets fall from my ears, and my hair is flowing all around me. Strands of gold beads, moons and stars are woven into it.

What would Dad say if he saw me now?

I can't stop thinking about Edith's words about my dad being killed and how I'd feel. I think I know the answer now. Sad, angry and lonely.

That's what Ace must be feeling. I need to speak to him. Absolve the guilt in my guts. Tell him I'm sorry.

I don't want to go to this ball. Not with everything that happened today. I just don't get its purpose. But there's this nagging voice in my head, not Wonder, that tells me I must go.

The maid places a lacy midnight blue mask on my face. It's delicate with little stars scattered all over it and one big crescent moon on the left side, near my ear.

"Perfect," the maid says, and tears flood her eyes.

I turn around. "Why are you crying?"

The maid shakes her head. "I don't know why I'm crying…"

"I don't understand."

"Neither do I." The maid sniffs and moves me away from the mirror. "Let's get going."

It's getting there that's the problem. I've never walked in heels; I'd rather walk a tightrope and fight my father than wear these shoes. They pinch my toes and the whole walking on a slant is stupid to me. I don't need to be taller. I'm fine as it is.

They said it's just down this hallway. After a few minutes of walking, a large red double door comes into my view.

"*Come get me quickly,*" Wonder says. "*Danger is approaching.*"

Not again, not now. I don't want to fight another Behemoth. I've learned that Wonder, whoever he is, tends to be right, but I don't understand his obsession with me having the crown.

Ace appears out of thin air in a flourish of rose petals. His eyes are puffy and red. Upon spotting me, his eyebrows raise and then lower as his gaze travels down my body before it fixes onto my hands. "Are your hands okay?"

"I'm fine." I hold them up. "There's no blood soaking through."

There's an awkward pause, but I know what I must do. The thing is, I've never apologized to anyone before.

"I'm sorry," I quickly say.

"I'm sorry," he says at the same time.

"Wait, why are you are sorry?" I ask.

"I was horrible to you. Why are you apologizing?" He buries his hands into his pant pockets.

I wrap my arms around me. "I was horrible to you. The White... I mean, Finn was very precious to everyone."

"I shouldn't have said what I said." He's not standing tall like he normally does. Instead, he's hunched over.

"I think I get it," I bite my lip. "I'm not the warmest of people. I can't help it. It's just been me and my dad..."

"You're nothing like the Pack members, I can assure you. Let's just leave it," he says. "What you did today was crazy, you know that, right?"

"Nothing my dad wouldn't do."

"But you did everything without magic."

That's technically not true. I know he pushed me with his magic to get me onto the Behemoth. Plus, if he hadn't reined in all the magical elements on his diamond armor, then it wouldn't have cracked. I wonder what type ended up being the final blow, given diamond is meant to be the strongest material.

"Come on, let's go pretend to enjoy the festivities." He offers his arm.

I like the way he thinks. "Yeah, let's pretend."

Reluctantly, I take Ace's arm. I can hear the music playing; violins, piano, drums, flutes and other instruments all merge together into a beautiful melody.

As we pass the doors Ace whispers shyly, "You look nice."

"Thanks," I say. "You look…"

"I'm wearing my usual uniform," he interrupts.

I laugh and the instant after, slap a hand over my mouth in shock.

"What's wrong?" he asks.

"Nothing," I gasp. It's the first time I've laughed out loud with Ace and it makes my heart lurch and warmth spreads across my chest.

"*This way, Lucina,*" Wonder says. "*Come, come quickly.*"

"What's wrong?" Ace asks. "Your cheeks are flushed."

I can't say anything about Wonder's constant calling in my head. It would only make me sound insane.

"This way, quickly."

Where to? *The crown*, I think to myself.

"The crown means nothing," Wonder continues. *"Come quickly."*

"Nervous," Ace says.

I nod. He walks me farther into the room and everyone's staring at me. The whispers start. I wish I could go back to my room and continue to get some much-needed rest, but Wonder won't leave me alone.

"I have to leave you, I have an errand to run," he says and then stops. "But I'll be back, so save me a dance."

"Okay."

I just want to run away from here. Once again, I wonder what my dad would think of me in this dress. He'd probably laugh.

"This way," Wonder says.

I'm going insane like the rest of the people in this castle.

"Lady Lucina," a walrus Beastian waiter says. "Here, have a drink?"

I stare at the tray. It has a dozen tiny milk bottles on it, with pink bubbling liquid in them.

I take one and find Candy and Hatter standing in front of me.

"Didn't I tell you that dress would like nice on her? You never listen to me." Hatter walks up beside me.

"She's so beautiful," Candy says.

"Be careful."

I scan the room, but nothing sparks my suspicion.

"Everything all right, dear?" Hatter asks.

I nod. My go-to reaction to most situations these days.

"You seem flushed," Candy says.

All the eyes on me are making me uncomfortable, and I wish Hatter and Candy had provided me with a dress that didn't draw as much attention as this one. A simple one would have sufficed, though I think I'd still have a lot of attention on me despite my outfit, what with all the bruises and bandages.

The room is filled with people in outfits ranging from delicate to ridiculously absurd. Hatter is dressed all in green. Unlike me, he likes to stand out. There are so many people in this room, it's unbearable. I've never seen so many jammed together so tightly. And the voices... It feels as if I can actually hear their thoughts.

"Look at her."

"She looks familiar."

"Who is she?"

A hand waves in front of me—it's Candy. "Where did you go just now?"

"Overwhelmed," I manage to say. That's an understatement.

"Why don't you dance?" Hatter says.

"I can't," I reply. More like I never tried.

The music seems to be getting louder and, with it, the voices in my head intensify.

I really want my dad. Yeah, he's not great at the emotional stuff, but neither am I. Also, there seems to be problem with my mental state and with him here, I know

I'd be okay. He'd do something. I know he loves me; he just has a strange way of showing it. If he were here, I also wouldn't feel as out of place. I'd at least have someone to accompany me in my thoughts of this ridiculous event.

It's too much. The lights, the chandeliers, the food... everyone. I'm not cut out for this.

"Come on, I can teach you?" Hatter holds out his hand.

"You can do it, Lucina, it's in your blood."

"Dad can dance?" I query, bemused by the whole statement.

"Pardon?" Hatter seems taken aback.

"Nothing."

Candy grabs his hand. "Come, darling, let's dance. Lucina is tired, she needs her space."

"Of course," Hatter nods. "We'll talk to you later, Lucina."

I don't know how much time has passed, but I've found myself in a corner, desperately trying to block out the voices in my head. I can't seem to understand anything that is going on around me and within myself.

"Lucina, please listen, there's not enough time."

I shake my head.

"Dance with me?"

Ace is standing before me with his hand out. He gestures with his head to the dance floor.

"I don't know how."

Ace winks. "It's not hard, just follow your heart."

Cheshire said that to me before. Maybe Ace is lying about knowing him? Yet there is something about the way Ace is looking at me that spreads warmth across my chest.

Those sharp features have gone, and softness has replaced them. Like I'm a delicate rose.

More importantly, there is silence in my head. No voices.

And with that, my hand touches his. He's warm and his fingers are soft. He guides me to the dance floor, and I can't see anything but him, surrounded by the bright light.

The music stops briefly, and a slower song starts to play. He spins me and then places my arm around his neck before placing his around my back. I gasp at his touch. His bare fingers on my skin. Something I'm not used to. He lifts up my other arm and our free hands intertwine.

The nerves in my body take over as his feet begin to move. He whisks me away into a dance I do not want to be a part of. I stifle my own movement, hoping Ace will give up and understand that I have two left feet. He laughs and forces me along. A few stumbling motions later, we collide into another couple.

"Hey, watch where you're going!" The man calls out. It's Hatter and Candy.

"I'm sorry." I feign an apology and curtesy.

"First time dancing," Hatter says and smiles. "The trick is to not give up."

Too late, the humiliation has got to me, and my cheeks are hot. Voices come out of nowhere and escalate in my head.

"*That girl, she can't dance.*"

"*Pretty to the eye, but no substance.*"

"*Knave's daughter, she is. She's got his feet.*"

They can make fun of me, but not my father. Before I can make my escape, Ace grabs my sleeve. He gives me an encouraging smile.

"Where's the queen?" I ask.

"Who cares? Relax, Lucina," Ace says. "Give into your heart, stop overthinking it. Just have fun."

I don't know how to have fun. I'm the Knave of Hearts' daughter. While it was hard to accept, at first, I can't deny it. The longer I've spent here has only proven what everyone else said about my dad. None of that takes away from what he taught me, and how I grew up. Fun, for me, is and always will be fighting or making a sword. And I have Dad to thank for that.

I glance around the room and everyone's back to doing whatever they were doing before. No eyes on me.

Ace holds out his hand, insistent even after that embarrassing incident. His blue eyes plead with me and my chest pounds. It's not painful. More like an encouraging beat.

I place my hand on his shoulder once again. After a few beats go by, we begin anew.

I allow him to take the lead and the next thing I know, I'm matching his movements with such ease. We move as light as air, passing the twin stairs leading up to the stage. The music of the orchestra carries us between the colonnades and the hanging flower arrangements. We prance and twirl to the jovial waltz as if we were born to dance to it.

I think I'm smiling. I'm not sure, as I feel a strange sensation in my heart. It's something very new to me. It reminds me of being a little girl opening presents on my birthday.

The orchestra's melody comes to an end and Ace pulls me close to him. "See? You can do anything as long as you listen to your heart. It will never steer you wrong."

There's a bang and I jolt. Not another attack. Above in the skyline, I find beautiful flower patterns. Fireworks, not an attack.

"Hey, this was quite fun," he says, gazing over my shoulder. "But I have to go, the queen wants me."

He's about to leave when he takes my hand and places it on my heart. "Listen to it. Don't be scared of it."

I can only bring myself to nod as he leaves me on the dance floor. Warmth crushes over my fingers where his hands had touched mine.

"Lucina." I recognize the voice.

I turn and lower my gaze. "Yes, Candy."

"You are a wonderful dancer," she says. "Where did you learn to dance like that? Certainly not from your father."

"From here," I say and place my hand on my heart.

Chapter Thirteen

A trumpet bellows. The Red Squirrel appears at the top of the stairs dressed in a black tuxedo. Heads whip around. The room switches from carefree conversations into an eerie silence.

She's already replaced Finn. What's wrong with her? It's only been a few hours. Doesn't she have any compassion? Does she even care?

No, of course not. She beheads individuals without a fair trial when beheading shouldn't be the answer. No wonder everyone's questioning her. She's a terrible queen.

"Hear ye, hear ye," he shouts out. "May I have your attention, please?"

"Hurry up," a female whispers from behind the door.

I think it's the Duchess. "Stop being so slow."

The Red Squirrel wrinkles his nose. "I would like to introduce our honored hostess, the Queen of Hearts."

The doors open and the queen steps out in a scoop neck cardinal red dress. Its corset is embellished with lace flowers and petals, and its cathedral train has sequins flashing down the side. Her arms are fully covered in billowy netting and her nails are bedazzled with actual rubies. Her hair is pulled up into a spiraling tower of curls, streaks of gold running through it, leading to the Heart Crown—the tiara.

My breath hitches. The crowd goes wild at the queen's entrance. Their cheers and whoops resound thunderously through the ballroom. The queen bats her eyelashes and softly waves her hands. The Duchess and the Pack follow behind her.

One of the servers scurries over. The man swallows, his eyes flicking down the hall. "We didn't expect you so soon, Your Majesty."

Without looking, she grabs a cocktail, her lips pouting into a dainty sip. The queen blots the corner of her lips with a napkin provided by the Duchess.

The crown sits pathetically on her head, so small. It shines under all the spotlights, the little ruby crystals twinkling at me. I clench my jaw, trying to control the bizarre feelings bubbling within me.

'That's not her crown," Wonder says.

Watching Alice raise her hand to silence her adoring subjects makes me angry. It bubbles along with the pain I have from the fight with the Behemoth.

She doesn't care about her people. It's all about her. If

anything, she likes the idea of seeing people miserable. I mean, it's absurd. She's having a ball after all that devastation, she separates couples, marrying them off in mismatched pairings, and she beheads people on a whim!

"There's more to your anger," Wonder says. *"You can't see it yet."*

"Thank you," Alice says, her voice all sugary sweet. "I'm so happy you could all make it here tonight."

"She is not she. Look at her." Wonder's voice rises with fury.

The queen is perfect, from her figure, to the angles on her face, to her posture and her skin. I swear it's carved from the same marble as the pillars in the room.

"My citizens, the Heart Kingdom's capital, Atria, has suffered a devastating attack from the Diamond Kingdom. They came into our home, destroyed our buildings, hurt our people, *my* people. But today, we will celebrate." The queen's voice is loud and clear as if she's standing right next to me. "Though we are on the verge of war with the despicable Diamonds, I refuse to back down and cower. Our traditions will not be interrupted, we will go on. We will celebrate and after all this, we will show them we are a force to be reckoned with. We will show them the extent of our power."

The crowd roars.

Extent of our power. I repeat those words in my head. What an odd phrasing? It's not about power, it's about doing what's right for Wonderland.

There is something arrogant in the way she talks, the way she carries herself, that doesn't sit well with me.

"She's exposed. Look at her."

Exposed. How?

"Look!"

At Wonder's insistence, I stare at Alice for what feels like the longest time. Nothing appears different; her blue eyes are sparkling, her smile is still wide, and her teeth are so perfectly straight.

Then the crown on her head catches the light as the spotlight falls down onto the queen and I gasp. I blink to make sure what I'm seeing is real. I shut my eyes, to make sure I'm not imagining it all, then open them again.

"Lies can't be hidden from the heart."

The queen continues to speak, but none of her words reach me. A different woman stands before me.

"I told you." Wonder's voice is full of glee. *"You finally see her for what she truly is."*

Alice is a woman with long, wavy gray hair that's tied up in a bun at the back of her head in a desperate attempt to hide the obvious bald spot. Her old, wrinkled skin sags down her face. She has age-spots that make her skin seem like it has been stained with tea and her jowls hang a good inch below her chin.

"By my sword," I whisper.

She's an illusion and the longer I stare, the more her true features are revealed.

I search the expressions on others' faces to see if they are seeing what I am. They are all still enraptured by the queen.

My search stops on Ace, who's leaning against a wall, his gaze on me. When our eyes meet, he straightens up and a slow smile spreads upon his lips. I turn away from him. Is this what I'm not seeing?

Conversations from my first day here resurface. They talked about people using magic to amplify their features and they also mentioned how the queen made rare appearances.

The puzzle starts to fit together—she makes less appearances. I wasn't seeing all of it, just like Ace and Edith said.

"Take the crown."

The crown on the queen's head twinkles as she continues to prattle on about something.

"It's not hers."

I know, because monarchs of Wonderland don't age. But what am I supposed to do about it?

"Take it. "

How?

"Your heart."

I place a hand over my chest and start to breathe.

"Call for it."

"Come to me," I whisper under my breath.

The crown on the old queen's head swirls and floats up into the air. The gold slickens, melts and becomes larger, the rubies grow and one of them takes a heart shape.

Alice blinks, confusion flashing over her face. A beautiful tall crown has now emerged with large rubies glimmering all around it.

"Take it."

A blast of air shoots past me, whipping strands of my hair against my face. Screams fill the air, and the crowd scatters in panic and confusion. The violent air pushes everyone to either side. I plant my feet firmly and refuse to budge as the wind rages through. It's bitter and cruel against my flushed cheeks.

The Pack members come to Alice's aid and form a circle around her. The Pack member with the whip, Three, tries to grab the crown with its weapon. The whip is zapped by lightning and goes back and slashes its owner.

The crown continues to spin, omitting an obscene amount of light.

The wind rotates around the room, whistling in high-pitched sounds. Streaks of light splinter throughout and a deafening crack of thunder follows. The crown rises farther up into the air.

"What's going on?" Alice screams.

The floor begins to shake, and it rocks beneath my feet, yet still I manage to stand my ground.

A tingle fills the air, and the room is haunted by magic.

"Ace!" Alice shouts, tugging onto a member of the Pack.

Ace appears in front of her and disappears, taking her and all members of the Pack out of the room. The crown starts to spin faster.

"Call for it."

At a curt flick of my fingers, the sharp tang of magic streams from the ground, into my toes, and all around my body. It pulses warmth beneath my skin.

This is unlike any other magic I've come across. It feels right, so pure. How can this be?

The crown flies over to me, still spinning. It hovers over me, stops spinning and lowers until it softly lands on my head.

The wind disappears until it's nothing more than a mere breeze. The room is destroyed, chandeliers are smashed on the floor, statues have fallen over and only a handful of people remain standing.

Voices cry out. And this time, there is no confusion, there is no confliction; the words are all the same.

"All hail the true Heart."

"All hail the true queen."

There may be no confusion in the voices but there's too much confusion within me.

Looking around, the world seems different, as if there's more color.

Hatter walks over to me, tilting his head. When his gaze meets mine, he smiles, revealing bright white teeth. He steps forward and kneels in front of me.

"Finally," he chokes out in a whisper, tears pricking his green eyes. "Forgive me, we couldn't tell you. Those of us who knew, we couldn't do anything—the magic bound us, stopped us from telling you outright. I almost gave up even when you came, I couldn't bring myself to have hope. I should have never doubted. You must understand, we've lived in so much pain."

"What?" The word comes out like a croak.

Hatter stands. "The crown never lies."

He delves his hand into the inside pocket of his jacket and pulls out some sort of compact. He opens it up and it's a mirror and then he turns it toward me. I'm met with red eyes.

"They're red again." I gasp for air, feeling myself go dizzy. "What does this mean?"

"You know what it means." Candy appears from behind a pillar. Her hair is a mess.

The gaping pit in my stomach balloons with mounting horror.

Candy looks over at Hatter. "She needs to get out of here."

Hatter nods. "Ace can only keep Alice at bay for so long."

"We don't have long." Candy grabs my hands. "I really wanted to tell you. Poor Edith tried, but couldn't."

"Lucina!"

I recognize that cry. Edith runs into the room; her lilac dress is ripped short and she has a sword in her hand. "The Pack are coming for you."

Hatter grabs my hand and waves Edith over. "Get her out through the secret passages."

Edith nods and grabs my hands and smiles widely. "Come, Your Majesty. Can't believe I'm finally allowed to say it."

"Protect her with your life," Hatter tells her.

Edith nods. "Always."

She takes me over to the back of the room where Daniel is.

He, like everyone else, smiles at me. "Stay safe, princess." He presses his hand onto a black tile near a pillar and curses. "Dammit! It's stuck."

Hatter comes running along and pushes at it with Daniel. After a few moments, the tiles slide over, revealing a hatch. Daniel fully takes over and grunts, pulling at it until it finally swings open.

A dark tunnel looms before me.

"I don't understand," I say, my fingers trembling. "Why is the crown on me? Why do I have to run?"

"You know, sweetheart. You are the true ruler of Wonderland. I'm not the one who should explain this to you. There's another." Hatter cups my face, and his hands are warm and sweaty. "Get her out of here."

"But why..."

"Because you're not your full self yet and until you are, we will protect you."

I glance back. Everyone has gathered weapons from the walls. Some are using trays as shields, bottles as swords.

"I can fight..." I begin.

"No, not yet," Hatter says. His green eyes begin to spin, turning gold. "Now go."

My feet are already moving on their own, and then I'm climbing down the hatch. There is so much more I want to say. I'm struggling to find the words. Nothing is coming out of me. It's as if my breath has been taken away and my body is moving on its own. I continue down the ladder of steps with Edith following me.

"Follow your heart," Hatter shouts after me.

Darkness takes over as I go farther down the ladder.

Chapter Fourteen

dith scurries ahead down the dark passage where the temperature continues to drop. The faint light comes from small crystals hanging on the sides. The lights flicker, casting an ominous glow throughout. I drag my hand across the wall, the jagged teeth of the stones, picking up cobwebs and dust.

"Hurry up, Lucina," Edith cries out.

It's not my fault. It's these stupid heels. I'm like a newborn gazelle, struggling to maintain my balance. Unable to bear this torture anymore, I lift my dress and move my feet up and down until the heels begin to slip off. I swing each leg and my shoes hurtle forward, almost hitting Edith.

"What is wrong with you?" Edith snaps. "Stop messing

around and get a move on."

"Where are we going?"

"To get you out of the capital," Edith scoffs.

"Why are you helping me?" I ask. "Don't you hate me?"

Edith stops in her tracks and makes a disgruntled noise. "I don't hate you."

"Really?" I roll my eyes.

"I don't," she hisses, refusing to turn around. She straightens her shoulders. "I know it's not your fault, okay? Now just drop the subject and keep moving. We have far more important things to worry about."

Edith moves on and all I can do is follow.

"Does anyone know about these tunnels? Will they find us?" I ask. She may have asked me to drop one subject but it's not going to stop me from asking questions.

"No," she grunts. "Alice and her people don't know about the secret passages."

"But what about everyone else? Will they be safe? Shouldn't we help them?"

"They don't matter." Edith spins around and places her cold hands on my bare shoulders. "If we're to get separated or we come under attack, you must promise to leave me behind and get to safety."

"That's absurd."

"I don't matter, only you matter, so you must promise me." She trips over her words in her desperation. Her eyes glisten as she shakes me. "You are Wonderland's one true ruler and only you can save us. I know this is all a lot to take in and it's all so confusing, but you must survive, or we're all doomed."

"I..." I stutter.

"Promise!"

"Okay," I nod.

"Say it." She shakes me.

"I promise."

"Good, it's binding now."

"What?"

Edith's eyes flash with worry and her nails dig ever so slightly into my shoulders. "You must listen to that voice inside you, you understand?"

"You know about Wonder..."

"Who?"

"The voice who keeps talking to me."

She gives a pained smile and takes her hands off me. "I don't know the specifics, but I know every ruler has it. It never guides them wrong... or so we thought. It doesn't matter, we have to go."

"But how can I be Wonderland's ruler?" I ask.

Edith drops her gaze, frowning, and starts to move. "It's not my place to tell you, and we don't have the time. But it will be explained soon enough, so stop talking and keep moving."

She rushes on ahead and I trail behind her. The tunnel grows narrower and narrower until we come to a short, wooden staircase. Edith takes my hand and helps me up the stairs.

"Everyone is going to be okay, right?" My heartbeat rages in my ears.

She sighs and shrugs. "I'm sure they will be fine." Even in the dim light, I can tell Edith is lying. Her breathing is heavier and she's pulling on her earlobe.

As we reach the top, we encounter another hatch. Edith carefully pushes it. It lets out a squeak and rattles as it opens. She pops her head out and scans the area.

"The coast is clear," Edith asserts.

She gets out and then helps me, grabbing parts of my dress in order for me to squeeze out. We're greeted by fruit trees, perfectly aligned and glowing under the moonlight.

We're at the orchard, so it means we've travelled quite a distance.

"They're going to cover all exits," Edith says, still inspecting the area. Her breath comes out shallow. "We need another route out. One they don't know about."

"*Run!*" Wonder shouts.

The tiny hairs at the back of my neck rise. "We need to go, now."

The clanging of metal armor grabs our attention. It's a Pack member, number Ten. It's at the other end of the orchard and before we can avoid its detection, it has seen us.

"Run!" Edith tells me and brings up her sword.

"No," I tell her. "Do you even know how to use a sword?'

"A little." Edith pushes me back with a hand. I almost fall over. "If you don't run, then we are all doomed. Do it for me, do it for Wonderland."

"No! Let me fight, I'm good."

"I know, but you're not complete yet."

"Complete?"

"Not now." Edith pushes me again, and tears start streaming down her face. "Please run, don't let our deaths be in vain."

"I'm not going anywhere." I refuse to let her be a martyr.

She narrows her eyes on me, shivering and clenching her jaw. "I command you to run as per your promise."

The air falls heavy with magic. It spreads above us like it's glitter and twinkles like the stars in the sky.

"No!" I gasp as my legs move on their own. Magic is forcing me to flee the scene.

"Run, this way," Wonder cries out.

Before I can ask which way, a path lights up on the ground in front of me. My feet slip outward on the wet grass as I dart around from tree to hedge, to tree, to the pebbled walkway and back to the grass. The cold evening air shocks my throat and lungs as I inhale deeper, faster. My ears perk up at every sound.

My heart drops when there's a scream. It's so sharp and tortured, the hairs at the back of my neck rise. I want to stop, but I can't. It has to be Edith. Her screams echo as my legs refuse to listen to me. Anger rises up and hot tears slide down my face, stinging my eyes. My feet swish against the grass. I have no idea where I'm going, but my lungs burn, and my legs feel like lead. I want to stop and take a breath, but the magic prevents me from doing so.

This is just a bad dream, I tell myself. It can't be real.

"Come on. This way."

I follow Wonder's light to the maze.

"I can't go in here," I whisper, remembering Ace's words. I can't quite stop, the magic still propels me on, so I'm left running on the spot.

"You couldn't then, but you can now. It's safe."

There's no point fighting Wonder or the magic Edith

has used. Deep down, I've known all along. It's all my fault for denying it in the first place.

I rush forward into the tall hedge maze. The pebbles crash against my feet like water rippling. The shade of the hedges appears darker against the faint light of the moon. The colors of the garden are not as vivid as they are from my bedroom window. Glancing upward, more clouds emerge, and they remind me of clustered dust. The overpowering scent of roses takes over but the crisp smell of lemon wafts through in small bursts.

As I run along, my hand reaches out and touches the red-as-blood roses. I'm expecting the soft texture of velvet, only to be met with the slippery texture of rubber. It's not real, just like Cheshire said, though he didn't say it in those exact words.

I gasp—but the smell! I stop and bend down to smell a rose. Sprinkles of liquid squirt onto my nose and even manage to find themselves up my nostrils. It burns, making me tear up once again.

"Keep running."

I do as Wonder says and soon find myself in the middle of the maze, staring up at the statue of a man.

"Who is that?" I ask. "Why are we here?"

"The King of Hearts."

He seems molded from a different cast, with an androgynous appearance uncommon to most. The moon's light shimmers on the stone like lacquer on wood. I close my eyes as a glint of light shines onto them. When I open them again, I see the statue's irises are bright rubies.

"Blood. Place a drop of your blood on the statue."

"What? Why?"

"*Please.*"

Again with the politeness. I'm such a pushover.

"Where?"

Strangely, I'm already moving. I take the brooch off my dress and use the pin on it to prick my finger.

"*The heart.*"

With a little stretch of my arm, I place my bloodied finger on the statue's heart. Nothing happens. Then I hear the reverberations of the iron cogs turning and the ground around the statue collapses slightly. I step back and a circle of light beams from under the stone base; the statue rises and moves, and the stone scratches against the other stone. I clench my jaw at the scraping sounds.

There is a tunnel—it goes straight down for some way, appearing to have no end. I search around for a ladder.

"*Jump.*"

Really? In this outfit?

"*Jump.*" Wonder is more urgent, almost desperate.

Jump to my doom. Yes, perhaps I am going mad since everyone's mad here.

"*No, you won't die. I promise.*"

I clench my teeth together. The dark has never bothered me, neither have heights. It's the unknown that bothers me.

"*Please jump.*"

I will regret doing this and so I close my eyes, curse under my breath and take a leap of faith. Either I'm falling down a deep tunnel or at an incredibly slow rate. I come to understand it's my puffy underskirts. They're acting like an umbrella, floating me down slowly.

My ballgown proves to be more of an asset than a hindrance. In addition to the unexpected help with the descent, a sudden light emits from the gold on my dress that allows me to see in the dark.

On the sides of the tunnel, I find cupboards filled with cups and saucers, herbs and spices, cutlery, and so much more. There are also bookshelves filled with titles I have never heard of. Odd titles like *Pride and Prejudice, Frankenstein* and *Great Expectations*. Colorful pictures and maps hang upon pegs. The maps are not of Wonderland. I may not have any sense of direction, but I know what a map of Wonderland looks like and I've never heard of the locations these depict: Africa, Europe, Asia, South America.

This reminds me of that dream I had where I was falling, and I heard Cheshire and Ace talking.

Down, down, down I go.

Will the fall never end?

I see a jar labelled *orange marmalade*. I've never tried it, so I gingerly open the lid since I have eaten nothing at the ball. Placing my finger in the jar, I scoop some of it out and dab it on my tongue. It's sharp, tangy and all of a sudden, bitter. Never again. I quickly put the lid back on and place the jar into one of the cupboards I pass.

Down, down, down.

I continue to fall and I'm getting pretty fed up.

I catch glimpses of pictures of a cat with the name Dinah written under it when suddenly— Thump! Thump! Down I crash onto a pile of clothes.

Why are there clothes here? I pick up a pair of trousers and dump them in disgust. I dust myself off and I'm shocked there isn't a scratch or a bump on me.

I tilt my head up. It's dark overhead and before me is another long passage.

Great! Wasn't there an easier route?

"Don't give up."

Despite the breeze, the passage is warm. I go forward and turn a corner and before me is another long dark hallway. As I walk down it, the candles ignite, one by one, and I find I'm walking on a red carpet. With more light, I can make out pictures on the walls.

Each picture has a portrait of a different man or woman wearing the Heart Crown. Each one is uniquely beautiful in their own way. My heart thuds against my chest. It's getting warmer.

I follow the pictures, taking in each individual I pass. It's odd they are all young in appearance and they all have bright red glowing eyes. The same red eyes as mine.

I shake my head to clear the thoughts and continue on. Now is not the time to ponder. There's a light at the end of the passage and as I get closer, I discover a golden drawbridge.

That's odd. There's no moat or anything else around it. Why put it there?

I take a step forward and the drawbridge comes down. My stomach churns. I can't stop now and so I press forward. My feet clang against the gold, and the sound reverberates around me.

As I step into the opulent room, I'm met with an absurdly large chandelier hanging from the ceiling. It almost touches the ground.

"Lucina," some man cries out and gasps. "My Lucina."

The room is cavernous with countless doors, all of different sizes, colors and shapes. Where's the person who was calling out for me?

"*Go. You're safe. I promise. Hurry.*"

Wonder's words give me the courage to continue. He hasn't strayed me wrong so far.

I rush down the room, past all the randomly placed doors and past a ginormous three-legged glass table with a golden key on it. It must be around fifty feet tall. I don't understand the logic for it.

"Lucina!" the man cries out.

I continue along what feels like an endless room. And suddenly I find a man, slumped down and chained to a huge red door, about twenty feet high. He's the physical manifestation of the statue I came down from—the King of Hearts. He hasn't aged the slightest, but his face is tired, and his hair is disheveled.

He gasps and holds his hands out.

I kneel to meet his gaze. "Are you the one who's been speaking to me?"

"No, that is Wonderland," he says. His eyes soften. "You look just like your mother."

"I don't understand. How do you know my mother? Why are you down here? I thought you were dead."

"Lucina." He takes a long breath, and his eyes are steady upon my face. "You're my daughter. You're the Princess of Hearts, the true heir to Wonderland."

I lean back and blink at him in confusion. I catch the

plates on the floor with discarded food; it smells like croissants, and his chains are old and rusty. He's been here for a while, so he's most likely delirious.

I shake my head. "My dad's the Knave."

The king lowers his head and scrunches his face. "That's what... We had to protect you. If Alice found out, she would've had you killed. Just like your mother."

He spits Alice's name out like he's eaten something rotten.

None of this makes any sense. I rub my head to try to process, but all it does is add to the confusion.

"Lucina, we have little time and if I don't give you the first piece of your heart, Wonderland will be destroyed." His eyes soften and he stares at me with watery eyes. "There are so many things I want to say to you. I've thought about this moment for so long and now I can't seem to find the words. But what I really want you to know is how much I love you and how there isn't a single moment that I haven't thought about you."

I pinch myself. Am I having some strange dream? This can't be real. I'm just a weird girl from a village that no one has heard of, with a father who scowls a lot.

"Your mother transferred you into Midori, a friend of hers, who like your mother, was from the Spade Kingdom." He wipes his eyes with his thumbs. Midori gave birth to you."

"Transfer?" I feel lost in a storm of confusion. "How is that possible?"

"Magic," he says and his gaze hovers over my hands.

"Of course." I roll my eyes. "But how did this all happen?

"You have pianist hands like your grandma."

I lift up my hands. They aren't like Dad's, which are burly. The only thing Dad and I have in common are the callouses.

"You're even more beautiful than I imagined." He grins. "You take after me."

A laugh spills out of me. "I'm covered in bandages, cuts and bruises still from the fight with the Behemoth."

"Yes, I know I must sound corny." He smiles. "But you're beautiful, bandages and all."

Dad never said that to me.

"Listen to your heart—you know I'm not lying. You wouldn't be able to speak with Wonderland if you weren't my child. And your eyes are red like mine." The king holds out his hand with deep longing in his eyes. The chains jingle at his movement.

No, none of this makes any sense. Wonderland is not a person.

"No, I am Wonderland. I am Wonder."

But my eyes weren't red, not until now. I can't even comprehend…

"The crown has chosen you," he goes on.

I'd forgotten about the crown. My hands go up and touch it; heat radiates into my fingertips. How has it stayed on?

Thump. Thump.

My heart pounds so loudly that my ear drums could break. I grab my chest. What's going on?

"Lucina, touch my hand. Let the truth flow through you," the king says. "Your mind is battling your heart. Let your heart in."

What do I do? Every heartbeat gets stronger and louder. I can barely hear anything.

"You can trust him."

What other choice do I have?

I stretch out my hand and the tips of my fingers tingle as I get closer to him. A feeling like no other courses through me. A feeling I've never understood. As our fingers touch, an energy, no, a *power* floods inside me. It's like fire and ice all at once. Thoughts, feelings, emotions flow through me and none are my own.

For a while, I can't decipher what it is and then the realization dawns on me: it's Wonderland. The people, the plants, the buildings, the sky, the sea. It's all in me.

The King of Hearts stares at me with soft eyes, ones of love. He's my father. He wasn't lying. His whole life rushes through me and not just his, but every monarch of Wonderland. Their joys from new life, their pains from death, their differences in appearances and values, their loves—all of it is mine to view.

It's so much. It's too much.

I hurl forward and snatch him in a hug, holding him tight as tears flow freely down my cheeks. It all makes sense.

"Lucina," he says, his voice ragged. "I've got a lot to tell you."

"What is it?" I pull away from him.

"You need to reclaim the throne. Alice can't rule, she's not the rightful heir and because of that, the magic is dying. When the magic is completely depleted, Wonderland will cease to exist."

"How did she come to rule in the first place? How did you get imprisoned?"

"It's such a long story." He closes his eyes, leans back and sighs. "It's all my fault. Your mother and Cheshire warned me. Even Mads warned me. But, I didn't listen. I like to see the good in everyone, even from a heart I can't read."

"What happened?"

He straightens up and looks behind me. "I suppose he'll be able to keep them at bay for a little longer."

"What?"

He takes my hands and holds them tight. "You may know that Alice is not from Wonderland, so I have no idea what she's thinking or feeling. The first time she came, she was a child, and everything was fine. She really seemed to like Wonderland. The second time she visited, she went to the Red and White Kingdoms and all was well. Then she came back a third time, as a young woman. I had been married to your mother for two years by then, the happiest years of my life. At first, everything was fine. Then little discords started to happen."

"What do you mean?" I'm enjoying the warmth of his hands. Dad's never held me like this. He's never hugged me.

The king pulls a face. "First it was simple miscommunications, then the strange rumors started to spread, which led to outright lies. Then the civilians I devoted myself to turned against me."

"I don't understand how Alice could do this."

His clutches my hands intensely. "She twisted them with her magic. She won the public over with it. Providing them with their deepest desires and supplying their egos. Problem is her magic is from a dark place and it's dangerous. She knew this and so taught everyone how to use magic and from there it started to drain Wonderland and me."

"How did she teach them how to use magic? I mean, couldn't anyone else have taught them? Why hasn't this happened before?"

"When you twist hearts, the people and magic become corrupt and Wonderland crumbles. The only way to set everything right once more is for you to take the throne."

"But why me?"

"Your blood, my blood, we are essentially Wonderland. Our Ancestor, Arexus di Fortem ex Coeur created Wonderland and in doing so he bonded himself with it. Thus, Wonderland's life exists due to our blood." He kisses my hands. "All you need to know is that Alice's blood is poisoning Wonderland, especially since she's not from here. Someone else will explain more, but I need you to know that everyone was bound by magic and they couldn't tell you about your real heritage."

"Edith tried to tell me, so did Cheshire." I gasp and start shaking. "Oh, my, everyone tried to tell me, even Ace. No wonder he was angry at me over the White Rabbit's death. That's why Cheshire told to me to look and to listen."

I feel so stupid now. Edith wasn't insulting me that one time, either; she was trying to tell me the Knave wasn't my father.

"It's okay." The king grabs my face. "It's not anyone's fault. Magic forbade it. I suppose it was for your protection."

"Did Alice bind everyone with magic?"

"No," he says, his voice is grave and quavers. "Alice

doesn't know about your existence. It was another."

"Who?" I please.

"I can't tell you." His voice breaks. "Magic has bound it."

"This isn't fair." A single tear slips past my eyelashes, rolling hot down my cheek.

"Don't cry, sweetheart." He rubs the tear away and presses his forehead against mine. "You've got to be strong. I know it's hard, but you have to be."

I gasp; my throat burns.

"It's okay. There are others who can help you. Cheshire, for instance. He's been your mother's pet since childhood, and you can trust him. He will help you."

"Where is he?"

"Alice had him blocked off from the Heart Castle, but since Alice's magic has been waning, he's been managing to get through the barriers, though not for long. And the last time he was here, he used a lot of his magic on you. He's just resting up."

"But why?"

"Because you're part Spade and part Heart, both your magics were conflicting, but that won't be a problem anymore..."

I suddenly think of my dad.

"What about my dad...I mean the Knave...I mean Dad, I don't know... Where is he? Why isn't he there? Is he okay?"

The king's lips make a strange shape, and the words slur out of him. "He's a tactician at heart. He's thinking of what to do. Trying to find the best way to save you without alerting Alice to your real heritage."

"But he's okay."

"Yes, he's fine." The king shifts his gaze. "Anyway, you have to find the Spade Kingdom."

"What? Why?"

"Your mother was originally the Queen of Spades." He closes his eyes. "She gave up her position to be my wife. I should've made her stay in the Spade Kingdom. If I had, she'd be alive. Her brother was right. I ended up being her downfall."

Tears prick his eyes, threatening to spill over. I don't know what to say. Curiosity burns at me, demanding he tell me, but on another hand... I don't want to know. Another time. Not now.

My eyes lock onto my father's dirty chains and it dawns on me.

"How long have you been here?" I spit out, staring at his disheveled form. "Why hasn't someone tried to rescue you?"

"*Watch out!*"

"Watch out for what?" I speak.

My father looks at me apologetically. "You'll get used to Wonderland talking to you. One perk of being a Heart monarch. It becomes comforting, I promise you."

I stare at the chains on my father's wrists and ankles and follow them as they all go into separate holes through the door. Why don't they open the door and...?

"You can't undo them, Lucina, not yet," he says. "This door isn't real, it's just a way to syphon my power to keep Wonderland alive."

"Then how do I save you?" I scream.

My whole life has been a lie and they expect me to sit back and do nothing. I need to save him. No, *them*. Both my fathers. The king and the Knave.

He smiles and lowers his head. "You have your mother's determination and temper, but I have little time. I'm dying."

"No, no, no," I cry out. "I've just found you. I can't lose you, too. Please, no."

"Lucina, listen. I can't sustain Wonderland much longer. You must take the reins and rule, but you can't without your heart. Once you have your heart, you can save me."

I find myself laughing. "What? I have a heart."

"Well, technically, you do. When I talk about your heart, I mean your lifeforce, your essence, what makes you the Princess of Hearts," my father continues. "We took out your heart before we placed you in Midori. We split it into four pieces when we recognized Alice was a danger. I have one piece, the Spade Kingdom has another, the Caterpillar knows of one's whereabouts and the last piece is with the Jabberwocky. You need the other three pieces before you can go to the Jabberwocky."

"*Danger!*" Wonder cries out.

"But if I didn't have a heart then I'd be emotionless, right?" Ace had accused me of being heartless. Could this be why?

"No, you'd be the same person, but we don't have time for this." He pulls his hand into his chest and a little crystal heart appears. "This is the first piece of your heart."

I stare at it. It shimmers and shines radiantly like a

small glittering sun. It's a red diamond that beats. That's my heart, but it's nothing like I imagined it would be. Then again, it's not normal for anyone to see their heart.

"I have to find the Jabberwocky." There's a tremor in my voice. The monster that everyone fears. "Isn't it dangerous?"

"No, she's loyal to true Heart royals." He smiles and holds the heart out.

I stare at it, frozen once again.

"Sweetheart, you must go to the Spade Kingdom. Your uncle, the King of Spades, will guide you from there," he says.

"I don't want to leave you. There must be another way..." I stutter. I've just found him.

"You can save Wonderland," he says.

"I can save you..."

"*Save everyone.*"

I shake my head. "I can't leave you. I've just found you, and I have so many questions."

"You must if you want to save me. Go to the Spade Kingdom."

I shake my head. I won't leave him.

"Remember, you have the Heart Sword," he says, his wide eyes filled with hope.

"What sword?"

He leans forward, his voice a whisper. "The one you used with the Behemoth."

"But that disappeared." My breath comes out heavy.

"You just need to call for it," he says with a serene face.

This is absurd. How does a sword just appear? How

am I supposed to get to the Spade Kingdom? I don't know where to go or how to begin.

"Don't worry, you will also have help," he continues and gestures with his head to look behind me.

A gust of wind brushes over me and I turn to find Ace. Genuine fear stabs at my stomach.

"You can trust him," the king says quickly. "He, like you, has his own desires to protect Wonderland."

"I will protect her with my life," Ace says and turns to me. "But we must go. Alice finally knows of Lucina's true parentage."

My father's face softens, and his eyes glisten. "Lucina, take this piece of your heart and go save us all."

I give a reluctant nod and take the heart from him.

"Place it in you," he says. "It will be odd at first, because you're not used to the feeling, but you'll gain access to some of your power."

I stare at the heart and feel it beat in my hands. Then those feelings in my chest were…

"*Me,*" Wonderland tells me. "*My heart.*"

All my life I've felt different from everyone, that something was missing.

The reality was I had no heart. It's not like I didn't have any feelings, so I never thought about it. And I never would've known what was missing if it weren't for these events.

With one quick thrust, I slam the heart into my chest. I choke and my back arches. The pain is sharp, sizzling. It lasts only for a moment. Heat spreads from my core to every single cell in my body.

My bandages fall off. The aches in my body disappear.

"How?"

"The magic of the moment has healed you." My father smiles.

Images and voices flash before me. I see everyone at the party, including an annoyed Alice. She is shouting at everyone. Hatter and Candy are calm, staring at each other in an unspoken conversation.

Another vision flashes. The Pack are nearby, in the hedge maze.

"The Pack are coming," I say.

"Go," my father says.

He kisses my forehead and, in that moment, it dawns on me—I can't leave him. I cling onto him tightly.

"I won't leave you," I whisper into his ear.

"Ace, get her out of here," he commands.

Ace yanks a pack of cards from his inner pocket. He throws them and they flutter around us. He tilts his head at me. "Come, Lucina."

"No," I say. "I need to be here with him."

My father lifts his hand, and a strong force pushes me away from him. I stretch my arm out to him.

No, I don't want to leave him. Please, not yet.

"I love you, my sweet girl—"

My father's words are cut off as a gust of air sends the cards out of orbit and they form a dome around us. The wind tugs at my hair and at the hem of my dress as the cards draw in.

"Hold on tight, it's going to be a bumpy ride," Ace says.

It's already a bumpy ride.

Chapter Fifteen

ie after lie. That's the essence of my life. It's got me questioning everything. What's real, what's not? When I finally get the truth, it's ripped away from me yet again. Instead, I have to save everyone, save them from Alice and her tainted blood.

The roaring of the wind reminds me of a large waterfall. It thrums against my chest and ears. It tears at my hair and I refuse to close my eyes, seeing as I've had them closed for so long from something that was right in front of me.

I don't look like my dad—Jack, the Knave. I'd just always presumed I took after my mother, a Spade. The Spade part is right, but the woman named Midori who I thought was my mother isn't. Turns out, that's the former Queen of Spades.

A shiver sets down my spine as I recall the stories I learned from school about the former King and Queen of Wonderland—my parents—are not true. Those same stories that my dad—or not dad—dismissed profusely. Telling me it's all lies without backing them up. It all makes sense, in hindsight. Yet it's in hindsight we get to see what we actually are, and I'm a lie.

The wind turns to a howl, then a sigh and, lastly, a whisper.

Finally, my feet are back on ground. I hold out my arms in an attempt to regain my balance and ease my queasy stomach.

After a few deep breaths, I manage to gather my bearings.

Trees tower over me, the largest I've ever seen, with dense foliage. The sky eludes me as black shadows hang over the entirety of the forest.

"Take me back!" I demand. "Take me back, right now."

"I know it's hard, but you have to let him go," Ace says. "If you love him, then you have to leave him to save him."

I collapse to the ground. "What about Hatter, Candy... Edith?"

Ace scrunches his face. "I know you don't want to hear this, but you're actually saving them."

"Saving them," I spit out, getting up from the dirt ridden ground. I shove him in the chest. "They're dead because of me."

Rage courses though my blood, heating my whole

body. Everyone tried to tell me, and I was oblivious. Am I that stupid, that self-absorbed? Why didn't I push Dad— no, the Knave—for answers? Why did I settle?

I'm so angry at him, why isn't he here? How could he leave me all on my own to go on those trips? What were they even all about?

Ace's jaw tightens. "Hatter and Candy are fine, Edith is..."

"Is dead." I screech, forcing myself to look anywhere but at him. "I heard it, I couldn't even help her. And the king, he—"

"Edith's not dead. She's not in the best condition, but Hatter is tending to her," he says. "And the king will be fine. He's endured far worse."

My head snaps toward him. "Why didn't any of you try to save him?"

"We tried."

"Then why didn't you try *harder*? For that matter, why didn't you tell me any of this! You had plenty of opportunities." It's so much easier to blame him, than to blame myself for everything I haven't seen. Everything that's been right under my nose all along.

Ace scowls at me. "I did try. I was trying to lead you to the crown all along, haven't you figured that out?"

A twig snaps, interrupting our squabbling.

A second later, a sharp voice cuts through the air. "Ace."

"Rhyme." Ace jumps in front of me.

"The name's Joker."

A young man emerges from the shadows. He's wearing

close-fitted black trousers tucked into worn leather boots, a black tunic belted at his hips, and gloves, also black. Half of his face is hidden by a white mask. His skin glows like amber, and his one visible eye is green and rimmed in thick kohl. He has spiky white hair and is wearing a black hat that hangs at three points, each tipped with a small silver bell that made no sound to alert us of his presence.

That's the Joker everyone talks about. His color scheme is a little dark.

"Let us go," Ace says.

The silver bells on his hat ring as he tilts his head. "I do as Queen Alice wishes and the message she's giving me is that she wants that girl. The pretender with the crown."

I've completely forgotten about the crown. It doesn't feel like it's there, but when I reach up, it's definitely still perched on my head. I'm surprised it hasn't fallen off from the teleportation.

"Alice is not the true queen!" Ace shouts. "She's destroying Wonderland, you know that?"

Joker goes to his back and pulls forward a huge black mallet. "Give me the girl and no one dies."

A pack of playing cards appears in front of me and surrounds me, forming a ring. Blue light emits from the cards and covers me from head to toe.

"Always playing Hide and Seek." Joker steps forward. "I'll just have to force you out."

Joker lifts up his mallet and starts spinning around on the spot. With each

spin, he gets faster and faster till the surrounding trees start to creak and the dirt from the ground whips up into the air, semi-blinding me. The barrier around me is strong, protecting me from everything, including the wind.

A gigantic column of air violently twists around Joker. The column moves closer to me and I try to run, but I'm limited in my movements by the barrier. Ace has disappeared to who knows where and all I can do is stand in place. I hate not doing anything. In case all else fails, I pull my dress up, searching for my trusty knife.

I catch some flashes of blue light as I search. The tornado Joker has created bumps against my shield, but it doesn't break it. I continue to fumble for the knife, and I manage to get it, holding it up.

I can't see anything but air, with some flashes of red and black. Where is a sword when you need one?

"Help us, Rhyme," Ace pleads with Joker over the raging air.

"The name's Joker," he shouts.

I narrow my eyes and briefly catch sight of Joker swinging his mallet. Great, there is a fight going on and I'm not involved.

I catch the mumbles of voices and this time I squint my eyes; I manage to make out either Ace or Joker, battling one another. I want to tell Ace that the mallet is a slow weapon, so he needs to use his speed to his advantage and also aim for the legs. But I know my cries are in vain.

"Wonder," I call out.

Wonder has been very quiet. Normally, he would warn me about any danger.

I get no response. I stomp my foot on the ground. Standing around doing nothing is frustrating. I can't even see much, unless I squint and then I only catch small glimpses.

An earthy, floral and sweet smell hits my nose. A loud whistling sound catches my ears. I follow the sound to my right and light whizzes past me and into the tornado. A thunderous boom follows. Smoke spills out of the tornado and up into the night sky. The raging winds slow down. I press my fingers against the shield, my gaze locked onto the waning smoke.

The air begins to clear; the trees are slanted or pushed back, but still rooted in the ground. They form a crater, and Ace and Joker are situated in the middle. Ace is holding onto his shoulder with a single card left in his hand. Joker stands beside a tree, breathing heavily, his mallet head on the ground.

"You know that she's brainwashed you!" Ace's voice cracks through the air. "She destroyed your family."

Joker sneers. "All families are doomed."

"Tell that to Finn."

"I don't need to hear another lecture from him!"

"You won't be getting that anymore." A shadow of grief clouds Ace's eyes. "He's dead."

Joker's face contorts. He'd been about to roll his eyes before Ace's words. Now, his sneer slips, he frowns, his lips become a thin white line, and then he bursts into laughter. His face is constantly moving, a new expression every time. There is a battle going on inside him, one I don't understand.

"You're lying," Joker hisses finally.

"No, I'm not," Ace says. "You know that attack with

the Behemoth, the one Alice arranged for the city? Ten used a powerful magical attack and the Behemoth countered it. Finn and some other card soldiers got hit instead. They all died."

Alice planned that attack. So, the Behemoth was talking about her. She set the creature up. I knew it. She's basically Finn's killer. Biles rises in my throat.

"No, no, no," Joker repeats over and over. His hands grip his white hair, and he steps back. "How could he be so stupid? Why didn't you save him? Where's Ten?"

Ace stands his ground. "I didn't expect the attack to be countered with a simple swipe."

Joker twists his head; a single black tear rolls down his cheek. "The queen wouldn't allow this to happen. She can surely bring him back."

"You know she doesn't have the power to do that."

There's a long silence as Ace and Joker face off, staring at each other. Then bells ring, and Joker turns his attention to me.

"But she can. Just give her to me." Joker holds out his arm. "I can make this all go away."

"Never!" Ace yells. "I will take you down, Rhyme, because she's worth saving. She will unite Wonderland again; she will heal us all and it's what Finn would have wanted."

"Ace," he whispers. "If I don't take her, she won't be able to bring back Finn. You know there's a time limit in which she can bring back the dead."

"She doesn't have her full heart, so she can't do anything, anyway," Ace says.

What are they talking about? I don't have that type of power. No one can, right?

Ace continues, "You know if you take her, Finn would be angry."

Joker's mouth opens and closes several times. He scratches his head. Finally, he lifts up his mallet. "I'll let you off this time, but only for Finn." Joker closes his eyes; bells start to chime and, like the wind, he disappears.

"Are you okay?" Ace says, running over to me. He snaps his fingers, and the barrier disappears. "We have to go now. We have to get you to safety."

"What was that all about?"

"It doesn't matter now." Ace steps in front of me. "Joker is not rational, and he might change his mind."

"He won't come back, he's hurting."

"He won't come back," I say.

"How can you be so sure?"

"Because Wonder says so."

"Wonder? Oh, you mean Wonderland. Your father mentioned him to me." Ace raises his voice in question. "Look, I can't risk it. Let's just go. Hatter and the others are keeping the soldiers back, but we don't have much time."

"You were right," I tell him, clutching the chain on my chest. "I'm heartless."

"No, that's not true." Ace looks at me with sad eyes. "And I'm sorry for what I said before. I know it wasn't your fault, there was no way all our cryptic pointers could've made sense, especially when you don't have your full heart. I know it's a lot, but we need to get going. We can't let them get you because if they do, then everything we've done will have been in vain."

I bite my teeth together and run a hand through my hair. I can blame Ace, I can blame Edith, I can blame everything and everyone. But at the end of the day, this is all my fault. I should have paid more attention to everything, and then we might not be here.

"I'm sorry, but..." Ace starts.

"It's fine," I choke out.

No, it's not, but I have to press on. I take a few steps forward; I manage to place my hand on a nearby slanted tree and vomit. My throat burns as the contents of this morning's breakfast—bacon and eggs—spill onto the forest floor.

"Lucina," Ace cries out.

I swipe my hand back at him. I don't want anyone near me as I purge everything, from a lifetime of lies to a bottomless pit of self-loathing at my own stupidity. At the same time, I mourn for my parents. All of them. I stumble back, lean on the tree, wipe my mouth with the sleeve of my dress and take a deep breath.

"It's a normal side effect of travelling with magic," Ace says. "I didn't think."

No, this is a side effect of the truth.

Chapter Sixteen

Ace goes over to the tree that is practically horizontal, placing a hand on the bark. A spark of magic leaves him and goes into the tree. Blue light engulfs it, making it appear as if it's glowing.

The magic moves into the roots of the tree and into the roots of the other trees nearby. A trail of blue light glistens around us and magic reverberates in the air. The trees start to curl forward, aligning themselves back up to the sky. The one I'm leaning on pushes me forward and moves to the center of the clearing.

Within seconds, the trees return back to normal as if magic never touched them in the first place.

"What are you doing?" I ask.

"I need to clean up the area. We can't leave any traces for the Pack to follow us."

"Where are we?" I say, a little too quickly for my own liking.

"Farthest Forest," Ace says. "Come on."

Farthest Forest is what I like to call a dead zone. An area that has nothing to offer, just like me.

I can't be queen. I don't know how to be queen. Dad never taught me that. Never taught me etiquette; it was all about war and the way of the soldier. But I know I must push through that, too, and figure out a way to rule. Even if I don't know how. For my family, for Wonderland.

With a heavy heart, I plunge through the forest, brushing against what might as well be every leaf and branch. I climb over huge roots spread like an eagle's wings, duck under branches and step in ankle-deep puddles of water. There's no light and not a single sign of life; no singing birds or creatures scurrying away.

How could anyone live here? I keep my thoughts to myself. I don't want to spur a conversation; I'd rather bathe in the haunting silence. And remember ever single detail of my father, the king, just in case it's the last time I see him.

Twenty minutes pass and my stomach starts to rumble.

"We're almost there," Ace says.

I don't reply. I'm too tired. I want to go to sleep and wake up to find out this is all a nightmare. But it won't happen. The hem of my dress is soaked wet, my bare feet hurt, my limbs are weary, and my stomach continues to betray me by growling.

Dreams like this don't feel so real.

The mist grows thicker and becomes more of a dense fog. I can't see anything besides Ace's figure in front of me. It's as if someone took an eraser and removed the surroundings.

"You were all trying to tell me the truth from the beginning and I wouldn't listen." I break the silence and stop.

"Don't stop moving. I'll try and answer all your questions," Ace tells me. "It's not your fault. Your heart not being there stopped you from seeing; I just got frustrated. I thought when you put on the crown, you'd be better, since it was supposed to give you the essence of your heart, but I expected too much."

I recall him saying he'd been trying to lead me to it. "What do you mean?"

"The crown rejected Alice and I thought that by it accepting you, it would change everything like that." He snaps his fingers. "But at least the crown has accepted you."

I reach up to touch the crown again. It's still there, even though it doesn't feel like anything's on my head.

I continue to follow him. "The king—my father—said that magic was used to bind people from telling the truth, but everyone kept telling me things. Only, they didn't make any sense."

"The magic in Wonderland has become corrupt. It's so unstable. People aren't the same. The laws of magic have twisted."

"Why?"

"Because Alice is on the throne and it's meant to be you," he says. "Also, no one in Wonderland should be using magic. Your bloodline created the magic, so it makes sense that it's yours alone. Your blood keeps the magic pure. I know the other kings and queens have a little magic which was bestowed upon them by the Heart monarch, but that's separated from your bloodline. But because everyone is readily using magic, it corrupts their minds and they have no sense of who they are, what is happening or what they are saying. If they knew or understood Finn's death, they'd be mourning."

"It's weird," I tell him. "I feel this stab of sorrow when you say his name. I didn't feel it before, but I did feel sadness whenever my dad left. How could I not have a heart and still feel?"

"I don't understand Wonderland myself, but I think it might be due to your lineage. You're still the Heart of Wonderland, you're just not fully tapped into it yet."

So, what am I? Am I a person, a thing or a place?

"I have so many questions."

Is having a heart meant to be complicated? If so, I don't think I can handle it.

After a few minutes of walking in the clouds, Ace stops. "We're here."

The biggest tree I've ever seen stands before me. It's so big I can't see where both sides of the trunk end as the mist engulfs them. But one thing with Wonderland is everything is not what it seems, and I know there is more to this tree. The tingling in my heart tells me this.

"Follow me," Ace says, and he walks through the tree, disappearing from my sight.

An illusion.

I take a hesitant step. I hold out my hand, tentatively

reach forward toward the bark, and my hand goes through. As I slip past the illusion, I am greeted with the inside of a tree. Bark surrounds me and there's a gigantic red door with a shiny silver bell next to it.

Ace taps the bell, and it rings.

Moments pass and the small latch high up opens. "Who's there?"

The voice belongs to a child.

"Everett, it's me, Ace."

The child, Everett, giggles. "What's the password?"

"We don't have time for this!"

"Password." Everett snorts and laughs. "No exceptions."

"Everett, we really don't have the time." Ace rolls his eyes. "The princess is here."

"The princess!" Everett squeals.

The door swings open and the smallest little white rabbit greets us. Like the White Rabbit—no, Finn—he wears a waistcoat and a blue jacket. A tiny pocket watch hangs on his side.

The little rabbit hops forward and his jaw drops. "It's really you. The princess."

The word "princess" echoes around us.

More conversation occurs but I don't listen. Instead, I take in my surroundings, noticing a few creatures, people, beastians and duezans appearing behind Everett; their jaws also drop.

Ace walks on and I follow. We're walking over a bridge, filled with light from paper lanterns. As we cross over, it dawns on me that this village is in a tree. It's so tall, the sky is out of sight. There are so many floors and everyone above us is staring at me from buildings or platforms high up. Each house is beautifully crafted, with leaf roofs and round windows, all lit up with lanterns.

I've never seen anything like this. I'm impressed with the ingenuity of this place. They even have ropes and wood providing bannisters and walkways.

Voices flood into my mind once more. Heartbeats flutter in my ears and the thoughts of these creatures surrounding me crash into my head.

"It's her."

"Wonderland's savior."

I wonder why it's happening now. Is there a way to turn it off?

"The real princess, she has the crown."

"Her eyes are red; she is the real deal."

I need to see my reflection again, to confirm it all. There's a fountain and I rush past Ace and Everett, holding the skirt of my dress up, exposing my dirt-ridden feet. I stare into the fountain's pond—my eyes are indeed red again.

I can see the king in me, in the high cheekbones, the aquiline nose. Now that I've met him, I can also see him in the smaller things—the way I hold myself, the tilt of my head, the grooves in my forehead when I get annoyed or confused. It's an odd sensation. Up until a few hours ago, I didn't even know who he was, other than his name and a vague recollection from history classes.

Now he's my father, and everything's changed. He's not just a king, he's family.

"Father, Dad," I utter, and I realize I'm not just referring to the king, but the Knave as well. I take a seat on the edge of the fountain. What do I do?

The burn of tears scalds my eyes, but not a single tear drops. There's so much I want to do—scream, shout, grab a sword and slash everything. But everyone's staring at me and I can't.

Staring at my reflection, I take in the crown on my head. It's so big, I can't go anywhere without everyone noticing it. I go up to remove it, but a bright glow surrounds it. When the light disappears, the crown has turned into a hairband with a red ruby shaped like a heart on it.

A brown, white-patched rabbit wearing an apron comes over and gasps. "Oh, you poor dear, you're going through a lot."

I simply nod, since the words just won't come out.

"Bunny," Ace calls out.

"Ace, go put the kettle on," she says. "Everyone else go into the house. Let me tend to the princess."

"But I want to help, Mommy," Everett says.

"Everett, go inside and help Ace," the brown rabbit says and gestures her head over at the rest of the villagers. "And the rest of you, be on the lookout. We must protect our princess."

Everyone starts moving around while I remain still, staring at my reflection in the pond.

"My name is Bunny," she says and takes my hand. It's comforting having her soft warm paw on me. "My father is— was—the White Rabbit. No, Finn. It's all Alice's fault we call him White Rabbit. She refused to use his real name."

I don't know what to say. Nothing surprises me anymore.

"I'm so sorry," I choke out. "I should have intervened quicker."

Bunny shakes her head, and one of her ears flops to the side. "You couldn't have done anything."

No, that's not true. I could've figured this all out earlier.

"How did you find out about your dad?" I gasp. "It's not been long."

"Ace sent me a message." Bunny lowers her head briefly. "You can cry, sweetheart. You have all the reason to."

"*She wants to cry.*" Wonder says. "*She misses her dad.*"

"You can cry, too," I tell her. "I know you miss your dad."

"I've cried enough, but I'll probably cry later when the children are asleep."

Bunny gathers me close, rocking me in her arms, but the tears refuse to come. Although I deny myself the cathartic cry, I do find comfort in her embrace.

I don't know how long I allow her to rock me. Minutes, maybe longer. Then something strikes me—a question I still haven't gotten an answer to.

I pull back from Bunny's embrace. "Why didn't anyone try to help my father?"

Bunny lowers her head. "None of us are strong enough to help him. Also, your father wouldn't allow us to, even if we tried. He's always been like that, thinking about the greater good. He made a deal with Alice. If she touched any member of Wonderland, he'd..."

"What?"

She avoids eye contact. "Kill himself."

"But Wonderland would die without him!"

"Yes, that's why Alice gave in to his demands."

My fists clench together so tightly, my nails dig into my palms. "What does she want?"

"I don't know," Bunny says. "I think she wants everything. And greed never satisfies anyone. It's a never-ending well where one will fall forever."

"I still don't understand how she took over."

Bunny lowers her head. "When Alice corrupts anyone with her magic, the king's bond with them weakens, as does his power within Wonderland. And so, people who use his magic weaken him."

"But how did they learn to use his magic?" The king mentioned it, but I need more information. I need more time with him, too.

Bunny's face may be calm, but her voice is meek when she speaks again. "Alice first tainted them with her blood magic. Then they fed off your father, as we are all connected to him. They forgot their real ruler. Hatter, my dad and myself tried in vain to get everyone to remember. But now they are beginning to see the truth and Alice's influence is waning."

So, Alice must have corrupted my dad, the Knave, and made him sign the contract. Dad left to get away from her. It all makes sense. It's all because of Alice—she's the reason I didn't get to know my real parents.

"My poor father. How well do you know him?"

"We grew up together, and he was my best friend. Finn was his butler, adviser and teacher. Valentine and I would play tricks on my dad all the time."

"Valentine?" I whisper. I know that name.

"Your father's name. It means strong and healthy," Bunny says.

How untrue that is. I continue to dig my nails into my palms through both the anger and the need to feel, to know that this is all real and not just some twisted nightmare.

"What about the Knave? I thought he was the king's best friend."

"That's true as well." Bunny fiddles with her fingers on her lap.

"I get that he wouldn't want the help, and none of you were strong enough, but what, exactly, were the obstacles?"

"None of us can get in," Bunny says. "Royal blood is needed or Alice. The only other person who got near him was Ace, but he couldn't undo his chains, no matter how hard he tried."

I'm so confused. There are so many questions and I don't know where to begin. What do I ask?

I want to know more about my mother and father. I want to know more about Wonderland's downfall. I want to know where my dad is, but the only constant I have is Ace. I want to know why he could go see my father when others couldn't.

I jolt up. "I need to see Ace."

"Are you sure? Don't you want to talk some more?"

I shake my head.

"Okay," Bunny says hesitantly. "Follow me. "

I follow her through the streets to arrive in front of a domed-shaped house that's short and sprout. It's two stories high, with wooden, framed sash windows propped open with sticks. The brick work is mud-like. To my surprise, I find a small rose garden with carrots planted in the front. It's baffling that something is growing inside of the tree.

"This used to be our secret hiding place—Valentine and mine's." Bunny speaks as if she can read my thoughts. "He knows I love gardening. So, he created it to be my own secret garden. Who knew that it would become a refuge?"

"He could do all that?" I blink. Will I able to do something as grand as that? I can't see it.

Bunny opens the door and I walk inside. There, I find little rabbits everywhere. One on each of Ace's shoulders, one on his head, several running around him, and two of them climbing up his legs.

This is not a good time to talk to Ace, especially with these children present.

"Ace, did you get me a present?" one of the rabbits asks.

My head almost bumps into the low ceiling.

"Greet your princess, you naughty rabbits," Bunny declares.

All the little rabbits' gazes fix on me. Each one has different colored furs and eyes, all are different sizes and body shapes but as they stare at me, they all appear the same. All wide-eyed and for a brief moment there is silence.

"It's the princess!" A little girl black and white rabbit squeals.

Just like that, I'm swarmed by rabbits. Some of them climb on me, like they did with Ace moments ago. I have two rabbits on either side of my shoulders and two on my head, two struggling to climb up my skirt and three under my skirt.

"You're so pretty," a small boy ginger rabbit says from my left shoulder.

"She has red eyes!" A tiny girl gray rabbit shrieks. "They are so shiny, like jewels. I want them."

She stretches out her paws. One of the rabbits on top of me bats her paws away.

"Don't touch the princess!" I recognize the voice as Everett's. "She has to save Wonderland and she needs her eyes."

"Get off the princess," Bunny raises her voice. "She needs to rest up before she sets off again."

"No go," all the little rabbits say in union.

"Yes." Bunny continues to use the full range of her vocals. "Ace, Everett and the princess must go."

"Everett's going. No fair!" Another echo of tiny bunny voices.

"I have the best tracking skills and I'm not immature like you lot," Everett says from the top of my head.

"And you're a scrappy little thing," Bunny says, tilting her head over to Ace. "Your cover is blown. Now we can't get any information from inside the castle. Also don't use your magic as much. You've been overdoing it lately."

Ace sighs. "I won't. Besides, Lucina has access to some of her magic, which is much more stable than mine."

"I can't use magic," I contest.

"Yes, you can," he says. "You'll learn to use it eventually."

"Why can't you use magic?" I ask. He's used it numerous

times over the past few days. He even summoned a dragon. Why stop now?

The room falls into silence.

Wonder? I ask internally.

"I can't."

"You're talking to Wonderland, aren't you?" Bunny says with a smile.

"Yes," I reply.

The little ginger rabbit grabs my head. "Can you ask Wonderland where the buried treasure is?"

"No! Ask Wonderland if I will be pretty?"

"That's silly. Ask Wonderland where the best carrots are?'

"Children!" Bunny raises her voice. "Get off the princess and get back to bed. And don't bother her and Ace. Everett, double check you've packed everything. Princess, come eat and then we'll get you some new clothes and make sure you get plenty of rest."

"Thank you."

Bunny ushers me over to the dining room, which is surprisingly big. The furniture is small scale but proportionate to the room. There is a long mahogany table and I take a seat on a cushioned chair. The walls are painted ochre. A tall red case provides a pop of color and displays small pictures of Bunny and her family, pottery fashioned as animals, and books.

I don't get to analyze much more as Bunny brings over a bowl of delicious smelling food in her hands. My stomach growls and the combination of what I believe to be root vegetables mixed with sage, thyme and onions. My mouth salivates at the amazing aroma.

"It's beef and butternut stew with mustard mashed potatoes and parsnips." She holds out the bowl. "I hear you weren't well earlier so I added some ginger, it should help to ease your stomach. I'm sorry, princess. This must be very hard on you with everything that you have just learned," she says. "I wish you could stay longer, but you must start your journey to collect all your heart pieces quickly."

"I understand."

I don't have time to waste. I have a father—no, fathers—and Wonderland to save. Talking to Ace becomes secondary as my body gives in to extreme hunger and tiredness.

Chapter Seventeen

he morning comes too soon; I'm all bleary-eyed and my head is methodically pounding. No conversation is getting through.

Bunny has kindly given me an outfit I can fight in. Loose black trousers, knee-high boots, a chestnut top with a middle corset to protect my core from attacks and leather fingerless gloves. All I need is a sword and I'll feel better.

We're outside Bunny's home and everyone is fussing over something. Because of it, I can't talk to Ace, or ask him about the king.

It's still hard to grasp that my real father is the king. My heart acknowledges him as my father even though it feels guilt toward the Knave. The Knave raised me. I can't just turn my back on him. But my heart yearns for my father, the king, in a way it never has for the Knave.

"I'm so excited." Everett squeals in glee. Bunny checks his backpack for the third time.

His squeal goes straight to my head and makes me flinch and grit my teeth. I know it's because I'm tired.

Everett's siblings continue with their incessant talking:

"It's not fair."

"Why can't I go?"

"I can distract the baddies with my cuteness."

"I can throw Beatrice at them."

As cute as little rabbits are, they're the most irritating beings in existence. Worst of all, I can hear what the little devils are thinking and it's all about food, especially carrots, or shiny things.

Last night, they took to my ballroom dress because of its sparkles and made it into a play mat. And by the Underland, did they fight over it! It's in pieces now, and to think I thought I had ruined it.

As we move into the square, the little rabbits' cries escalate, and I can't even hide that my head is throbbing. Numbly, I try to massage the side of it in an attempt to ease the ache.

"We want to go," the little rabbits sob in union.

"Stop it, all of you!" Everett shouts. "We have more important things to worry about than your complaining. Wonderland is disappearing. We will all cease to exist without it."

"I want to go," the little brown girl rabbit whines.

Everett slaps his hand on his head.

"If you don't let the princess and everyone go, then no

carrots for any of you," Bunny raises her voice.

The whining suddenly stops and beautiful silence washes over my ears. I glance over at Ace. His eyes are on the ground, and a sudden feeling of apprehension tightens in my stomach. He looks more tired than I feel, which is saying a lot.

"I heard we have to go to the Forest of Illusion. Are you sure you know how to get there?" I give Everett the once-over skeptically. He's half the size of my boots.

"Everett may be small, but he's got a sense of direction and the best nose for danger out of anyone," Bunny says with pride.

As we make our way to the bridge—the exit—I catch a familiar voice singing.

Wonder? No, Wonder doesn't have that voice.

"Journey to the deep,
The climb will be steep,
Each must do their part,
To find the inverted hearts,
Together we will go,
To my original home."

An upside-down crescent moon appears, revealing Cheshire on the railings of the bridge to the village. He's plump and blue and upon further investigation, I can see his stripes are indeed purple. It's the first time I've seen him in the light.

"Cheshire." Bunny smiles. "It's been too long."

"Where have you been?" Ace grunts, trying to stop one of the little rabbits from getting into his backpack.

"Regaining my energy and diverting attentions," Cheshire says. "The Pack are indeed effective at what they do, but they're stupider than the Tweedle twins."

As I stare at Cheshire, I'm reminded of the king, my real father. He told me I could trust him. "You're not speaking in rhymes anymore."

"Because I'm no longer in that accursed castle."

I approach him. "You were my mother's pet."

"Hikari," he simply says and walks closer to me without getting off the bridge's railings. "Her name was Hikari di Schwarz ex Coeur."

"Long name," I say.

"When she was the Queen of Spades, it was Hikari no Kuroi Kokoro. Hikari is the Spade word for light, hence why the king and queen chose the name Lucina for the princess," Cheshire says. "Now, let's be on our way. No more dawdling."

I've always known my name means light, but I never knew why it was chosen. Knowing that makes me feel better because it shows there was thought behind me. That I was wanted and loved. And knowing a little more about myself is much better than nothing.

We set out through the forest, maneuvering through the dense maze of trees. Two hours ago, the trunks of the trees were very thin. Some weren't much wider than my arm, and they made our path an ever-constant zigzag. Now, the trees are dense enough to block out the sun. The floor of the forest is a thick mat of decaying leaves, a soft cushion to our feet.

There are so many questions ruminating through my

head. All I want to do is talk to Ace and Cheshire. Only, they're both walking ahead of me and talking with Everett about where we're heading.

I'm finding it really hard to keep up with them. It's unusual for me, I've always been an athlete. But yesterday really took its toll. I feel like my entire world has been turned upside down.

I used to recognize the girl in the mirror, but now I don't. I used to be comfortable in fighting clothes and now I wonder if I'll ever be comfortable in fluffy dresses. And I have so many questions going around in my head that I can't concentrate. I feel ashamed that I've lived in such naivety, not knowing what's been going on with Wonderland.

Inner voices bombard me, and the only voice I can take is Ace's.

"He's different."

And what does that mean?

"Not my place to tell."

Ace pulls back and waits for me; Cheshire jumps over and goes to Everett's side.

"Princess..."

"Lucina," I say. "Call me Lucina."

"Are you okay?" He asks.

"I..." I stutter. I've been waiting so long to talk to Ace that I just don't know where to begin.

"I only ask because with you gaining a piece of your heart and being transported like you did last night, it must have taken a massive toll on your body."

"Is that what it is?"

"Have you been feeling under the weather?" He frowns.

"You should have told us. We would have taken more time to rest."

I shake my head. "We can't afford to. Wonderland and my father need me."

"But if you're not well, then Wonderland is not well. You're bonded."

"I don't understand. Isn't Wonderland still bonded to my father?"

"Yes," he says. "But it's also now linked to you and the more pieces of your heart you get, the stronger the link."

"Why can't you just teleport us to the Spade Kingdom, then?"

"Because I can only go to places where I've been or where the Pack have been. Now that I'm cut off from them, I can't go where they go."

The questions bubble up inside me and I blurt out, "I understand everyone else's motivations, but yours are not so clear."

"Isn't saving Wonderland enough?" He raises his eyebrows.

"No," I say. "We all have ties to Wonderland, whether through friends and family. I don't know what ties you."

"You're right," he says. "But I'm not willing to share that with you. And don't bother asking Wonderland, it's not in his jurisdiction."

I narrow my eyes. "What?"

"I'll tell you one day, just not now."

"Okay, I can deal with that. However, you have to answer one thing?"

He tilts his head. "Depends."

"If you can teleport anywhere and you can teleport to

my dad, then why can't you save him? I know Bunny says the chains can't be broken, but you have powerful magic."

Ace winces and pulls a face.

"Everyone has kept so many secrets from me, I can't take it anymore. I understand when it comes to your personal life that you need privacy, but this is something else, and it affects me. I have a right to know since, as you said, I am Wonderland and Wonderland is me. Magic is part of Wonderland and magic is part of me."

"Touché, princess." He sighs and gestures with his head for me to take a seat on a bunch of rocks. He calls out ahead. "She wants to know about my magic."

All their faces instantly drop.

Cheshire disappears from Everett's side and appears on my shoulder. "She does have a right to know. Princess, if you feel stressed, then you can stroke me. It was what your mother used to do in stressful times."

"I'm okay." I hold my hands up.

"I don't bite." Cheshire licks his paw. "Most of the time."

It makes me not want to touch him even more. An uneasy silence forms. The only sound is Everett, who is still ahead sniffing, and Ace pacing a small patch of grass.

Ace stops in his tracks and breaks the silence. "Your father gave me my magic."

"What?" I utter with a gasp.

"I used it to infiltrate myself into Alice's camp."

"I don't get it. Why you?"

'That's where it gets personal and I don't have to answer anything personal as you said earlier," Ace interjects and turns away from me. "However, I will answer your other question. I can't save your father with his own magic. Also, teleportation uses a lot of magic and so using it affects your father as my magic is linked to him. Essentially I sort of… drain his lifeforce."

"What?" I shriek.

Cheshire falls onto the foliage with thud. "Abrupt much?" he purrs from below.

I ignore him, my entire focus on Ace. My voice rises, full of emotion. "Why did you use it yesterday then?"

"Because your father commanded it," Ace says. "Just like you're connected to Wonderland, I'm connected to your father."

"You used magic on the first day we met, from the Glass Coast all the way to the Heart Castle!" I find myself yelling. "That must have used a tremendous amount of magic. I mean, the Glass Coast isn't exactly close by."

"It did," Ace says. "But your father was adamant I get you. And I need to use magic to protect you."

"*Danger!*" Wonder chirps in.

"I don't care," I snap, both to Ace and Wonder. I find myself walking right up to Ace's face. "You're putting his life at risk."

Ace says nothing and avoids eye contact.

Silence hangs heavy after my words. No one moves or speaks. Not even Wonderland.

The silence is eventually broken by the pitter-patter of tiny feet.

It's Everett. His jaw is quivering. "The Pack are coming."

Chapter Eighteen

told you." Wonder rubs it in.

Wonder likes to come when he pleases and not when it's convenient to me. It seems that like everyone else, he's in on the lies, too. I'm too angry to respond.

"What?" Cheshire's tail flicks and he disappears.

"I can hear them and smell them." Everett twitches his nose. "It smells like sweat bags."

"Oh, great," Ace exclaims and readies a card in his hand. "What direction?"

"Do you ever stop using magic?" My hands fly up.

Everett places his ear to the ground. "One o'clock. They're not far, so we can't escape them."

Cheshire appears on my shoulder, startling me. "He's right."

Great, no one's listening to me.

"Do you know which ones?" Ace asks.

"Excuse me..." I start.

"Four and Six," Cheshire says over me.

"Four is the master of sword combat, and Six is great with knives," Ace says. "That never changes, and you all know Pack members can be dangerous. I'll fight, but the rest of you..."

"I'm a really good jumper," Everett interjects.

"I have claws." Cheshire retracts them from his paws.

I let out a snort. "I can fight better than any of you. I was trained by the best, my dad... the Knave."

"I heard he's a right killer," Everett says.

Cheshire places a hand over Everett's mouth.

"Damn. I don't have a sword, or an axe." I check my outfit. "But I have some knives. Wait... I have the Heart Sword! All I have to do is call for it."

"Call for it, then." Ace crosses his arms.

"Fine." I scoff and hold out my hand. "Heart Sword."

A moment passes and the sword doesn't appear. What's going on?

I let out disgruntled laugh. "Heart Sword."

"Doesn't matter." Ace dismisses me and rolls his eyes. "You can't call the sword until you come into your own."

"How do you know that?" I gasp.

"Because your father told me," he says. "Besides, we're not putting you in any danger. Your safety is crucial."

"Sorry," Cheshire says. "I have to agree with Ace. Let him handle this."

I give him skeptical look. "What's he going to do? Use

more magic. Burn out my father even more."

Everett's ears perk up. "They're getting closer."

"Okay." Ace paces back and forth for a few moments. Eventually, he comes to a stop, places his hands on his waist and lifts his head up to the sky. "Got it. You three climb a tree and seek shelter."

"Just give me a weapon," I cry out.

"Up the tree," Ace demands. "Or can't you climb?"

I let out a long, hard breath and scrunch my face tight. Ace magically disappears out of my sight. This makes me want to scream. He's using magic, thus depleting my father's lifeforce. Why isn't anyone thinking about the consequences but me?

Sometimes you have to go against the rules. I stretch out my arm. *Come on, Heart Sword.*

"Why are you dawdling?" Everett pulls on my arm. "We have to hide."

"Come on, Heart Sword," I call out.

Again, nothing happens.

"Please stop doing that, it's embarrassing." Cheshire's whiskers twitch.

I stomp my foot like a petulant child. Ace is an idiot. I'm no princess in a fairy tale, I don't need saving. I'm here to save Wonderland.

Cheshire's tail flicks in my face and I remember I have him and Everett to protect. At least I'll be doing something.

"Come on, Everett."

I bend over, ready to pick him up and put him on my back, when suddenly he jumps. I mean, twenty feet high. How does he do that? He's up in a tree with no problem.

"It's just you and me, Cheshire."

"Speak for yourself," Cheshire says and disappears. I look up and he appears besides Everett, smiling that incredibly wide smile of his.

Okay, so I just need to protect myself. I suppose it wouldn't harm me to get intel on my enemy. I pick a tree carefully, one that is high enough and that has an excess of leaves to provide cover.

I climb up, sticking to the stronger branches close to the trunk. I enjoy climbing now but when I was younger, I used to hate it because the friction got to me. It used to be agonizing, requiring not only exertion but direct contact of my hands on the tree bark. However, Dad had me climbing every day and the more I climbed, the more my hands adjusted. I'm fast as well; in only a few short minutes, I've already gotten fifteen feet high up.

For a moment, I stop and survey the area. Where are they? No one is in sight.

Cheshire appears out of nowhere and floats in front of me. "Keep moving, princess."

"How do you do that?" I ask. "I thought magic is only in the royal bloodlines."

"Your grandfather gave me magic when I was a kitten." Cheshire licks his paw. "Now stop asking questions and get a move on."

I jump slightly and regain my balance. If he can float, then why has he been resting on our shoulders? He's not exactly light.

"Come on," he says. "Keep moving up."

At Cheshire's request, I climb further up. It's all about

the placement of the hands and feet. Also, it's about the distribution of weight. I climb higher and higher, but still searching for my opponent. Dad always told me, *"You always have to know what you're going up against before you fight. It will give you the advantage."*

"Can you see them, Cheshire?" I whisper.

I get no reply—he's disappeared again. Where does he go?

Scanning the area, I catch sight of them. Their faces are plastered with a magical hole in the shape of a wide grin. It's not like Cheshire's, he has teeth; they have nothing but an empty void. Their weapons are of high quality. The sword Pack soldier has a great sword, so it's using both hands due to the weight which will make its combat slow. The other soldier has double-edged daggers, one for each hand. I'm sure it's packing knives elsewhere. It may be speedy; I'll have to watch and see.

There's a rustle of leaves.

"Where are you, traitor?" One of the Pack members calls out.

I cover myself further into the leaves as he circles around.

The sky darkens and the wind picks up. I know that sound. It's Ace.

A harrowing cyclone of cards hits the forest, flying out from every direction; top, down, left, right. I wince as he uses magic.

"Don't worry, princess," Cheshire says, only his head appearing. "This only uses a small percentage of the king's power."

That does nothing to comfort me.

All I can hear are my father's words. *"I'm dying."*

I have to do something, so I push the branch of leaves out of the way and stare down. The Pack have a magic dome protecting them.

"Are they using my father's magic, too?" I ask.

"Not directly, but whenever anyone uses magic, it is part of Wonderland. With your father being Wonderland, they are effectively stripping at his lifeforce," Cheshire says.

So that means Cheshire is draining my dad, too. I'll talk to him about that later. That's if there is a later.

"This is not good." I start to climb down the tree.

"What are you doing?" Everett jumps down effortlessly to me.

"Protecting my father."

"Don't do this." Everett says.

A bang catches my attention. My head snaps to find Ace setting bomb cards off.

"Great. How is my father going to have a chance to live, if he's draining the life out of him?" I climb down some more, intent on putting an end to this.

Cheshire appears in front of me. "Princess, stop and think."

"I know I'm important to Wonderland, but..."

"I understand your need to save others," Cheshire interrupts. "Your father always rushed in and that was his downfall. His heart always spurred him on. If he'd listened to Hikki, maybe things would have been different."

Hikki... My mother's name is Hikari, is that her nickname? It's cute.

I stop climbing, but not because of that. "So, what I

am supposed to do? Sit back and watch? Maybe I should make a cup of tea."

"No, *think*," Cheshire says. "Your father is a Heart, but your mother was a Spade, and we Spades are known for our brains. You should always listen to your heart, but listen to your head, too. You have two of the most powerful royal bloodlines running through you. Don't waste them by neglecting one."

"Listen to him."

Now Wonder decides to speak up.

What can I use? Then I remember.

"Everett," I call out. "What's in your backpack?"

Everett hops down to my branch and holds it out. I dive into the bag, surprised at how full of everything it is. And it becomes evident that it's not a normal backpack, it's a never-ending one. I don't have time to go through all the contents. The grunts and clashing sounds cause my chest to tighten. Ace is shooting fireballs at them.

Come on, I tell myself.

I remember my dad, the Knave's, voice. *"When in doubt, always use the simplest techniques, you can never go wrong. When you get into the flow, the complicated stuff will come out. Then smash them with the deadly moves."*

My heart tugs.

I dive back into the backpack; there's got to be something that might be of use. A flashlight, a rope, some canned food, a whole load of carrots; underwear, clothes, pots, pans, cooking oil, a lighter, dynamite...

Everett has been holding out on me. What's a child doing with dynamite?

"I've got a plan and I need you two," I say.

I take out the rope, the dynamite and the lighter.

"Cheshire, I need you to tie the ends of these ropes to those trees over there." I point in the direction of the spot. "We're going to trip them up, then we use the dynamite to knock them out and make our escape."

Cheshire purrs. "Good idea, princess."

"What do I do?" Everett blinks.

"You're the bait," I say and take out a pan. "If you have any of your siblings' annoyingness, then this should be easy for you. Grab their attention away from Ace, and head toward the rope Cheshire is going to set up. We'll make it taut and trip them. I'll set off the dynamite and, boom, we're ready."

"I can be annoying." Everett giggles. "Just ask Mommy."

"Okay, let's do this," I say. "But before we go, Cheshire, is it possible for you to teleport me to those trees and bushes over there?"

Cheshire places a paw on his face. "Actually, I think I can. I used to teleport your mother all the time. Blood bond. I think because you're related, I can do it."

"Get me to those trees." I point, at the same time handing Everett the pan. "You go annoy."

Everett hops off the tree and Cheshire jumps onto my shoulder, which slumps under his weight.

A sweet, rich and syrupy smell wafts into the air. The scene disappears around me and within seconds I appear where I want to be, in the dense shrubbery.

"Wow!" I crouch on the ground with the dynamite. "That didn't feel like Ace's magic."

"I use Spade magic; it's intrinsic, unlike everyone else's," Cheshire declares and disappears with the rope to set up the trap. "My magic comes from *my* king, not your father."

That's nice to know. I start placing the dynamite sticks around the vicinity, mainly thin spaced. The way I've set them up should cause enough damage for the trees to collapse on the Pack members, but with minimal damage to the surrounding area. I don't want innocent creatures getting affected by this.

As I place the last stick, I remember that I need the lighter. How could I forget?

"Use your magic," Wonderland tells me.

"But..."

Magic corrupts people. It's probably why Dad hates it so much. I just can't make myself use it. I don't want to be crazy like everyone in the Heart Castle. I don't want magic to corrupt me or corrupt magic and, most importantly, I don't want to drain my father.

"You can do something as simple as light a match and it will not use you father's magic. This is your own magic. Separate from your father. Also, you can't be corrupted. You are magic."

"I don't know where to begin."

"See it in your mind's eye."

I move to a safe spot behind some bushes and crouch down.

"Envision it in your mind. Think of lighting a match. Press the match head into the striker. Quickly drag the match head along the striker. Think about the pressure you

need, and the fire will come. When Everett comes over, let off the spark."

"I still don't know how. It makes no sense."

"Think of the people you love—your mother, your father, the Knave and me. Think of what you need to protect."

Everett is on his way. He has somehow managed to irritate two members of the Pack. He's having no problem avoiding them as he jumps from one enemy to the other, making it difficult for them to attack as it could lead to them hitting one another instead.

He's moving so fast, he's like a blur. His mother wasn't kidding. It makes me think about his younger siblings and what they will be able to do in the future.

"Don't get distracted. Concentrate."

I try with all my might to set off the spark. I think of the match and striking it against the rough red strip, but nothing is happening. And seeing how close the daggers are getting to Everett makes my heart speed up. The daggers are missing him by inches. If anything happens to him, I'll never forgive myself.

One of Ace's card comes into view.

"Cheshire?" I call out carefully.

He appears. "Yes, my princess."

"Make sure Ace doesn't come into the trap."

"On it," he disappears.

I wish I could do that.

"You will when you gather the other pieces of your heart," Wonder tells me. *"Now concentrate."*

Damn, I should have asked him for a lighter.

"Trust yourself."

How can I, when everyone is in danger?

"Trust them like they are trusting you."

I don't trust myself. I don't really trust anyone because of all the lies. The only person I do trust is my dad, and who knows where he is?

I'm just so angry. Wonder is not helping, all I get are cryptic messages, and Ace won't tell me everything. Meanwhile, Everett and Cheshire are innocent in all of this. My body shudders and a warm energy whizzes through me.

The dynamite closest to me sizzles. A quick glance around confirms the other ones have set off, too.

I run out of my shelter. "Everett!"

The rabbit is flying through the air. I rush over to catch him in my arms and break out into a run. I only doubt myself for a moment, a doubt that soon evaporates when a thunderous boom erupts. I'm blown forward into the air.

My mind frantically thinks about the others. Did Cheshire protect Ace? Will I hurt Everett when I fall?

A honey-like smell captures my attention. It's delicious and reminds me of the cakes I bake for Dad. Wouldn't an eruption create a smoky aroma?

A sudden silence falls over the forest and I find myself floating in the air. Did I do this? Everything slows down, the air becomes cold and my body tingles.

A few feet away, shrouded under a tree's shadow, I notice a woman in a long black robe. I move my legs and even though I'm floating in the air, somehow, I manage to keep moving until my feet touch the ground.

Loud bangs break the silence. The ground rumbles and cracks spread across its surface.

For some strange reason, I manage to keep upright. I continue to run forward, refusing to stop. After about a minute, the ground stops vibrating. I eventually stop to turn around.

Where are the others? My breathing is heavy with panic, worry and fatigue.

An acrid smoke fills the air, which is not the best remedy for someone trying to regain their ability to breathe.

"Where is everyone?" I say out loud, still hugging Everett to my chest.

He buries his tiny nose in my shoulder. "You saved me."

Okay, he's just as annoying as his siblings, but he's so soft and warm that I don't pull back.

The forest is full of smoke and flames. Burning branches crack from trees and fall in showers of sparks onto the ground. Everett and I remain quiet; watching, waiting for something—anything—to come out.

Cheshire appears on my shoulder. "Ace is fine. He's just finishing off the last Pack member."

"What about the other ones?"

"*Dead.*"

My insides contract with anxiety and guilt.

"*Don't. It was your life or theirs.*"

I understand but...

"*Alice didn't think of this when she killed many citizens of Wonderland.*"

"You're right," I say out loud.

"Wonderland?"

I nod at Cheshire. "They're both dead."

"That was a good plan, though," Everett says from my arms. "Did you see my hopping skills?"

I find myself smiling. "Yeah, you were great."

Everett beams. "You were great too, princess, the way you landed."

"Time shift. Very powerful magic." Cheshire smiles. "I felt it, princess. You're much stronger than I anticipated. It's your Spade side."

"I saw a woman in a long black robe decorated with pink, blue and yellow butterflies," I tell him. "I couldn't make her out."

"Black robe?" Cheshire asks.

"Yes."

"Miku," Cheshire says. "Your mother's best friend and your uncle's—the King of Spade's—wife."

"Why didn't she help? Or at least take us to the Spade Kingdom?"

"She doesn't have the authority to leave the Spade Kingdom," Cheshire says. "So it was your aunt, not you who used time magic."

"She can manipulate time? That's powerful."

"She gained it when she married your uncle, but she can use it sparingly. You will be able to do more with it. But it has consequences for the user."

"And she did it anyway to save me..." My heart flutters. She slowed time down so I wouldn't fall.

"What are you two yapping about?" Everett asks.

"Yes, what are you two yapping about?" Ace says, appearing from the fire.

"Miku, the time priestess from the Spade Kingdom.

She came to the princess' aid," Cheshire says.

"Call me Lucina," I say. "All of you."

"Lucina and I are now besties," Everett tells Ace and hugs me again.

Unlike the cute little bunny, Ace is far from impressed. His expression is thunderous as he rushes toward me, closing the distance between us in the span of a few feet.

"What you did back there was dangerous!" His voice is low but filled with reproach.

"Using my father's lifeforce is too," I retort.

"You are too important to Wonderland." He rubs his temples. "When are you going to get that?"

"When are you going to understand I'm not a damsel in distress?" I bark back.

"If anything happens to you, Wonderland is gone, just like that." He snaps his fingers to illustrate his point. "Do you want to be the reason everyone dies?"

I growl. He's right, but I'm not going to let him know that. I'm not going to lose my independence for anyone or anything. I wish he could understand that.

I turn to Everett. "Which way do we go now?"

Everett points with his left arm. "North east."

"Let's go, then," I say and place Everett down on the ground.

I start walking, ignoring Ace. He has no right to lecture me. I helped them and, more importantly, I helped my father.

Chapter Nineteen

re we there yet?" I ask, feeling like a child.
The only reason I'm even whining is because I'm
sick of lugging around Cheshire on my shoulder.
I think someone's eating too much milk and cheese and
that's not good for his health. One of my first demands as
a ruler will to be to put him on a diet.

"Through the Forest of Illusions, then across the flower
fields and over to the Obsidian Desert," Everett replies with
a grin. "So, not far."

Great! I wish we could move faster. I don't know if the
king will last that long. He looked terrible; eyes gaunt, skin
deathly pale. There are still so many questions I need answers
to and trying to get them from this lot is as painful as me

trying to forge a diamond. It's not only that; I want the opportunity to get to know the king, to find myself in him.

It's a moonless night and because of that it's so dark, I can barely see. The only source of light comes from Ace and Everett. Ace is holding up a card that provides us a little halo of blue light and Everett has on a head torch.

"Okay, time to set up camp," Ace says. "We are getting close to the Forest of Illusions, but the last thing we want is to sleep in there."

Why not?

As if reading my thoughts, Cheshire answers, "The forest has a mist that's dangerous enough when we're awake, but it's worse when you're asleep."

"Does it create illusions? Is that why it's called the Forest of Illusions?"

"Originally, it was the Forest of Sweet Dreams." Cheshire yawns. "Then Alice came along, and the forest turned, twisted and now it feeds off people's insecurities. Now those who go in have illusions, usually about their worst nightmares."

Everett adds. "I heard that anyone who goes in never comes out."

"Then why are we going through it?" A tendril of reservation curls in my stomach.

Cheshire smiles. "It's the fastest route. If we go the other way, we're adding another two days onto our journey."

I shake my head in disbelief. "Aren't you all worried how we're going to get through it? Do we have a plan?"

"We will figure it out as we go along," Everett replies. "Besides, we have you."

"Really?" I raise my eyebrows. "Because when the Pack members were attacking us, you all shoved me to the sidelines."

"Because we need to protect you," Ace adds.

Cheshire purrs. "The more heart pieces you collect, the stronger you will become. At the moment you're a walking target, like a helpless guppy on land..."

"I am not a guppy!" I shout and grind my teeth. "I can fight."

"Yeah, so?" Cheshire licks his paws. "Princess, this is about who you are fighting for, not who you are fighting against. You need to stand back and come to terms with what is more important: your ego or Wonderland."

There is no reasoning with this lot. "Well, we at least we need a plan."

"You can't prepare for everything in life," Everett says with wide eyes. "Sometimes you have to just live in the moment."

That's pretty deep for a kid and he looks adorable saying it.

"I'm hungry." Everett comes over and rubs his eyes. "And sleepy."

And then he ruins his moment. This is why we shouldn't have brought a child along. I don't want to stop, but a quick glance around at everyone shows they're all exhausted, not just Everett.

And I hate to admit it, but I'm tired, too. Tired of constantly thinking, questioning everything. Tired of worrying about both my fathers and physically tired after the last two days of fighting and running with a severe lack of sleep.

In the end, I cave in. We need to rest up, but that doesn't mean I'm walking into the Forest of Illusion without a plan. One always needs to be prepared.

Ace sets his own backpack down and it falls into a heap on the ground, crunching a few twigs in the process.

"We will take turns doing the lookout. I'll take the first shift," Ace says. "I'm not feeling tired."

"I'm hungry," Everett says, munching on a carrot that I swear wasn't there a moment ago. "I can't live on carrots alone."

My stomach lets out an angry growl. Turns out I, too, can't just survive on carrots alone.

"We're not going to sleep right here, are we?" I say, pointing to the dirty, almost dead, grass. "Otherwise, we're just offering ourselves to the Pack."

"Of course not," Ace says and opens up his backpack. He pulls out a small velvet drawstring pouch—the one he'd used to draw a sword out of last time. The same sword that helped me fight against the Behemoth—the Heart Sword. "We'll be sleeping in this bag."

"Ooh," Everett says with wide eyes. "You will all have to sleep on the ground. Lucina and I will share the sleeping bag."

Ace rolls his eyes. "No, we can all sleep in it."

Cheshire stares at the bag. "I suppose we can cram ourselves in like sardines in a tin. Maybe we can each get a foot in."

"Seriously," Ace raises his voice. "You lot aren't even listening to me."

Ace opens the small bag and puts it on the ground. He places his foot in and it disappears.

"Come on, all of you," Ace instructs us. "Follow me."

He starts to go down into the bag as if he's going down a set of stairs.

"Fun," Everett says and jumps in after Ace.

Cheshire ushers me along and I get in. I'm expecting to be met with darkness as my head goes into the bag but light bulbs flicker above me. I was right—Ace wasn't walking *as if* on steps. There are actual steps!

As I hesitantly go down the spiral stairs, I end up in a small room. It has double bunk beds and one double bed that has my name etched on it in gold on the headboard. There is a small kitchen area and another little room, which I can only presume is a bathroom.

Cheshire appears on the bed with my name on it. "When did you get this?"

Ace takes a deep breath and says, "Your father gave it to me when he learned Alice was searching for the Knave."

"Why are you constantly draining his magic?" I find myself holding the wall for support.

"No," Cheshire replies for him. "This is a constant. It requires no further magic. I think this was your father's originally, but the king redecorated it."

"It's true," Ace says. "But you don't believe anything I say."

I scowl at him and fold my arms. It's because I've been fed so many lies.

"Now, now." Cheshire appears between us. "We're all hungry and tired so we're saying things we do not mean."

"I'll make dinner." Everett hops along to the kitchen.

Are they seriously going to let a child cook?

"I'll help," Ace mumbles and follows him.

He avoids me like I'm a disease. It's me who should be avoiding him, not the other way around. His ambivalence pulls at my heart.

I rage across the room and flop onto my bed. Cheshire jumps next to me and starts licking himself.

"Do you have to do to that in front of me?" I sneer.

Cheshire licks his lips. "It's been a while since I've had a bath."

I roll my eyes.

He sits back on his haunches. "I think you should learn Spade magic."

"Why?" I stretch out on the soft bed, releasing the tension from my body.

"Well, for starters, you can't call the Heart Sword."

"You know about the Heart Sword?"

"Everyone knows about it." Cheshire grins.

"Do you know how I can call it?"

"No," Cheshire says with disgust. "I know nothing about Heart magic, but I do know Spade magic won't drain your father. But, then again, using your Heart magic won't drain him, either."

"How come?" I sit up.

"Because when the first royal families of the other kingdoms were given magic by Arexus, the first King of Hearts, he purposely made sure their magic was separate from his, so they could govern their kingdoms freely." Cheshire rubs his paw against his head.

"How is Heart magic different from Spade magic?" I ask.

"Heart magic comes from emotions and feelings. Spade magic comes from logic. You're aware of what you're doing, and you understand it."

"So how does it work?"

"It works when one gets to know oneself," he tells me. "It's all about confidence."

"Is that why you're so cocky?"

"True, princess." He grins. "But I'm different, I've had time. I've been around for a long time, like your mother."

Finally, a chance to get know my mother. "What was she like?"

"Nothing like what the history books have said. She was the most elegant, beautiful and intelligent creature to exist. The day she became the Queen of Spades was the beginning of the golden era and the Spade Kingdom thrived."

"How did she meet my father?"

"Doesn't matter." He hisses and narrows his eyes at me. "I wish I'd been there. Maybe she wouldn't have died."

I've never seen Cheshire this hostile.

"Why weren't you?" I ask.

"My duty is to the Spade Kingdom and that overweighs your mother. I had to go back. The King of Spades became a father to twins, and he needed me."

"I have cousins?" I'm surprised to hear the delight in my own voice. To think, I've had more family out there and had no idea.

"Yes, four, in fact," he goes on. "The king had two daughters afterward. Their middle names are your mother's name... Dammit! I'm digressing. This isn't important now. Anyway, where was I?"

"Knowing myself?"

"Yes, yes." He nods. "You have to accept yourself for who you are; positives, weaknesses and all."

"Sounds hard."

"It is. Took me four hundred years to get it."

"Then how do you expect me to get it?" I bang my fist against the bed.

"Your mother came into her powers very quickly, a bit like one of your cousins. They just seemed to have an understanding of the world that sometimes I don't even get. But I'm hoping maybe your mixed blood might make it easier."

"Sounds like it would make it harder. Don't emotions conflict with logic?"

"Yes, but I think you have some acceptance of yourself and you can unlock some basic Spade magic. That alone is powerful enough. Let's do an easy exercise."

He spins his head all the way around and vanishes. Seconds later, he reappears, bringing with him a small rock. He places it on the bedside table, about sixteen feet away from me.

What's the point of the rock?

"We will use this rock," Cheshire says. "Now, what do you know about it?"

I rest my chin on my hand, already bored. "It's a rock."

Cheshire lets out a vicious screech. "Concentrate, Lucina. What have you learned about rocks? What is it made of?"

I grunt. I never really liked school. "Um, there are several types of rocks."

"And what is this one?"

I narrow my eyes. "It looks like granite."

"It's sandstone." Cheshire gives me a grave glare.

"How am I supposed to know?"

Cheshire twitches his whiskers and jumps off, hovering in the air. The rock comes flying my way. I catch it in my hands.

"What was that for?"

"Feel it!" Cheshire barks. "Get to know it. What does it *feel* like? What color is it?"

My fingers brush against it. It reminds me of sandpaper, when I use it to finish off wooden pieces. "It's soft but rough, and this one's tan."

"Yeah, and what do you know about it?"

I shrug.

"Oh, my. Please, I don't think I can handle another Nero."

"What?"

"Your cousin." He rubs his head. "Didn't you learn anything about stones in school or from the Knave?"

"You can build things with it, but water erodes it and if it does, moss, grass, small bushes grow in it, damaging the infrastructure."

Cheshire stretches. "This is good. Anything else?"

"It can be made up of loads of other things like shell, bone and coral."

"Okay, you know enough about it. What is its weight?"

"Well, it can vary, but this is one's pretty light."

"Good," Cheshire says. The sandstone comes out of my hand and goes flying back to where it was once was before. "You know this, so I want you to think about it logically and I want you to think about this specific stone. Think about its weight and how it feels, and then I want you to move it."

"So, you want me to go over there and move it with my hand."

Cheshire screeches yet again. "I want you to move it *with your mind*. Any moron can move it with their hand."

"Fine," I snort.

"Start by looking at it," he says.

I stare at the sandstone rock and mentally start to list off facts about it. *It's got a grainy texture, is as light as a letter, and has a tan color. Water will erode it over time.*

I have no idea how much time has passed, but the stupid rock refuses to budge. I stretch out my hand, and still nothing.

Cheshire watches the rock intently and I can see hope in him. I don't want to disappoint him. I've been such a disappointment to everyone so far.

I let out a large grunt. "How come I don't siphon off my father's energy?"

"No, that would be too dangerous." Cheshire shakes his head. "Having two Heart royals in one would be explosive."

"Then I'm just useless. I can't even move a stone."

"Lucina, please don't be so hard on yourself," Cheshire says. "This is my fault. I'm pushing you too hard. Maybe I'm pushing you in a direction that you're not meant to go in just yet."

This is the first time I've seen Cheshire be sympathetic. It's really strange, almost disturbing. I know I complain about him enough, but I can't stand to see him like this. It's like I'm letting him down. And he's done a lot for me. It's amazing how his faith in my mother doesn't waver despite her being dead.

The waft of cheese, onions and eggs grabs my attention and my stomach grumbles. Everett has already placed plates on the kitchen tabletop. There's a huge pie and in a big bowl next to it are baby potatoes, plus another bowl full of veggies.

"That looks amazing." I rush over to the table.

"I'll eat anything," Cheshire says and materializes at the table. "Your mother was an amazing cook, and also a great baker. She made the best lemon tarts of all time."

A gasp escapes me. "*I* make really good lemon tarts."

Cheshire smiles. "I will have to wait and see if they are good as your mother's."

To have something in common with my mother makes my insides gooey. I didn't think royals cooked. Too bad I'm too hungry to really sit and take the feelings in.

Ace comes over to the table but keeps his eyes on the food. I go for a few bites, trying to ignore the way he affects me. It's like being on a merry-go-around. One minute we're fighting, then we're okay, then we're fighting again.

Ace gives me a side glance.

I focus on my plate whilst trying to fight off the heat rising into my cheeks.

"I'm going up to keep watch." Ace takes a plate, plops some food on it and goes upstairs.

What was that about? I didn't even say anything.

Chapter Twenty

'm stuffed. The food wasn't the best I've ever eaten, but it's not the worst, either. I look over to Cheshire and Everett, who are busy stuffing themselves with pumpkin pie. At least I avoided desert, though it's tempting.

"What's wrong with you?" Cheshire purrs.

"Ace doesn't think much of me," I mutter.

"He didn't say that, Lucina." Everett places his fork on the plate. "He's just got a lot on his shoulders."

"Like what?" I run a hand through my greasy hair.

"It's not our story to tell," Everett says with downcast eyes. "It's a sad story."

A story I wish someone would tell me.

Cheshire sits back on his haunches. "Cut him some slack,

Lucina. That boy has been through a lot. You of all people should be able to understand that."

Everett picks up his fork and licks it. "Maybe it's because Lucina doesn't have much of a heart, so she can't empathize."

"That's not true." My elbows rest on the table. "I feel normal. Besides, I always felt for the Knave."

"The Knave is anything but normal." Cheshire burps. "Excuse me."

A hard knot of anger twists in my stomach. "The Knave is a little reserved, but he's a good man. He took care of me. He loves me. I wish he was here now."

Cheshire mumbles something. I don't catch it.

Everett scrunches his face. "My dad's been trying to find for him for ages."

"Your dad is searching for my dad?" My fingers curl into the tablecloth.

"He's not your dad." Cheshire raises his voice.

"He raised me!" I raise my voice right back at Cheshire.

"Yeah," Everett says, hopping down from the chair and ignoring Cheshire's outburst. "If anyone's going to find him, then it's my dad. It's where I get my great sense of direction from."

"So, when he finds him, he'll let us know?" I can hear the excitement in my voice.

"Yeah." Everett turns away from me with his plates in his hand. "I call Lucina's bed."

"You have your own bed," Cheshire narrows his eyes.

It's too late. After Everett shoves his plate in the sink, he hops into my bed and I'm too tired to argue.

I'm walking down a long, secret passage again, the same one I found my father in. I don't have a candle to shed light, yet my feet know what to do. I know I'm going the right way as the closer I get the smell of roses grows stronger.

Suddenly, the surroundings change and I'm walking on the softest clouds. The moon is so large that it's right in front of me.

"Lucina." My father, the king, appears from the clouds as if through a fog.

"Father!" I cry out and run over to him.

He takes me in his arms and hugs me without the restrictions of the chains to stop him. I've never had this feeling radiating in my heart; it fills every part of me with warmth. Dad, the Knave, has never held me like this.

The king—Valentine—strokes my head. There's a light in his eyes as he stares at me.

"How is this happening?" I pull back from his embrace.

"The dream world," he says. "We're both sleeping."

"How come you never did this before?"

"You didn't have a heart and last night my magic was greatly drained," he says. "It was safer that way. Now, Lucina, I need to talk to you about Wonderland—that is, the world, not the voice in our heads." He starts to walk among the clouds, and I follow. "Anyway, I wanted to tell you not all of Wonderland's inhabitants are bad, some are simply warped beyond their control. Try to save them, but if you can't, then you have no choice but to kill them. It's better they are put out of their misery."

That explains everyone at the Heart Castle. They were all crazy, even when they were calling me princess. And there was me thinking they were stupid... Joke's on me.

"How come everyone knew about me being your daughter, but Alice didn't?"

"Only some of them knew. The ones who still have some semblance of their loyalty to me. And again, it's down to magic. But now the rose-tinted glasses have disappeared from everyone's eyes, they're becoming aware of Alice's rule poisoning Wonderland. Also, remember, Alice is not from this world, so as much as she tries to claim my magic as hers, she can't feel Wonderland."

My eyebrows knit together. "What do you mean?"

"When someone dies, you will feel such sadness, but then it's counteracted when someone is born, as then you will feel happiness. These are the emotions of Wonderland. You see, our blood created Wonderland so essentially our blood is in everything and we are linked to it all. It's how we, the Heart monarchs, can hear all the thoughts and feel the feelings of Wonderland's people. As you grow into your power, you will be able to control it more."

"But someone dies or is being born all the time."

"Yes, and you'll probably feel a pang now and again. Sometimes, it's so unbearable that you can't move. That's what happened to me during the needless bloodshed that occurred in the Broken Hearts War. But when it's someone close to you, it will be a lot for you to take in."

"I killed the Behemoth and I felt nothing," I tell him.

"You didn't have a heart back then, though."

"What about the Pack? Three members died today; I didn't feel that, either."

The King's eyes harden. "The Pack are dead spirits. They're

not alive. They're poor souls that Alice constantly reanimates into wooden dolls using her cursed blood magic."

"That's disgusting." I spit out.

"Lucina, when you're in a dangerous situation with the Pack, I want you to call upon the Heart Sword."

"I tried." I throw my hands to my sides.

"What do you mean?" He cups his chin with his hand and the moonlight catches his ruby eyes.

"I tried to call it with the Pack earlier and it wouldn't come. Ace said something about coming into my own."

He takes in my worried expression and then he makes a sound in between a laugh and a gasp. "How could I forget?"

"What?" I stop and stare at him.

"There's a technique to calling upon the Heart Sword. Unfortunately, you have to figure it out on your own. I had to go through this rite of passage, too." He clears his throat. "I have so much to tell you, like how you have the power to heal those who became warped by Alice's influence. When you get your second heart piece from the Spade Kingdom, your power will grow, and it will continue to grow until you have all the pieces."

"I can't use my power well. I barely lit some dynamite earlier."

"You'll get better, you're still quite limited." He places his hand on my shoulder and squeezes it. "You'll get there."

"Like what?"

"You can't make people do what you want, and you can't use your magic for evil. Otherwise, whatever you do wrong will come back onto you. You can't make people fall in love with each other, you can't bring someone back to life, well, unless..." He trails off, his hand comes off my shoulder and he turns away from me.

"Unless what?' I run in front of him.

He changes the subject.

"What do you think of Wonderland—I mean Wonder?"

I frown. "Unless what?"

He sighs, breaking eye contact for a moment, before meeting my gaze once more. I'm getting the strong sense that whatever he's about to say, it'll have nothing to do with Wonder and everything to do with something unpleasant.

"I always wanted to have this conversation with my child, since there is no one else who gets to talk to Wonder apart from you and me. Unfortunately, I have something very important to ask of you, and it must take precedence over anything else. Please, be kinder to Ace."

"Wait, how do you know?" I shake my head in disbelief. Why does he have to bring up Ace? It's distracting me from my previous thoughts and questions.

"I'm connected to him and all of Wonderland."

"He's using your lifeforce!" I shout.

"And without him, I'd be dead." The king closes his eyes for a moment. "That poor boy has his own demons, too, and he could do with some kindness from you. That is what it means to be the monarch of Wonderland. Just like Wonder, you must be loving, kind and warm to all."

"It's hard."

"I know, especially with everything you have been through, but you have to remember you're not the only one. All of Wonderland has been damaged. Take Finn, for instance. I could hear him crying out for me every night and I could do nothing to comfort him. Now, he's dead and that's on me. When you gain more of your heart, it becomes easier to understand others; but at the same time, it becomes more painful. It hurts to see your subjects in pain of any sort. So, it's best you learn compassion now."

"He's using your power," I mutter.

Doesn't he get it? I don't want to lose him. I know people using magic is what's slowly killing him. And I don't want to be alone anymore.

"Yes, with my permission," he says. "And without his connection, I would be dead. Lucina, he keeps me alive. That boy gave me his heart."

"I don't understand this heart thing?" I ask as my stomach drops.

"Ace only gave me a portion, but that portion is linked to me so he can feel. But Ace's heart is filled with the sole purpose of saving everyone. It's so strong, nothing like I've ever felt. He's even willing to die for it. Die to put you on the throne."

"I had no idea," I say. "Why doesn't he tell anyone?"

"His story is a lot more complicated. If anything, the two of you have more in common than you think."

I turn my head, guilt pricking my chest. This entire time, I'd been thinking Ace is selfish in using my father's power, but it turns out he's only doing it because he wants to help everyone. I was so focused on the king staying alive that I didn't think about Ace. He didn't need to give my father his heart.

"You know what you have to do."

With that, my father disappears, and I wake up.

I'm in the small room again and I find Everett in my bed and Cheshire at the foot of it. I carefully get up in my long nightgown, pick up a baby blue throw blanket from one of the spare beds, and climb the stairs.

Ace is outside of our makeshift shelter, sitting down and leaning against a rock, his shoulders hunched over. He's staring at his cards, his eyes sad, as he shuffles them up, down, left, right and diagonally. He draws in a staggered breath. I've never seen him like this.

I clear my throat and walk over to him. His gaze faintly drifts in my direction, and his face hardens.

"What are you doing up?" He stops playing with his cards. "It's Cheshire's watch, not yours. You don't have a turn."

"And why is that?"

Ace's face is tense. "Because if they take you, that's the end of it. Obviously. No Wonderland, no nothing."

I maneuver the blanket around so I can sit on it rather than the ground, and I plonk myself in front of him.

"What are doing?" he asks.

"My father sent me," I say and look up at the sky.

A beautiful array of stars reflects the palest blue soft light. The occasional hooting of owls breaks the silence of the night.

"What did he say?" He narrows his eyes.

"That I should be nicer to you."

"You have no tact." Ace lifts his eyebrows. "You just come out with it."

I pause, forcing down the building rage within. "It's better than lying."

"I don't like lies, but there have been times I wish I didn't know the truth."

"Why?" I scrunch my face.

"I said sometimes," he says and rolls his eyes. "If I didn't know the truth, I couldn't do anything to save anyone."

"Like giving my father your heart," I blurt.

"He told you." He stares at me for a moment before leaning back and crossing his arms, then stretching his feet out on the dying grass. "No one but your father knows that."

I lift a part of the blanket to my lips for comfort. "Guess it's harder when you don't know what you've got till it's gone."

"Not having a heart doesn't change you as much as everyone thinks it does. Things just feel..." He pauses and thinks. "Slower."

"For me, it's more intense, having my heart." I place a hand on my chest.

Ace takes a deep breath. "You know, I'm like you in some ways. My mother died when I was young and my dad, he wasn't a part of my life."

"I'm sorry."

I couldn't imagine life without my dad and everything he did for me. Actually, what did he do for me? Other than teach me how to fight. Maybe Ace is right, and we do have a lot in common.

"I was in an orphanage for most of my life."

"I know you don't want to talk about it," I say. "But if I heard your story, perhaps it would help me understand you. Apparently, monarchs of Wonderland are meant to be kind and loving."

He snorts. "Your father is the most loving person I've ever met. He's one of the good ones."

I smile with a tight chest. As much as I love my father, I love my dad, too. "Do you know anything about my dad... I mean, the Knave, like where he is?"

Ace shakes his head. "I don't know much about the Knave. Not many people talk about him, which is a bit odd. Anyway, you father, the king, he's always worrying about you. He's always telling me."

"When do you have time to talk to my father?"

Ace cocks his head. "You know when my eyes light up blue? He's talking to me then."

"That's..." I try to find the words.

"Intense. I know a lot about him. He worries over his legacy, but I keep telling him you will be his legacy."

That's sort of sweet, but sad at the same time. "Don't say that. You make it sound like he will die."

"I won't let him die." His voice has a determined edge to it. "I have more to lose than anyone from his death."

"Your heart." I fumble with my fingers.

"I suppose, and then I'll die. We're interconnected, after all." Ace's blue eyes glow with sorrow and anger.

It's strange to think we're connected in so many different ways. There's still so much I want to ask Ace. But with his arms folded over his chest, I know he doesn't want to talk anymore. And I respect that.

I still don't understand all this stuff, but I feel like I'm becoming closer to Ace.

Chapter Twenty-One

he next morning, Ace avoids me. He walks ahead of me, and my feet struggle to keep up even as my mind spins circles around itself. Even Everett, with his tiny legs, is ahead of me. Then again, he's supposed to be the navigator.

The woods begin to evolve. The trees around us are getting taller, thicker, with more branches and leaves. I sigh, breathing in deeply the smell of pine needles and woodsmoke.

Cheshire materializes on my shoulder and he places his tail in front of my eyes.

I shove it out the way. "What do you want?"

"Always in a mood," he says. "No matter, I forgive you. I must say you're so much like your mother."

"How so?" My excitement tangles with a thread of sadness.

Cheshire's weight moves off my shoulder. He's in front of me again, floating. "Well, she was all work and no play until she met your father."

"How did they meet?" My hearts leaps at finding out more about my mother.

Cheshire rolls his eyes. "He came to visit the Spade Kingdom ten years after your mother became queen. Then he saw her fencing. At the time, he didn't know it was her, as she was covered in her lame—fencing outfit."

"Tell me more," I plead.

"He thought she was a man." Cheshire shrieks. "How dare he? She always had a beautiful, elegant frame. How could he think like that?"

I grab Cheshire's face and squeeze it. "Get on with the story."

"Me-ow!" Cheshire vanishes from my hands and he teleports five feet away, his smile disappearing. "That was mean."

I inhale deeply. "Just tell me what happened?"

"Your father challenged your mother," Cheshire snorts. "Idiot. She beat him with ease. The stupid Knave was crying foul like a buffoon."

"Dad was there, too." I lean in.

Cheshire's nose twitches. "Yeah. He overreacted and tried to fight your mother. She beat him, too."

"She did?" My heart flutters like a butterfly's wings.

My mother sounds so amazing. She beat both men! And while I don't know how good Valentine is with a sword, beating the Knave is an impressive feat. I can only do it on a good day.

"Oh, with ease," Cheshire scoffs and floats backwards as I walk along. "Then when your mother revealed herself, your father instantly fell in love. Chased her like a puppy for a year."

I shake my head. "So, she didn't feel the same."

"Not initially. Hikki found him amusing." Cheshire makes a guttural sound in his throat. "She had her kingdom to think about. But then things started to change. She was conflicted at the time. She loved your father and her kingdom. But eventually she gave up her home, her family, her people... her life."

There's something about the way he says it that makes me stop moving.

Cheshire continues to speak. "We, the citizens of the Spade Kingdom, are different to the Heart Kingdom. Hearts have this profound optimism; they trust their heart. While the Spades, we think deeply about situations; we trust our minds. So, it was strange to have her abdicate her throne. Hikki was loved by her people."

"Wow," I whisper. I don't know if I could do what she did.

"Hikki was a natural with her magic," Cheshire goes on. "I think you will be, too."

"Really?" I jump over a puddle.

"Yes, you just need to keep practicing."

Yeah, like how I have to practice getting the Heart Sword. Why couldn't things be easier?

"You have the blood of the most powerful Spade in

you." Cheshire places a paw under his chin. "You can do it. It will help you in this forest, for instance."

"How?" I walk across the forest floor. "Because none of you are sure what happens in this forest, other than citizens going mad? Then how do we prepare for the unexpected?"

"You will be able to know what's real and what's not," Cheshire says. "Why don't you try practicing some Spade magic as you go along?"

I nod eagerly. As we walk, I try to move leaves, branches and little pebbles by remembering what I know about these objects. My enthusiasm changes quickly into frustration and I end up yelling at Cheshire, who disappears.

We continue on, me trailing behind Ace and Everett, my feet stomping and rustling against the leaves.

Within a few hours, the leaves change from a striking blend of greens to copper and gold. It's as if the seasons have changed within minutes. The others walk ahead like there's no issue, so I trail behind them even more.

A thick, vaporous mist clutches around and in-between the forest's upper canopy. Soon, darkness takes over the forest as no light filters through. Mist seeps across and fog obscures the forest floor, to the point I can't make out my own feet.

For all I know, I'm floating above the ground, as my steps make no sound. In fact, nothing does. The forest is silent. No rustling of leaves from the wind or birds chirping. No snapping of twigs from scurrying creatures. No noise of any kind to break the complete stillness.

Something isn't right, and I don't need Wonder to tell me that.

I can just about make out Everett's outline, so I run forward. It's weird that none of the others have said anything about this oddity. The trees are now silver as if they have been bathed in moonlight.

"Everett," I call out. There is no reply.

The mist fog thickens till I can't see anything.

"Wonder," I call out. He probably won't reply because he's never there when I need him.

"*Watch out,*" Wonder's voice comes out as a whisper.

A shadow emerges from the blanket of white. A silhouette appears. I know that shape. That tall, thick build. It can't be.

I reach down to my ankle and swing out a knife just in case. One never knows.

"Lucina."

It's my dad's voice—the Knave. He's got a voice like a foghorn, husky, and I'd recognize it anywhere.

"Dad!" I take a step forward.

He comes into my view—big, burly, salt and pepper hair with a hideous beard. It's Dad. I want to tell him how much I miss him, how much I need him, let him know about what's happened, ask him why he never told me.

He must have come for me. I knew he would.

But as he emerges more into my view, I see bright red drops of blood. His shirt and breeches are torn and bleeding. He's panting, blood seeping from his abdomen, and he crashes onto the ground.

"Lucina, help me."

My heart pumps hard, each beat fueled by panic until my mind is overcome with thoughts.

I remember the time when Dad almost cut his arm off on the grinder. He didn't call for me, the stubborn mule. Instead, he bandaged himself and went to his room. Even when I tried to apply cream to his wound, he brushed me off, telling me only the weak used it, and demanding I get on with the orders. He was delirious for days, and ignored everything the doctor said. Told me if I called the doctor again, he'd kill them. He said he'd rather die than take the doctor's magic. After two weeks, he healed, but he still has a huge scar on his left arm.

Even if he were dying, my dad would never ask for help, he'd bark orders; even if he was dying. Whoever this is, it's not my dad. It's an illusion.

My dad disappears and my eyes open—I'm on the ground.

Cheshire appears next to me. "I leave you for one moment and look what's happened. I swear you can't cope without me."

The wall of fog and heavy clouds render the forest invisible. All I can see is Cheshire, because he's right in front of me. And then a part of me wants to whack him away.

Too bad, he's all I have.

I get up from the ground. "Shut up. If you want to help me, tell me what in the Underland is going on?"

Cheshire fades away until nothing but his eyes remain. They move left and right, circle around, and eventually stop.

His full body materializes again. "I have good news and bad news."

"What is it?"

Cheshire's head spins upside down. "The good news is

we have made it to the Forest of the Illusions—we're in it now. And the bad news is I can't find the others, so they've been affected the mist."

I lift up my hands. "What does that mean?"

Cheshire's head continues to spin around. "It means nothing to you and me. Spades barely get affected by mythical mists. You know, what with us having higher cognitive prowess and all."

"Funny, considering I was just in an illusion." My fingers go into my palm, and I dig my nails into my skin. "Okay, but what does it mean for everyone else? Are they hallucinating?"

"Oh, that." Cheshire's head stops spinning. His paw disappears from his body and it taps his head. "Well, this particular mist is well known for taking an individual to confront their greatest fears. They're dreaming, effectively."

My nails dig deeper. "Is there anything we can do?"

Cheshire purrs. "It means they must confront their demons. We confronted ours."

I let out a disgruntled sigh. "What do I do? Just stand around and do nothing?"

Cheshire rolls onto his stomach. "We could just leave the woods and wait for them outside."

My insides squirm and a hard knot of anger tightens in my stomach.

"By the way, what was your worst fear?" Cheshire asks, licking his paws.

"I'm staring at it," I reply. "We have to find the others!"

"You are so mean to me."

"Because you make it so easy."

Cheshire opens his mouth and closes it. "Do you think we can find them in here?"

"*Yes.*"

"Yes," I reply, happy to hear Wonder again.

"And how can you be so sure?" Cheshire mutters from somewhere behind me.

I can't suppress my smile. "Because Wonder says so."

"You're so stubborn, just like..." Cheshire trails off. "Let's find that little rabbit and boy with the jaded heart."

"Shut up," I scan the area. "Damn fog."

"If Wonder says you can find them..." Cheshire vanishes, sarcasm dripping in his voice. "Then why don't you listen to Wonder?"

"Fine."

Come on, Wonder, I think to myself.

"*Listen to you heart.*"

Not this again.

"*You can do it.*"

I close my eyes, trying to channel the magic within my heart. Warmth surges in my chest and spreads across my body. The energy threads through my muscles. My arms start to tingle, and a bubbly feeling fires through me. My heartbeat rises and falls with my breath until there's no sound, not even my own pulse in my ears.

The magic pours out of me, extending out into the world, spreading its warmth. I know everyone says my magic is separate from the king, but I still can't help worrying about him.

Moments pass, and nothing happens. I won't give up,

and I ask my heart with all my will to help me. More moments pass and I start to lose faith when the soft thud of a heartbeat grabs my attention. I gravitate toward it and it grows louder as I reach out.

A dash of crimson comes across my eyes.

"*I helped.*"

"Yes, you did," I say and open my eyes and dash forward. "Follow me."

The blanket of white mist starts to fade away and it no longer swallows the objects in the distance. The forest floor slowly unfolds as I press on.

It's then I see him—Everett! His little body is crumpled on the floor, next to a mossy log.

I speed forward and slide down toward him. I shake his body, crying out his name "Everett!"

"Everett." Cheshire jumps on the other side of him.

Everett doesn't move. Not good.

Cheshire waves his paw in front of his eyes. "I never thought I'd have to resort to this." He then slaps Everett's cheek. Over and over again, leaving the poor rabbit's cheeks turning crimson.

I grab Cheshire's paw. "What are you doing?"

"It's how my wife wakes me up," he says sweetly. "It's very effective, I'm never late."

"You have a wife?" I try not to laugh. How can anyone put up with him?

I have no time to waste on this. Everett needs my help.

"*Go into his heart.*"

What?

"*Use your heart to go into his.*"

How?

"Listen to his heartbeat."

"Of course," I say out loud.

Just like before, I close my eyes and search for his heartbeat.

"What are you doing, Lucina?" Cheshire growls.

"Getting Everett."

My skin goes cold and clammy and I drop to the floor. Everything goes black, then turns to white, and white melts away to reveal a party.

A very large party.

Chapter Twenty-Two

arties are a pretty new concept to me, since the only ones I've been to were at the Heart Castle. I only went to one party in my village and that was as a child. Dad hated it. He picked me up and ran home.

This party isn't normal, I can tell; unless everyone at it ate a growing mushroom, and that includes the furniture. The chairs, the tables, the bouncy castle, and the ice cream machine are all gigantic. Then there's me, this tiny little insect in comparison. Everything's ten times my size.

How am I going to find Everett in this? Also, if I do find him, how will he see me in this small state?

The loud music drowns out every other noise, even

making my skin jump. The bass from the drums and guitar thumps in time with my heartbeat as if they are one.

The sound is too much for me. I can understand why Everett would find this place terrifying. To top that off, everyone's talking over the roar of the music. I can't make out anything they are saying but their laughter rings in my ears and won't stop.

The room looks like someone puked color all over it. Huge bubbles float in the air and multicolored balloons drift around aimlessly on the floor among the discarded wrapping paper. Multicolored banners drape the walls. There's a stack of unopened presents on a large table in the middle of the room, wrapped in smooth, shiny wrapping paper.

The ground thumps and a group of screaming children run over to me. I'm going to be squashed like a bug if I don't get out of the way!

I run as fast as my legs can take me, which isn't as fast as I'd hoped. The children cover more ground in comparison to me and my tiny legs. I just need to get to the leg of the table closest to me and it should provide shelter from the children's feet.

But as I run, it occurs to me—this place is an illusion, like the one I had with my dad. None of this is real. So, by that logic, then they shouldn't be able to hurt me. They'll go through me.

I never touched my dad, so I really don't know if my theory is correct. But if I was in danger, Wonder would tell me—or so I'd like to think.

I'm not going to make it to the leg of the table and even

if I do, there's still the chance of being trampled. There's no choice; I turn to face them. A part of me wants to move accordingly, but then I remember how I woke up back in the mist. It's not real. It's like a dream, someone else's dream.

The children come running toward me. A rabbit child with shiny red shoes and white laces is first. I stand defiantly, staring at the foot that is about to go over me—I hope.

As it comes down, the world grows darker, but I don't move. I try with all my might to keep my eyes open. My breath comes out rapidly as I try to steel my nerves.

The child passes through me like a ghost. I breathe a deep sigh of relief.

The children loom around the table. Some kids come and go quickly while others hover around the table, filling their mouths with sandwiches and sweets. Glancing around, I become aware that everyone here is a rabbit beastian. I never knew there were so many different types. Some have long faces, some have chubby ones, some have long bodies and others have round ones.

Why can't getting my heart pieces be easier? Maybe we should have taken the longer route.

"Everett," I shout.

My voice can't be heard over the noise and it's like a squeak compared to everyone else's. Why is his illusion so much more complex than mine? I can feel the vibrations of magic here. There was nothing like that in my illusion, which was so simple. Maybe it's got to do with me only having a part of my heart; therefore, the illusion is incomplete, too.

It doesn't matter anyway. I have to find the kid.

I rush forward, no longer worrying about whoever gets in my way as I pass through them. There are so many people, it's overwhelming and it feels like the room is neverending.

"Everett!" I call out, over and over.

I'm not going to find him like this. I can't get anything right these days. I didn't win the fight with the block of wood, it's my fault Finn is dead, and I couldn't figure out that I was the princess of Wonderland when everyone was literally screaming it at me.

How am I supposed to figure this out when I can't even figure myself out?

"*When you're so close to it, you can't see it,*" Wonder breaks my thoughts. "*This is different.*"

"Nice of you to join me," I mumble.

"*You figured out on your own the illusion before was not your father, and that those children weren't real.*"

Big deal. Like that matters.

"*Trust yourself, Lucina.*"

A part of me wants to explode. As much as I want to shout and scream my lungs out, I know I have to focus.

I take a deep breath. Why is it so much harder to focus? It always felt so much easier before. Making decisions was crystal clear because I thought rationally.

I suddenly remember Cheshire and how he talks about Spade magic; how they think logically, just like I had with my illusion.

Everett's a kid. As a child, what was my greatest fear? I suppose there was the dark, but Dad kicked that out of me by making me camp out at night by myself. Then there was the clown who came into the smithy one time. He was just asking for directions, but his face scared me. So, Dad made me sit with him. It wasn't great; I kicked him in the leg, but I got over it. Dad laughed so hard that his laugh echoed through the smithy. Also, I used to be scared of Bandersnatchers, but Dad took me hunting one day for them and, again, I was cured.

Thinking back, my dad did everything to drive any fear out of me. He really was preparing me to take back the throne. Without him, I wouldn't be as strong as I am today.

It only makes his absence worse and increases my sense of loneliness. There's so much I want to say to him, to thank him for. I miss him so much. As a child, I hated being without him, and I still do. I wish he were here now. He's not the fuzziest of people, but I know he loves me, deep down.

Something snaps me out of my memories. Chimes of magic ring in my ears. A puff of black smoke appears before me. It unwinds and stretches out, forming a trail. I don't even think. I follow it, running as fast as I can. It weaves around furniture, balloons and discarded food. I rush through all of them to save time.

The path moves away from the children to the adults. It's crowded at first, but as I go on, the crowds grow thinner and at the end of the black smoke, I finally find Everett.

He's *very* small. He's always been smaller than me, but now he's half his size.

"Mommy!" he calls out. "Daddy, where are you?"

His head is slumped, his shoulders are sagging, and there's a black cloud that swirls around him.

"Everett!" I shout.

He doesn't hear me, and he continues to waddle his way around the room. Suddenly, he stops, and his eyes widen.

"Mommy! Daddy!" he cries out and dashes toward a table with very large rabbits on it. They are all drinking cups of tea.

I follow after him. Everett's fast as usual, but at least I know where he's going.

He gets to the table and calls out to the adult rabbits. They ignore him and, like Cheshire, they suddenly disappear.

His eyes shift from side to side again and glaze over with a glassy layer of tears. His pink nose twitches and he blinks. Tears drip from his eyelids and slide down his furry cheeks. He bites down on his lip tightly. My heart feels strange; it clenches at the sight.

He shrinks.

"Everett!" I cry out.

He turns to me. His lower lip quivers as words slowly make their way out of his mouth. "I can't find Mom and Dad. They've left me behind."

"No, that's not true," I tell him. "This is all an illusion, see?" I place my hand through the leg of a nearby chair.

"It doesn't matter." Everett's tears gush out. "Grandpa left, then Grandma, then my uncles and aunts and cousins, and then Dad."

"My dad leaves me all time," I blurt out, surprised I've said that. "But I know he comes back."

"Grandpa's dead, isn't he?"

I gasp. Didn't Bunny tell him?

"I saw Mommy crying, but I pretended not to." Everett sniffs. "I don't even know what he was like."

Everett continues to shrink until he's the size of a mouse. I have to go onto my knees now to talk to him.

What should I say, though? I always say the wrong thing in situations like this.

"Trust your heart."

I only have one quarter of my heart.

"But it's better than nothing."

I think back to Finn and memories resurface. On my first day in the Heart Castle, he treated my foot and it healed incredibly fast now that I think about it. Staring at Everett, I can see so much of Finn in him.

"He looked like you," I say.

Everett's head snaps up.

"And all he ever wanted to do was return to his family," I continue. "I remember him telling me that when I first met him."

"He did?" Everett perks up, his whiskers twitching.

"Yes, he really wanted to visit your family. Apparently, I even reminded him of your mom when she was younger."

"How?"

"She didn't want to wear a dress like me."

"Really? I never knew that. What else did he say?" Everett asks, his ears perking up.

"Well, I didn't get to know him well," I say, rubbing my head. "But he was always nice to me."

"That's nice," Everett smiles, and he starts to grow. It's not much, but it's something.

'That's it, Lucina."

What's it?

"Keep reassuring him."

I scratch my head as I try to think of things that will make Everett feel better.

"You will be reunited with your Mom and Dad soon, once I get back my heart. Your family will be together again. And I'll make sure no one will tear them apart ever again."

"You'd do that?"

"Of course." I rub my palms together. "It's sort of my job now."

Everett grows larger, to the size of my knees. He's much larger than he is in real life.

"You're the best, Lucina," he says and hugs my knees.

Everything vanishes around me, turning white at first, and then eventually black.

I open my eyes to find Cheshire pressed up on my heart. "What are you doing?"

"Trying to wake you up," he hisses.

Everett's body stirs on the ground and he yawns, slowly getting up and opening his eyes.

"Everett, you're okay?" Cheshire screeches.

Everett smiles and runs over and hugs me. "All thanks to Lucina."

"What did you do?" Cheshire grabs the collar of my shirt.

"I thought logically," I say. "It wasn't as hard as I feared."

Cheshire's paw vanishes and appears above his head, scratching it. "It must be the combination of your Spade and Heart blood that allows you to do this."

"A little of both." I place a hand over my chest.

Cheshire growls. "I'm glad you're embracing your Spade side."

I shrug. I suppose it all comes eventually. I wasn't good in the smithy at first. It was only through practice that I got better.

Everett rubs his face. "Why do my cheeks hurt?"

Cheshire shakes his head, giving me pleading eyes. "I have no idea."

"Cheshire slapped you," I say bluntly. "In his attempt to wake you up."

"What?" Everett's cheeks become even redder.

"I didn't use my claws." Cheshire reveals his claws.

Everett scrunches his nose. "That's so mean."

"It really was," I add.

"Quiet, child, and I'll give you a purple carrot," Cheshire says.

"Ooh, give me!"

Cheshire rolls his eyes and does a flip. A purple carrot appears. Everett takes it and munches on it.

No trace of his trials remains, he's as happy as before. In some ways, I didn't just reassure him in that illusion—I also reassured myself. That I *can* do something right.

I glance around the forest. The mist is still the same thickness, blanketing the ground. Why I expected it to be any different, I've no idea.

Now, to find Ace. Hopefully, he's not too far away.

My heart beats rapidly at the thought of him. And though I never know where I am with him, there's nothing I want more in this moment than to find him.

Chapter Twenty-Three

hat's strange," I say.

"What's strange?" Everett asks.

It's not something I want to explain out loud, since I really don't understand the process myself. Reaching out for Ace with magic is impossible, but that might be because my use of magic is so limited.

"Ace isn't normal," Wonder chimes in, telling me what I already know.

Everett taps my knee. "You're not in this alone, you can talk to us."

The mist is somehow getting thicker. It seeps the colors out of everything it touches; from the green of the leaves and moss to the browns of the tree trunks, branches and dirt ridden path. Everything has become the same stony gray.

And every time I try to reach out with magic, I get pushed back. Not like with Everett.

"Finding you was easy," I eventually reply. "I heard your heartbeat. With Ace, there is nothing. It's like the forest doesn't want us to find him."

"You're right," Everett says and lowers his head to sniff the ground, wherever that is. His pink nose twitches. "I can't smell him."

"The magic is stronger here," I say.

Cheshire pops in front of my face. "It might be because we are getting deeper into the heart of the forest…"

"Let me guess, the magic is becoming more unstable," I cut in.

I hold my hands out in front of me, worried I might walk into a tree. Even the sound of my boots crunching against the leaves and tapping against the soil is being drowned out.

"That's Wonderland at the moment." Everett says with a heavy sigh. "But shouldn't some stability be back with Lucina having a piece of her heart?"

Cheshire's head spins upside down. "With Alice still syphoning off the king, it's still unstable because technically he's still the true monarch. At least until Lucina gets all the pieces of her heart back and takes over."

"My heart," I whisper. Ace doesn't have a heart at all, unlike me who has a piece of mine. "Does having a heart really make such a difference to a person? Is that why I can't find him?"

There is a long, ghostly silence that stretches too much, until I can no longer bear the tension and break it.

"What's with the silence?" I say, turning back to find no one can face me.

Cheshire disappears, leaving behind only his tail that swishes back and forth. Everett stares at the ground and scrapes his foot back and forth.

"More secrets?" My voice is tight.

"It's not our secret to tell," Cheshire's voice booms out of the mist.

"You can't break a promise." Everett blinks.

"What promise?" So many feelings spring up inside of me at once—like I've been shot, and no one is willing to help me. My fists clench at my sides. I'm sick of these secrets.

"Ace is very private about his life." Cheshire reappears. "Even I don't know that much about him."

"And Cheshire knows everything about everyone." Everett nods. "I mean, he's got nothing better to do."

Cheshire hisses and reveals his claws in his front paws. "How dare—"

I grab Cheshire before he can lunge at Everett and he vanishes from my hands.

I don't know whether to laugh or cry. "Would you lot stop with all of this? Tell me the truth, it might the only way we can find Ace. Do you really want to waste more time here? We need to save Wonderland, and I need to save my father."

Several seconds of awkward silence pass.

Everett hops over to me and tugs on my trousers. "Don't be upset, Lucina, you know how important promises are."

"No, I don't." I shake my head.

Cheshire appears above my head. "Has that Knave taught you nothing?"

I jolt back a few steps. "Stop doing that! And I have no idea what you're talking about."

"Oh, my." Cheshire's hand vanishes and appears on his face. "Lucina, promises in Wonderland are bound in magic."

"Yeah, and if you break that promise, you get punished," Everett chimes in.

A vague recollection of Edith and my promise to her springs to mind... Ugh. I don't have time for this.

"Fine," I say through gritted teeth. "Well, you tell me what we're supposed to do to get out of this mess. We could be wandering this forest for hours or days and not find Ace."

"Ask for help."

"From whom? Not these guys." A muscle in my jaw twitches.

"What is she on about?" Everett says.

Cheshire says something to him, but it doesn't register as I focus on Wonder's voice.

"No, ask other citizens of Wonderland."

My head starts to throb. Not magic again.

"It's not magic, it's who you are."

"What do I do?" I ask, trying to block out Cheshire and Everett's voices.

"Reach out to them with your heart. Maybe you can find Ace through their eyes."

It's worth a shot. Anything is better than hearing my so-called team of experts squabble.

"How?"

"Just like before—concentrate. Become one with the land and call out to them."

I wish Wonder would make more sense. I still can't even make that stupid sword appear. Every time I use my magic, it's by accident.

"Is it? Think, Lucina. How did you feel during those times?"

Thinking back to the few times I used it, back in the woods with the Pack, with Everett, I was worried. It was all about protecting everyone. But I've always grown up with that logic. Dad drilled it into me. So, if that was true, when I met the soldier Eight, I should've used magic.

"You didn't have your heart then. Also, what did you feel?"

A hand waves in front of me. "Are you okay?"

Everett stares at me with his large pink eyes. Looking at him reminds me of the worried people in the capital, when the Behemoth attacked. All I wanted to do was save them from harm and feeling any pain or losses.

"I didn't use magic then, either," I mumble and drop to my knees.

"Why are you talking about?' Cheshire raises his eyebrows so high, they're off his body and floating in the air.

How do I do it?

"Heart magic uses emotions but not just your emotions. It uses other people's emotions, too."

It finally dawns on me. With Everett, I found a trail of his emotions, the black cloud of his sadness by focusing on my own emotions.

Why can't Wonder tell me things more simply?

Placing a hand on the ground, I dig my fingers in the grass. It's rough and shaggy, like uncombed hair. Instead of pushing out for emotions, I pull for them. Pulsing from my fingertips is a strange, bright light. I watch it flicker.

In the light I see a bagpipe bird—a very annoying bird that makes a blaring shrill sound that grates the ears. He's searching for berries in the forest. He disappears and a dog duster appears. This dog duster is brown and shaggy. Their sole purpose is to clean floors with their tails.

"The forest is very dirty today," the dog duster thinks while cleaning the forest. *"Something new has entered and disrupted it."*

The dog duster vanishes from the light, and new animals flock through; a badger, and a drum panda—a panda with a drum for a stomach.

A committee of vulture umbrellas appear perched on a dead tree branch with their flat, chicken-like feet. They gawk at something with their naked heads that range from a deep red to a blood orange.

The vulture umbrella farthest on the right tilts its head to the others. "Do you think we can eat it?"

"Only if it's dead," another vulture umbrella replies, flapping its light fabric-like wings.

"It looks dead to me," another vulture umbrella says.

"Then why is its body moving?" says the first vulture umbrella.

"I say we eat it," the one that flapped its wings says.

Show me what they are looking at. There is an authority in my voice I've never heard before.

The light moves—rather, shifts—and there is Ace on a floor of leaf litter. His chest moves ever so slightly. He's asleep, lost in some illusion like Everett.

Which way is he? I ask Wonderland mentally.

"East."

I'm about to get up when I catch sight of the vulture umbrella appearing beside Ace. Seconds pass and another one joins him.

"No, no, no." I shake my head.

"What's going on?" Everett asks.

"Ace is in trouble," I say.

"Where is he?" Everett asks with alarmed eyes.

I can't answer him as my gaze hangs on tightly to the light's image. More vulture umbrellas surround Ace.

This is bad. Even if I run at my fastest speed, I don't know if I'll make it in time.

My heart leaps and sinks. It drops as If I'm free-falling out of the sky as the vulture umbrellas draw closer. I need to be there now; I have to help him.

A warm yellow light wraps around me. It soothes my anxious bones and holds me up. In the light, I catch sight of a silhouette. It's taller than me—it's my father, the king. He extends his hand and I take it. He pulls me toward him, and the light brightens to the point it forces me to close my eyes.

When I eventually open them, I'm in front of the four vulture umbrellas circling Ace. One of them bends down, his beak ready to tear at his flesh.

"Back off, you stupid idiots!" I shout.

The vulture umbrellas leap up. A few of them hop away from Ace's body.

"Who are you?" One of them asks me.

"The Princess of Hearts," I say, feeling the lingering warmth of my father's presence.

They start talking to each other as if I'm not there and I'm struggling to tell them apart since their monotonous voices, appearances and poor mannerisms are all the same.

"I didn't know there was a princess."

"Did Alice have a child?"

"I don't know what goes on outside this forest."

"I heard from a sawfish that trouble is brewing in the capital."

"Why would a fish talk to you?"

They're truly the stupidest creatures.

Ace lies still in the leaf litter and my heart begins to beat thunderously against my ribcage. I rush forward, shooing the vulture umbrellas out of the way.

He looks so serene when he's sleeping. There's no sharpness in his eyes, no anger, and no conflict on his face. It suits him. He appears so childlike with his almost-feminine features, silky blond hair and refined beauty.

"We can make a deal. If you want him, we can share," one of the vultures says, peering over Ace on the other side of me.

I brush him back with my hand. "No one is eating him and if you want to put up a fight with me, then I'll gladly show you my knife." I pull out my knife from the inside of my boot.

One of the vulture umbrellas flies up and settles onto the dead tree branch. "You can all die; I want to live. I'm a lover, not a fighter."

These creatures are so odd.

"She only pulled out a knife," one of them says.

"Do you really want to mess with me? I'm the Knave's

daughter," I say with gritted teeth. These idiots are wasting my time.

The vulture umbrella behind me speaks up. "Wait, so Alice and the Knave had a daughter?"

"That's disgusting, no!" I try to keep my voice's pitch from going too high. "My real father is the former King of Hearts, but I was raised by a different father—the Knave."

"I don't understand," one of the vulture umbrellas says.

I wish I could differentiate between the four of them, but I can't, and it's confusing me.

"You don't understand anything, Tor. I heard about this," one of the vulture umbrellas behind me says. "My dad used to tell me the story of how the King of Hearts had a daughter that somehow was passed on to the Knave."

I lean forward and place my knife back. "Do you know any more?"

"No, he used he tell the story around my bedtime and I always fell asleep because my dad has one of those voices."

Why am I even bothering to talk to them?

"They can help."

How?

"Right, I need to get into his...soul. Using magic." I hesitate, trying to find the right words. "And save him. But the last thing I need is you four pecking on him or me."

"That sounds heavy," the vulture umbrella from the tree says.

"How is that heavy?" I gasp. No, I will not engage with them. "I need to save him because if I don't, Wonderland will cease to exist." It's all true, even if I can't tell them about Ace's heart being tied to the king.

The four vulture umbrellas stare at me with brows that dip in confusion. I briefly explain my story to them—with a few omissions—and end nicely with, "Wonderland will blow up."

All four vulture umbrellas' mouths drop.

The one vulture who hasn't spoken opens his beak. "Then what are you doing talking to us? Save him."

"Then don't peck me!" I shout.

"Why would we peck you?" The vulture umbrella from the tree asks.

"Because I'm going to lose...consciousness..." I begin, but their blank faces tell me I need a much easier explanation. "I'm going to go to sleep in order to pull him out of his sleep."

"So, will you go to sleep in his place?" The vulture umbrella behind me says.

"No," I say with gritted teeth. "I will wake up, too."

"Erek, Grifilet and Tor, let her do what she needs to do," the quiet vulture umbrella says. "Don't worry, princess. I, Gawain, and my companions will not peck you. If anything, we will protect you when you're down."

"Thank you," I say and kneel beside Ace. "Wait, he doesn't have a heartbeat. How do I get in?"

"What?" Gawain squawks.

"Then can we eat him?" The vulture umbrella beside me asks.

"No." I pull back his beak. "He's still very much alive but... he's...."

How do I say this without giving away Ace's secret?

"I see." Gawain pushes one of his friends out of the

way by opening up his wings. He wobbles toward me and whispers, "Sounds like heart transference. He'll still have a heartbeat, but the actual essence is elsewhere."

"Really?" I whisper back worried that I've let Ace's secret slip. Well, at least the umbrella vulture doesn't know Ace's heart is with the king. "But I didn't hear it before when I was searching for him."

"Perhaps it's due to his proximity." Gawain nods. "Physically, the heart is gone, but the essence is still there. You can't fully take someone's heart."

"Thanks," I say with mild surprise. "How did you know that?"

"My granddad," Gawain says. "He's very wise. Taught me a lot. He's always talking about the old Wonderland, the one before Alice. He believes that the true heir will come and save us all. I thought it was all stories, but you're living proof they're not."

"She could be lying," one of the others says.

"No," Gawain raises his voice. "Her eyes, they're red, the mark of true Heart royalty. And that headband, it's the Heart Crown reshaped. But then again, I don't expect any of you to understand since you never went to school."

The other vulture umbrellas duck their heads.

"I didn't like school," the one up in the tree says.

"I'm sorry, but I don't have time for this," I say. "It's bad enough I have to use magic, but I've been separated from the rest of my group and I have to find them after this."

"What do the rest of the group look like?' Gawain asks.

"A little white rabbit and a grinning cat," I tell them.

Gawain turns to the other vulture umbrellas. "Boys, I

need you to find a bunny and a cat. Get them out of this forest to the side where the flower fields will be."

"You'd do that?" I place a hand over my heart.

"Of course," Gawain says. "I would tell them to bring your group here, but they'll probably get lost. They're not the brightest apples."

"Thank you," I say.

"See? You can do it."

"No, we should be thanking you," Gawain says. "You will save Wonderland."

"I hope so." A long sigh leaves me.

"No hope. You *will* do so," Gawain says with a nod. "Now get your friend out of that trance. These three will get your other group out and once you've woken your friend, I'll help you two exit the forest."

I nod and smile, then take Ace's hand and search for a heartbeat.

Chapter Twenty-Four

step onto the smoothest road I've ever seen. It's wide, flat and matte-black, and the edges have neat yellow lines. The buildings are strange; some are stone, some are brick; some have spires, some have slanted roofs. It's strange. It reminds me of Wonderland, but I know it isn't.

I walk by a building with giant posters on the upper walls. One has a green-faced woman in a black hat, a woman in white whispering in her ear. Another poster has a star and a man on the top point of the star.

People walk on the sidewalk; I rush over to them, but their faces are blurry.

"Excuse me," I say. "I'm looking for someone…"

They walk right through me without any acknowledgement. I tap a finger on my forehead and remind myself this all just an illusion. A very strange one. I need to find Ace, and soon.

As I explore, I find smaller alleyways and cobbled streets that remind me of Wonderland. I turn and pass the biggest shops I've ever seen, each with strange names that make me wonder what is in them.

A loud roar erupts, and I jump. The biggest red contraption appears. It's like a carriage made out of metal but with no horses to pull it. How does it move, and so fast, too? It heads toward me with bright lights that appear out nowhere. Is that magic? I move out of the way and it passes me, only to disappear down the never-ending road.

I push my questions aside and continue to search for Ace, but he's nowhere to be found. This isn't like Everett's illusion, where everything was contained in one room.

Great, another maze for me to find Ace. The vulture umbrellas helped me last time, but I've got nothing here.

"Wonder," I shout.

"This is strange."

"Yep," is all I can say. "What do I do?"

"You can still use your magic here."

Follow the heartbeat, I tell myself.

I have to concentrate and think of Ace with his honey-blond hair, his angled face and sharp eyes. A soft beat touches my ears. It's faint, so I start to move. After a few minutes of trial and error, I manage to feel Ace's heart pounding in my ears—*duh-duhn, duh-duhn.* As I keep moving, it grows louder to the point where I can hear his breath.

Fifteen minutes pass and the hairs on my arms stand to attention, chills running down my spine.

"Ace," I call out.

There is no response. He's got to be here somewhere.

Finally, I find many stationary metal carriages and Ace standing outside a pale-yellow building that says, 'The Eagle and Child' on it and has a plaque with the same message.

I rush over to him. He's pacing up and down the area very slowly. He's wearing odd clothes; rough black trousers, with a white shirt with no buttons and a shiny black jacket. His shoes are ridiculous—the same texture as his trousers, but with a toe cap made of white rubber.

"Ace," I cry.

He doesn't reply, nor does he see me. I wave my hand in front of him, but still nothing. His pupils are larger than normal. He continues to walk past me, nudging my shoulder without a care.

"Ace," I repeat, rushing after him.

He's mumbling something. "I need to fight..."

I can't catch the rest of his words because he gets quieter toward the end. His voice perks up again. "She's the most important person but I can't..."

His voice drops again. This is getting frustrating. How do I help him when I don't know his problem?

"Maybe I can go into his heart."

'That won't work because he doesn't have it. You can feel his heartbeat but not his emotions. Besides, he appears broken to me."

He really does. The area under his eyes is dark and his skin has a sickly hue. Maybe he's sick and I need to get him some medicine? I shrug it off, knowing it's a bad idea and continue to follow Ace's mumbling.

"Need to save her..."

"Why can't I do anything?" I ask again.

"I need to be free..."

I stop in my tracks. He wants to be free; why is he not free?

Then I remember—he needs his heart. The one my father has. He's obligated to do all this because of my father. By giving him his heart, he's stuck. He can't be free. He's stuck helping my father.

"*But Ace gave it to your father. He wants to save Wonderland.*"

"I know, but maybe he needs it back," I say to Wonder. "To save whoever this 'her' is."

Ace continues to pace up and down this strange street with its bright colored shops and odd buildings.

"But how do I give him his heart? It's with my dad."

"*But none of this is real. Use your magic. You can do it.*"

I gasp. "That's it, Wonder! I can create a heart with my magic, claim it's his and everything will be back to normal."

"*You can give it a try. If giving him a heart doesn't work, we can try something else.*"

I cup my hands together and focus on them. I think back to my own heart. It was only a tiny piece of it I'd seen, but it was beautiful; so shiny, so red, so full of life.

I narrow my eyes and concentrate on creating. Sweat pours down my forehead and salty beads invade my eyes. Ignoring them, I push forward, focusing all the energy within me into my hands.

My breathing accelerates and my chest becomes hollow, but the heat intensifies everywhere. More sweat dribbles down me and I feel the energy leaking out of me like a hole in a watering can. But thinking of Ace and what he's done for everyone, including the king, urges me on. Moments pass and the magic stops, and I slowly open my hands—a heart lies between them.

Relief washes over me, and I rush over to Ace. He scratches his head, his eyes transfixed on nothing in particular.

"Ace!" I shout.

He doesn't react and so I have no choice. I kick him in the back of the leg. He stumbles slightly but somehow manages to maintain his balance. I kick him hard, then rush forward and kick him in shin. This time, he falls to his knees.

"Sorry," I say, though a part of me enjoys kicking him. Not because it's him, but because it allows me to let out some pent-up anger.

I hold out the heart in front of him. "This is for you."

My breath hitches as I wait for his reaction.

He doesn't move. I knew it wouldn't be this easy.

Then there's a slight twitch in his eyebrows, his pupils get smaller and his eyes soften.

"What are you doing here?" He blinks uncontrollably and his lips slowly move. "Are you giving me your heart?"

I freeze as Ace slowly gets up. A smile spreads across his face, transforming him from the moon into the sun. Both beautiful, but in different ways.

"Wow." He tilts his head slightly, and a soft blush spreads into his cheeks. He places his hand on his face. "I didn't expect this…"

"No, you've got it wrong," I say trying to keep the heat off my cheeks. "This is *your* heart."

"My heart…" He stutters and his smile falters.

I hold it up to him. "Yes, so you can be free."

He takes a step back. I frown and the silence between us draws on. I hold up the heart again.

His lips curls and his hands come forward and push mine back. "Keep it away from me."

"But why?" I ask. "This is your heart."

"No!" he shrieks and gives me a glare of palpable disgust. "I don't want it."

"But Ace…"

"I don't want it!" he yells.

The steel chairs and table outside the green shop that says 'Café' start to rattle and move like several carriages have passed by them. The building shakes and cracks appear beneath us.

Please don't let it be another Behemoth, I don't have the energy to fight one. My limbs are heavy from using magic.

"It's not a Behemoth," Wonder tells me. *"It's Ace. He has become disillusioned."*

"What?"

"Lost the plot."

Ace's pupils widen again, and he drops to the ground, bringing his knees to his chest.

"What do I do?" I say and drop the fake heart.

Ace's face twists into fury and he kicks it with his right leg. It hurls off onto the smooth road where the metal carriages run. Ace pulls his leg back to his chest.

"Ace." I drop down next to him.

The shaking around us intensifies.

"I can't save her!" he shouts at me and buries his head into his knees.

The buildings in the distance begin to move likes waves on the sea, rising and falling. Each new wave grows faster and stronger, causing buildings to crumble into their own foundations.

"You need to get out."

Wonder doesn't need to tell me twice. I lurch forward and grab Ace. If he's not going to come willingly, then I will force him back.

I take a deep breath. I'm so tired from creating his heart, but with Wonderland at stake, I call out with everything inside me to save us.

A hot light comes through the sky—it smells like roses. It's my father.

Chapter Twenty-Five

My father pulls me out as I hold Ace in a place full of nothingness, just pure white. Ace fades from my arms, slipping through my fingers and disappearing. My heart twists and worry ripples through my blood.

"He's safe," my father says.

He's only a silhouette in the light but I can feel him, and it makes me feel safe. The way I was with my other dad, the Knave. My hand instinctually reaches out for him. Just a little more time of this warmth, love and security. Before I can touch him, he vanishes and everything goes ice-cold.

"Lucina," a familiar voice calls out. "Lucina."

The white fades to black and I open my eyes with a flutter. Ace is crouched next to me. His eyes are tight as he bites his lower lip. I try to move, but my body is stiff. It's never been like this before. Again, I try to move, but everything is slower.

"I can't move." My voice is on edge as shock goes through me.

"What? How? Why?" Ace grabs my hands.

Gawain tries to move my right leg but pain soars through like I've been struck by millions of needles.

"You have depleted your magic. It has taken a toll on your body. You just need rest, and your magic and body will be restored."

"Oh great, stupid magic," I say. "I've depleted my magic and Wonder says I need to rest. We don't have time for rest."

I think of my father, who was with me only moments ago. He helped me when he shouldn't have and here I am, being a complete utter waste of space.

"You saved me." Ace's eyebrows draw in together tightly.

"No...yes. Dad saved us, and now I can't move."

I bang my fist onto the ground, only to produce a soft thump. The area is more visible as the fog has become a mist.

"The boy can carry you." Gawain leans his head in and tilts it to Ace. "Just follow me, I'll be in the air."

"Gawain, he can't pick me up." A bitter laugh comes from my throat. "Look at him, he's so puny! There's no muscle on him."

"I can pick you up." Ace speaks up, his anger a quiet undercurrent.

"But can you carry me?" I laugh.

"Yes, I can." Ace stands. "Besides, you're not exactly full of muscle."

"At least I have muscle," I say, wishing I could lift up my arms.

"Would you stop arguing?" Gawain intervenes. "You need to rendezvous with your friends. Pick her up, boy."

Ace kneels down with his back facing me. "Come on then, get on."

I slowly lift my arms and place my hands onto Ace's shoulders. He takes a hold of them and pulls them over his shoulders, so they dangle in front of him. My chest is now against his back. He picks up his bag in the process and hands it to me. Luckily, it's not too heavy.

He starts to stand, grunts, then pushes through and lifts me. My upper body flops against his back. My head lands against his shoulder, brushing his soft hair. He hooks his own arms under my legs, picking me up completely. His touch is warm through my clothing.

Ace tries to get a glimpse of me over his shoulder. "You're surprisingly light."

"Why, did you think I was fat?" I tease.

"Perhaps," he says in a mocking tone.

"Hurry up, you two," Gawain says and opens his umbrella wings. He starts to float up into the air and as he does, he pushes the mist back, clearing the area.

"That's amazing," I say out loud, thinking about his innate skill.

Gawain smiles and tilts his body to the east. He glides across the air, and the mist disappears wherever he moves.

Ace pulls his arms up, lifting me a little higher. He crosses my hands over each other, then takes a deep breath and begins to walk.

He gestures with his head to Gawain. "How did you meet him?"

"Trying to find you," I say. "Used magic there, too. No wonder I'm so tired. And there I was thinking I was an infinite source."

"You will be when you get your full heart and the more pieces you get, the more magic you can sustain."

Gawain is flying ahead, concentrating on finding us the path out of here.

Ace's uniform has a strange texture. It's smooth yet rigid, not like the clothes he wore in his illusion. I know that illusion of his is private, but I saw things I can't unsee. Those smooth roads, the metal carriages, the strange shops and those people with no faces.

I lean into Ace more, relaxing my head. "What did I see in that illusion?"

Ace lifts his head, tensing. The mist has all but disappeared thanks to Gawain. The sun is setting and it's an orange-pink glow that makes the fully leaved trees appear like cotton candy. My stomach starts to rumble.

Ace digs into his trouser pocket and pulls out a small purple packet with strange writing on it. He tears it and stretches his hand back. "Here, have this."

"What is it?"

"A chocolate cake bar," he says. "Your stomach's rumbling."

"Oh, I can't."

"Eat it," he commands. "You need the energy, and I can't stand to hear your stomach squelching as I walk."

I take the package off him, peeling it back to reveal a deep shade of brown. It

smells like sugar. I take a bite and the moist chocolate melts in my mouth, sticky with chocolate frosting on my tongue. I smack my lips together.

Ace keeps walking and I stop caring about everything else as I slowly devour my treat. And I mean slowly. I savor every bite. I've always been a slow eater, something that got on my dad—the Knave's—nerves.

As Ace walks, I push away any leaves and branches that come our way with the little energy I have. After an hour or so of walking, my ears perk up at the sound of trickling water. There's a brook where the water flows between the rocks. A bone fish jumps out and kicks its tails upstream. We end up following a small creek through a series of moss and lichen covered rocks.

"You saw my world," Ace whispers after a while, sounding hoarse.

"Your world? What in the Underland are you talking about?"

"It's what you saw in my illusion." Ace stops walking. "I'm going to share some things with you, but don't you dare tell anyone."

"I won't, I promise." I take my head off Ace's shoulder.

He sets me down on the ground, leaning me gently against the moss-covered rock. He moves away toward the brook, getting out a small flask and filling it with water. He calls to Gawain and the vulture swoops down. They share a quiet conversation I'm unable to hear. Gawain bobs his head and flies off.

"What are you doing?" I ask Ace as he comes back.

He holds out his flask. "He's going to come back in thirty minutes. I told him we needed some private time and to go rest for a bit, get some food, have a drink."

Sweat drips off Ace's face. He's done a good job carrying me with those puny arms of his. He deserves a break, too.

I take the flask. "Thanks."

Ace sits down next to me and leans back against another moss-covered rock. "What you saw in that illusion was my world, the place I'm from."

"What? You're not from Wonderland?"

He shakes his head. "I'm from a city called Oxford in England and that illusion, it was my home."

"Does everyone know you're not from Wonderland?"

"Only some of them, like the Hatter, Cheshire and so forth."

So that's the secret Cheshire and Everett wouldn't tell me.

I think back to the illusion. "You have metal carriages with no horses?"

He frowns, scratches his head, then his expression clears. "Oh, you mean cars. Yeah, they're a fast mode of transportation but terrible for the environment. That's not what I want to talk to you about, though."

Ace's eyes dart everywhere to avoid looking at me.

I lean over to him. My muscles are still tight but have loosened. "You can tell me anything."

"The only person who knows this secret is your father."

He inclines his head back against the rock. The forest is darker, and the night grows closer.

"I promise not tell anyone," I say, trying to help him feel comfortable.

"It's not that." He lets out a bitter laugh. "I'm afraid—you'll never talk to me again."

"Was my father angry with you when you told him?"

"No," he says. "If anything, he was really sympathetic and kind."

"Then I shall also do the same," I declare, leaning back.

Ace doesn't say anything, and I find him staring at me with an unreadable expression.

"What?"

His eyes find my lips. He leans forward, growing so close that I can hear his heartbeat and my own. They beat together in perfect union. Slowly, his fingers brush against my lips and they tingle. A strange sensation goes down my spine. Heat flushes into my cheeks.

"You had chocolate on your mouth, it was annoying me," he says.

My lips feel warm from the ghost of his touch. I wince, cursing the chocolate for embarrassing me so much.

"So, you were saying?"

"Oh, that." He sighs and leans back. There is a heavy pause. "You see, I'm from a world unlike Wonderland, the same world Alice is from."

Shock spreads up my spine and I sit up. "What?"

"It gets worse." He gives me a quick glance out of the corner of his eyes. "Alice is my relative."

"What?" More shock jolts through me, but this time it

feels like a slap that reverberates across my face.

"She's my great, great—some more greats—grand-mother," he tells me.

"How is that possible?" I suddenly remember how Alice appeared old without the crown on. "She's been covering her age with magic."

Ace makes a strange sound. "Time also works differently where I'm from. It moves much faster than Wonderland."

"Oh, I see," I scratch my chin. "Then why are you going against your great, great whatever grandma? Surely she's family."

"She's not my family. Not anymore." His eyes focus on me sharply. "She cursed my family."

"How?"

Question after question slips off my tongue. I'd have thought, given how our last conversation ended, that he would shut down again. But he doesn't. On the contrary, much as I can see the strain on his features, it's almost like telling me all this is cathartic for him.

"To come back to Wonderland, she did a blood curse," he continues with narrowed eyes. "You see, she came to Wonderland as a child and then returned back to my world. Got married. When she had children of her own, she wasn't content. Always thinking back to her beloved Wonderland and its King of Hearts."

I say nothing and let him elaborate.

"Alice was a seven-year-old girl when she came to Wonderland. She was a stupid, bored little girl sitting on the riverbank with her older sister. Then everything changed when she saw a talking, clothed white rabbit with a pocket watch run past. She followed it down a rabbit hole and came into Wonderland, where everything was peculiar and wonderful. She met so many characters, from a dodo to a duchess to a cat to a caterpillar. She heard a story from the mock turtle and gryphon and went to the maddest tea party in all of Wonderland. But she was taken with a handsome king."

Ace takes a breath, then lets out a sigh. For a moment, I fear he won't continue, but then he picks up where he'd left off.

"Luckily, Alice's stay didn't last long. She returned to her world, always thinking of the handsome king. Eventually, she returned to Wonderland through the Looking Glass, but landed in a different kingdom. Again, she returned back home, with no king by her side. Years passed, Alice married and had three boys, but they were nothing to her. She yearned for Wonderland and its handsome king. She tried everything to return but couldn't because Wonderland had locked its doors to her."

"How? Why?"

Ace shrugs. "I don't know. I don't understand how Wonderland works."

I study his face, looking for answers. He's quite handsome, I realize suddenly, with his high cheekbones and mesmerizing blue eyes.

This is not the time. I need to focus on my mission. "Then how did she get here?"

Ace's face is stark as his eyes focus on something far-off. "She stumbled upon a book which told a story, one that was eerily similar to her experiences in Wonderland. She found the writer and asked how he knew of her story. It turned out he was actually a resident of Wonderland but was trapped in our world. You see, the writer was a disgruntled soldier who yearned to rise in the ranks of the nobility in Wonderland. The king banned the writer for his attempted assassination of the Knave, the king's dearest friend. He came to this world, angry and full of contempt for Wonderland and then he found Alice. Learning of Alice's ability to enter Wonderland and her love for the king, the writer saw an opportunity. He twisted Alice with his magic and used her blood to have her return to Wonderland. He even taught her how to manipulate the king and his citizens with magic. Unfortunately, magic comes at a cost. And Alice's magic draws from her bloodline so whenever she uses it, it drains life from her children and her children's children, and so forth."

He finally returns my gaze.

"I'm sorry."

His lips press into a thin line before he says, "It's not your fault."

I give him a nod and Ace continues to speak. "Her successors all die young. She has only two of us left, me and my sister, Kate. We don't have much time, Lucina. She's draining us. She will kill me, but I don't care as long as Kate survives. She's only thirteen, she has so much time ahead of her. I can't let Alice live, but I can't kill her because of the wall of magic she has up. Only you can break through that wall."

"This is a lot to take in." And even more pressure on my shoulders. I rub the temples of my head, recapping the events of his illusion. "So why don't you want your heart back?"

"Because I'm safer without it." He sighs, his eyes softening. "We share our lifeforce and so I keep the king going while he slows down my energy drainage."

"But wouldn't my dad be double-drained?" I swallow. "From Alice's blood magic and everyone using his?"

"No, he's immune to the blood magic because he and Alice don't share the same blood," Ace replies.

My shoulders sag with relief and it occurs to me. "Does Alice know you're her... great...grandson?"

At last, he smiles and the sorrow in his face disappears. "She's a narcissist. She wouldn't notice if a big blue whale was in the room."

I cover my mouth to stifle a laugh.

"Your father was the first person I met in Wonderland, then Finn." Ace clears his throat, and the sorrow reappears. Finn's death has taken such a toll on him. "I suppose it was fated that way, that I'd come through one of those doors to your father."

"You've been through a lot," I say.

"So have you."

"No," I shake my head. "I've lived in ignorance for most of my life. You've had to suffer without any parents, afraid you'll die young."

Gawain's squawk captures our attention.

"It's time to move on." Ace stretches his legs out and gets up. "But I can stop this, if we can find your heart and return Wonderland back to you. After which Alice must be killed."

It feels strange that he'd want a family member dead even if they're distantly related, but at the same time, it makes sense. Hearing his story also makes me wish I had more time to talk to Ace. It's nice seeing this side to him, and his vulnerability is refreshing.

"Alice has done this all because she is in love with my father."

"In the beginning, yes, but now she craves power." Ace stretches out his body. "Come on, we have to get to the others."

Ace picks me up again.

"But what about that writer in your world?" I ask.

"Don't worry, he died a very long time ago."

The energy has returned to my body. I really should let Ace know, except I'm enjoying being carried around while eating another of his world's chocolate bars—another treat follow-ing more rumbling from my stomach. He's been lugging me around for two hours, with two fifteen-minute breaks.

The forest is even more beautiful at night. According to Gawain, the magic releases into the area and creates a beautiful shimmer. But it's not as beautiful as it once was, when the forest would be lit up in blues and pinks and purples.

All it does now is shimmer like glitter, but it's beautiful in a romantic way.

As I rest my head against Ace's shoulder, I feel content. It's a big deal for him to reveal everything to me. The walls he's put up are gone and it's nice to get to really know the person behind those sharp eyes.

"We're almost at the exit of the forest," Gawain tells us.

"I wonder if the others are out of the forest," Ace ponders out loud.

I hope so, but I don't have much faith in the other vulture umbrellas. They're not the brightest of creatures, but I've learned not to judge a book by its cover, like with Ace. Never would I have imagined he'd be able to carry me for so long. He smells like sweat and cinnamon.

Ace speaks up. "You've got a lot of callouses on your hands."

I laugh. "That's what happens when you train with the Knave. I only wish I could call the Heart Sword."

"Unfortunately, can't help you there. All I know is the king told me to lend it to you for that one fight, and that when you came into your own, it would come to you at all times."

"Great," I mumble and change the topic. "What was your life like before Wonderland?"

"School," Ace replies with a grunt. "Studied all the time. At school, at home and in between breaks."

"Is that all you did?"

"Mostly," he says. "But I spent a lot of time trying to figure out how to get into Wonderland so I can save Kate."

"It must be nice to have a sister." My arms tighten around him. "I wonder if Alice hadn't come if I'd have any brothers or sisters."

"You wouldn't have any," Ace says.

"Excuse me?" I jolt up from his shoulder.

"I didn't mean that in bad way. It's just, there can only be one Heart heir at a given time."

"What?" My voice comes out raspy.

Gawain swoops down and interjects. "Yes, only one Heart can rule them all. Two Hearts will create conflict."

"Oh." I can't hide the sadness in my voice.

Ace lets out a short chuckle. "Siblings aren't that great. Kate used to love dressing me as girl. Also, she used to force her cakes and biscuits on me. It would've been nice if she could bake. Instead, I was forced to eat cakes with a soggy bottom on a regular basis."

"What's a soggy bottom?" I snort out a laugh.

"A cake that has not been cooked enough," he tells me. I catch a wisp of a smile on the corner of his lips. "I mean, all she had to do was follow the instructions."

"I can bake and cook," I tell him. "I'll make you a cake sometime."

"That would be nice, princess." He clears his throat. I see a smudge of crimson on his cheeks.

"Lucina!" I shout out. "Don't call me princess."

"Okay, Lucina."

"I'd love to meet your sister."

He laughs softly. "Maybe you can teach her how to bake."

I bury my head into his shoulder and try to hold back my laughter.

The scent of fresh grass catches my attention. A little ahead, the forest opens into a vast grassland.

"Princess!" Cheshire shrieks, appearing in front of Ace. "Are you okay?"

"I'm fine," I say.

"Then why is he carrying you?" Cheshire's turquoise eyes narrow on Ace for a moment.

"I used too much of my magic," I tell him.

Cheshire snorts. "This is why I'm telling you to embrace your Spade heritage. If you can balance the use of your Heart and Spade magic, you wouldn't get so tired."

He's right, but I can't seem to connect with Spade magic. No matter how much I try.

The eruption of hysterical laughter interrupts our conversation. "What's going on?'

Cheshire twists his nose in disgust. "Those stupid vultures are having tea with Riddel."

"How dare they?" Gawain squarks. "They know they're not supposed to have fun without me."

Gawain flies off at full speed.

"Oh, no." Ace rubs his head. "What type of tea?"

"You really don't know want to know. Come on." Cheshire begins to fade away. "Everyone's down this hill."

"Who's Riddel?" I ask.

"Hatter and Candy's daughter," he mumbles. "Rhyme. I mean Joker's sister. She was meant to join us earlier, but she had another mission."

"What mission?"

"Hatter sent her to gather intel from the Diamond Kingdom."

"That's good," I say.

With everyone gone, awkwardness fills the air.

I speak up to fill the void. "Hey, I think I should get off now."

"Are you sure?" he asks quietly.

"Yeah," I say removing my arms off Ace. It's strange, because it's hard to let go of the warmth his body emits. "I have enough energy."

Ace holds my legs tighter. "Are you *sure?*"

"Yes," I say. "Besides, we're going to rest now, and I need to check if I can move."

Ace lowers himself and lets go of my legs. My feet touch the grass. I wobble at first, but I adjust quicker than anticipated. Ace stays close to me and holds out his hands just in case I fall. It's like I'm a baby walking for the first time.

Ace continues to walk backward, afraid I'll fall. Normally, I'd be angry about this. I'm fiercely independent, another trait instilled into me by my dad, the Knave. But there's something about Ace's kindness that makes my insides tingle.

Going downhill is harder, due to the constant need for me to slow down. Plus, it hurts my joints. But Ace is there to catch me.

"Forty-six cups of tea on the wall,

Forty-six cups of tea!

Take one down,

Smash it around,

Forty-five cups of tea on the wall!"

"What is that?" I ask.

Ace frowns in the direction of the noise.

As we approach the camp, a fire is lit, and logs have been placed around it. There are a few tents, too. There's a girl—whom I presume is Riddel—seated on a log with a huge mug in her hands. She's waving it around frantically, some of it spilling onto the ground. The vulture umbrellas dip their beaks into the mug and laugh.

She sits there serenely in a mid-knee purple top and shorts, turquoise coat and stockings with black ankle boots. She's pretty, with bright green eyes, white hair pulled back in a ponytail and her skin is bronze with warm golden undertones.

Everett somersaults, back and forth, higher and higher, all with such ease. He's not stopping.

"Keep going, little one," one of the vultures cries out.

"What's going on?" I ask, walking up and holding my hands against the warmth of the fire.

"The princess!" Riddel screams and gets up. She falls straight down. The vultures all laugh, causing Riddel to go bright red.

"Are you drinking magic mushroom tea?" Ace asks.

Oh, no, she wouldn't, would she? Magic mushrooms really mess with your insides, making you grow one minute and shrink the next. They're not good for one's sanity.

"No, no." Riddel giggles. The vultures all laugh with her, with the exception of Gawain, who's drinking his tea. "It's just mushroom tea with a little magic in it."

Ace rolls his eyes and points over to Everett, who is still spinning and somersaulting. "He'd better not have had one drop."

"Nope." One of the vulture umbrellas hiccups.

"Want some, princess?" Riddel picks up her teapot with great eagerness.

"No," I say with a forced smile.

Ace pulls the velvet drawstring out of his bag. "The rest of us are going to sleep. Riddel, you're staying out here, all night. You've been banned from coming in."

"Okay," Riddel says with a sheepish smile.

Ace opens up the bag and manages to grab Everett. "It's your bedtime."

Everett's flops his head against Ace's chest. "Okay, Mommy."

"Lucina, after you." Ace gestures with his hand.

I nod and step into the bag.

Chapter Twenty-Six

O pening my eyes, I'm met with white fur and bright pink eyes. It's Everett, he's staring at me.

"You're awake." Everett hugs my face. His soft fur tickles my nose, causing it to twitch.

"Princess, are you okay?" Riddel leans over from the foot of my bed.

"Yeah," I lie.

My body feels like the energy has been sucked out of me by some gigantic leech. Every single one of my muscles aches and as I stretch, there's an uncomfortable clicking in my joints. It sounds much worse than it is.

"Really?" Ace grumbles from afar. "Because you've been asleep for over twenty hours."

Twenty hours? I jolt up from the bed. "Why didn't any of you wake me?"

"We tried," Everett says.

"We can't let you use your magic like that anymore." Ace is seated at a table with a large paper on it.

Yeah, because the other alternative of people draining my father is a *great* idea.

I purposefully ignore him and throw the aqua bedcovers off me. "Is that a map? Do you have a plan?"

As I stand, my knees creak. It's like I'm an old lady.

"Hi, princess, my name is Riddel Hatter. It's spelled R-I-D-D-E-L because my name itself is a riddle within a riddle." She says it all with a wide smile, holding her hand out to me.

"Her father can't spell," Cheshire adds from my bed, where he's curled up in a ball.

"He can," Riddel protests. She turns back to me, smiles and curtsies. "I'm yours to command, Your Highness. I am here to help you."

"Didn't you drink magic mushroom tea yesterday?" I narrow my eyes on her.

Riddel lets out a strange sound, a mixture between a laugh and a sigh. "You see, I'd just come from the Diamond Kingdom and my cousin thought it'd be funny if he swapped my chamomile tea for silly tea."

"That doesn't sound funny to me." I place my hands on my hips.

"He's half Club," she says.

I shrug. "What does that mean?"

"The Clubs are tricksters by nature," Cheshire yawns and rolls onto his back.

I walk over to the table where Ace is and stare at the map he is studying.

"Where's the Spade Kingdom?" I ask.

Ace frowns and points to an area in the Obsidian Desert. "We think over here somewhere."

"We think?" My voice comes higher than I anticipated. "That's not good."

"The King of Spades denounced all kingdoms when they sat back and allowed Alice to take the throne." Cheshire stretches his arms.

"Um, princess." Riddel creeps over. "The sources we spoke to believe the Kingdom's there."

"Oh, great," I mumble and give Cheshire a deadly stare, as he rolls all over my bed. "Cheshire, don't you have any idea where it is?"

Cheshire vanishes from my bed and appears on the table. "I got stuck here in this terrible place when the king closed off the Spade Kingdom and made it disappear. I couldn't go back as I had to ensure your safety. My poor wife can only visit me once a year. Do you know how hard that is on a marriage?"

"Your wife visits?" I spit out, wanting to pounce over and wring Cheshire's neck.

"Someone would marry you?" Everett gasps and pokes Cheshire on the nose.

I manage to hold back a laugh.

"Oh, pish posh," Cheshire says. "She can't reveal its location. No need to make such a fuss."

"We're not far from the desert," Ace says. "We might as well try."

"It will be okay, princess," Riddel says and goes to her belt. A teapot is hanging on one side from it. "Let me make you some tea."

I give her a skeptical look, especially after the tea she had last night. "I'm not so sure."

"I am rather parched, now that you mention it," Cheshire says.

"Trust me, this is no average teapot," Riddel says and flicks her finger on the handle. Out of the lid comes out a tiny brown mouse in a loose yellow dress. The mouse can barely keep its eyes open.

"Is it killing time?" She asks with a squeak.

Did the mouse just say kill? That tiny thing can't do anything.

"Not yet," Riddel says. "Meet the princess."

"Nice to meet you, I'm Hazel." The mouse bows with the lid on its head like a hat and smiles at Riddel. "Wake me when it's time to kill."

"The princess needs some tea to recharge." Riddel smiles. "Don't underestimate Hazel."

"Hazel's teas are the best according to Mommy," Everett declares, and he jumps from my bed to the table. "But Mommy won't let me have tea."

"I have just the thing," The mouse retreats back into the pot and a whole bunch of noises occur. It sounds like metal crashing against metal, like back in smithy.

The afternoon sun blazes on my back and sweat trickles

down. So much for Ace saying we're close. We've only just arrived at the flower fields and it's not even a field; it's like a jungle, and the heat is unbearable. The flowers tower over the land and I don't know how long this supposed field goes on for. In the haze of the sun, the flowers glisten.

The ginger tea Hazel made earlier really has kicked in. It's slowly melting away every ache from my abused limbs and it's loosening my muscles, previously locked hard with tension.

Ace stands in front of us. "Okay, everyone. We have to be careful now. The flowers have been corrupted by Wonderland's magic and they will whisper crazy things to you. Ignore everything they say. It will mess with your mind."

"What were flowers like before Alice came?" I ask.

"I don't know," Riddel says.

Everett also shrugs.

"They would sing beautiful songs that would help heal and soothe any problems." Cheshire purrs, floating in the air. "They loved the king; apparently, they used to put him to sleep when he was baby. After Alice came, they became very vain. They didn't like your mother too much but that was because they were jealous of her beauty. Everything is about appearances with them."

"Reminds me of the girls from my school," Ace mutters.

My school life didn't have any of that. There were only seven of us children in the village, so we all shared the same class. I finished when I was fourteen and then Dad loaded me with books and forced me to work at the smithy.

We walk into the flower fields—no, jungle. I still can't understand how it can be viewed as dangerous.

The sun passes through any minor hole it can reach and illuminates the greenery. I find this place an assault on all my senses. The heat and humidity presses on my skin, creating more sweat that trickles down my face. Insects, birds and larger animals create an annoying cacophony. The leaves' smooth texture keeps brushing up against me, so I'm left constantly swatting them away. The air tastes both sweet and fresh, like flowers in a tea, blooming on my tongue. I can't view any of the flower buds as their heads are too high up, but the sky is an array of colors.

"Is it me or is the smell overwhelming?" Riddel says in a nasal voice.

"It's a bit strong," I admit.

Riddel sneezes and she takes out a handkerchief and blows into it. She sneezes again. When I turn to her, I find that her eyes are red, and her nose is running.

"Tea," she gasps and pulls at the teapot on her belt. It unclips and she opens the lid.

Hazel, the little dormouse, pops out, and her mouth drops. "Oh, dear Riddel, you have hay fever. I've got something that will help."

Hazel goes back into the pot. Strange banging noises occur within, again reminding me of metal clashing. Suddenly there's a deep growl and a puff of smoke wafts out of the teapot.

"Hay fever?" Everett wrinkles his nose. "How? You're always outside."

"I don't know." Riddel sniffs.

"Hatter doesn't like too many flowers, always preferred herbs and vegetables." Cheshire taps his chin.

"It's the pollen," Ace says. "She's not used to this much. It's a lot."

"Ready," Hazel says from inside the teapot.

I'm still trying to process how the tea is made in there with Hazel *in* the pot.

Riddel takes out a cup from her bag and pours tea into it. The smell of berries and honey wafts into the air and Riddel takes a sip.

"Maybe we should let her rest up for a bit," I say, wincing at Riddel who can't stop scratching her nose.

"No way," Ace says. "The longer we stay here, the more susceptible we are to the flowers."

"It's true." Riddel chugs the tea down and then takes a deep breath. "I think it's working, but I want out of here."

Hazel lifts up the teapot lid. "If anyone else would like some tea, I can make it for you."

Everett stares at the dormouse. "You're smaller than my sister Angora."

"Ooh, how about an Earl Grey..." Cheshire starts.

"No," Ace says. "We don't have time."

I nod in agreement. "Come on, everybody. We need to get out of here."

Riddel closes the teapot lid and we press on.

It's been over an hour since we've been in the flower fields and my feet are soaked in sweat. I can feel it sloshing inside my boots. Still, I continue to hike, pushing the gigantic leaves out of the way.

Riddel stops every now and then to have some tea. It seems to help her.

Everything seems fine, until Everett comes to an abrupt halt. I hurry to catch up to him.

"What's wrong?"

"I'm so tired," he says with droopy eyes. "I think we should go to sleep."

Out of everyone last night, he got the best sleep. He didn't have to do a watch and he slept in my hair. He likes the smell of it.

"You can't be tired now, you have to direct us," I say, bending down to tap his nose.

"But the music is soothing." Everett sways back and forth like he's on a rocking chair.

"What music?" I ask.

"No, no, no." Ace comes running over. "The flowers are affecting him."

"I can't hear any music," I say.

"Neither can I." Ace says. "I don't know how their singing works."

"My nose!" Riddel screeches. Green liquid oozes out of her nose and her eyes are red all over, drooping with liquid.

"What's happened to Riddel?" There's a strange shrill tone in my voice.

"I don't know," Ace says. "Seriously, we need to get better intel."

"What do I do?" Riddel whines and pulls out a handkerchief from her pocket. "It's so disgusting."

I turn to find Everett slumped on the ground, one side of his face pressed against it, and his bushy tail up in the air.

Ace picks him up. "He's lighter than Cheshire and you."

"Watch it." I teasingly raise my fist. "Maybe Cheshire will know what to do about Riddel. Cheshire, where are you?"

There's not a single sound. Now that's odd.

Even odder is Riddel going over to one of leaves and wrapping herself in it. "Ooh, nice wardrobe."

I raise my eyebrows at Ace. "It's the mushroom tea from yesterday, isn't it?"

"No, it's the flowers." Ace stares at Riddel with amusement.

"Mersey!" Cheshire squeals next. "I've missed you."

"I'll get Cheshire, you sort these two out," I instruct. The moment after, I dart through the flower stalks.

It doesn't take long for me to find him; he's hugging a flower stalk.

"Oh, great," I say. He's been affected, too. "I wonder who he thinks he's hugging?"

"His wife, the love of his life," a saccharine female voice says.

"Don't listen," Wonderland warns me.

"A bit like you and Ace." She giggles.

Heat floods into my cheeks. "No, we're nothing like that."

"But you wish there was something more."

"Shut up!" I cry out, a part of me wishing I could cover my face.

"He likes you, too." There's a bunch of giggles.

I ignore them and make a grab for Cheshire. My fingers brush his fur until the stalk grows and moves higher up, pushing Cheshire farther out of my reach.

"Lucina likes a boy." A bunch of female voices giggle.

Maybe I can use my magic. Only problem is, I've not

fully recovered from my last use and let's face it, my magic is temperamental. The natural way is the best way.

Groaning, I realize I have no choice but to climb the stalk to retrieve Cheshire. So I wrap my legs around the stalk and start to climb.

"He tried to kiss you," the saccharine voice returns.

"You mother was killed by your father," a little girl's voice says.

"I will never believe anything you say," I tell them as I continue to climb up.

What a stupid thing for them to say. There's no way I'm believing that. The king loved my mother.

The leaves begin to rustle and the flower stalks around me start to move.

"Danger."

Oh, no. I should have kept my big mouth shut.

"Alice wants you dead and will make sure you die in our flower bed," the saccharine female voice says.

A rose head comes down and there's a face in the middle of it. Giant leaves grab me like hands, lifting me, bringing me closer to her. Her stalk is full of thorns. I struggle to break free as the leaves wrap around me like a tight blanket.

Ace and Riddel are shouting at each other in the background. Something must be going on with them, too, meaning I can't rely on them to help. This is my battle.

I think about the sparks I created with the dynamite. That's all I need to create a distraction and get away. It's not that much magic. I need a sword. Dad, the Knave, always said I was born to hold a sword. And Cheshire said my mum was best at it; it runs in my blood.

The Heart Sword, I must call for it.

"Heart Sword," I cry out.

A few moments pass and nothing happens. Damn. Why won't it come? I'm going to demand a weapon after this. A proper weapon, not a pan, or rope or dynamite.

"Don't focus on that. You are a weapon. Focus on an emotion and bring forth that fire."

I'm so new to emotions and the only one I can think of is sadness. I start to dwell on all the bad, the Knave and the king, my father. The image of my father trapped in that horrible place, losing all his energy, his spirit.

"Harness it. Take it, manipulate it and make it something new, something magical."

My body begins to glow and a spark appears, like tiny, crackling fireflies.

I drop to the ground with a thump and the flowers desperately try to take out the fire with their leaves. Strangely, I feel a stab of pain in my heart as if I've been pricked with a sword, but nothing hurt me.

Cheshire comes flying down and floats above me. "What you saw earlier wasn't me."

"Not now," I tell him.

Many flowers surround me. A daisy, a daffodil, some petunias and some tulips. Their faces are menacing, and their teeth look ready to bite.

I think of my father again, chained up to that large, red door.

Energy surges through my body, flowing like a thousand rivers, cascading violently and crashing on the shore. Sparks come out and surround my body like a ring of fire. The plants and flowers back off, some even hiss.

Why are they hissing?

I move closer to them and they close their eyes. They can't deal with the light. That's not normal. Plants all need light to grow.

My father wasn't kidding when he said Wonderland had been warped. The plants are doing the opposite of what they are meant to be doing.

I can use my fire to stop this.

"*No!*" Wonder screams.

There's a strange screech and I spin, coming face-to-face with a bright green stalk. Its bulbous mouth is right above me, but it's too late to do anything. I'm picked up and flipped off the ground. Next thing I know, I'm trapped in a greenish purple tube. Everything becomes fuzzy and liquid hits my skin. Thankfully, it's only water. I hope.

"The plant has eaten Lucina!" Cheshire shouts.

"Cheshire, get me out!" I scream.

I remember my knife and try to pull it out of my boot as more water fills the tube. Throughout the space my heartbeat pounds loudly, echoing in my ears.

"This cat has claws," Cheshire yells from somewhere outside.

There's a rumble and I fall back onto my bottom, my pants drenched in water.

"*Try to save them,*" Wonder says.

"How?" I screech.

"*Heal them,*" the king says in my mind.

"Father!" Even though he's far out of my reach, he's still there, diligently trying to protect me and give me advice. He should conserve his energy. "How? What should I do?"

"*Avoid death,*" he says. "*We're not Alice. Don't let our citizens suffer.*"

"Lucina!" Ace calls my name from the outside.

More water comes down, swallowing me as it comes up to my waist. Everything becomes blurry. My vision is all red. I am not an instrument of death. I will not be Alice.

Power stirs inside me, sucked in from the world around me. I try to imagine it, the sensation of something flowing, filling me up. It's calm, loving and all giving. The power surges into me like a flood, and I gasp.

"What's going on?" Cheshire calls out.

I place my hands on the walls of the tube, close my eyes and call out to the flowers. White light blinds me.

I'm sorry you've had to go through all this. All the pain, the sadness. I will not let you succumb to Alice's whims.

I dig deep into myself and travel through the plant, down the stalk and into the roots, into the soil and toward the seeds. I'm at the beginning of the flowers' lives and I reach out to them. The world is new and full of possibilities.

"Push, little seed, push up into the light," I say out loud.

More light bathes all around me. Warmth seeps out of me. A soft tingle rolls out of my fingers and humid air rushes out. The mix of moist earth and fresh flowers fills my nose. Magic rolls along my body like static.

When I open my eyes, I'm not in the plant anymore. The large flower fields are gone, everything has gone back to its original size and the flowers are still there, surrounding us. They bloom around us. Their colors have deepened, and their faces appear out of the petals with bright smiles.

"Princess," a red rose cries out. She is small, about knee-height.

I rush over and fall onto my knees and cradle her face in my hands. "I'm sorry."

"You saved us, princess," the red rose says. Her voice is softer and younger.

"You did it!" The flowers all cheer.

"Thank you," I manage to utter. "But I should thank you."

"Why?" They ask in union.

"I was reminded that I have to save life, not destroy it," I say.

My heart beats uncomfortably under my ribs as my stomach churns, and sweat pours down my cheeks. I'm so tired, but I can't let anyone know.

The pitter-patter of footsteps is behind me.

"You did this?" Everett asks with wonder in his voice.

"Wonder and I did," I tell him.

"How?" Ace says. "You shouldn't be able to do this. Not with your heart still incomplete."

"Love is the greatest magic," I tell Ace and stroke the other flowers.

"Wow, they really love you," Riddel says, trying to get out of a hug on her ankles from the leaves of a nearby petunia.

"And everything and everyone else." Cheshire bats away the affections of a daffodil.

"Your father would be so proud," a yellow tulip says.

My insides sting at the mention of the king.

"Princess, we know you're worried about your father," one of the pansies says.

When I renewed them, we intertwined lifeforces. I got to know everything about them, and they got to know me.

"The princess is hurt," a daisy says.

"She's very weak," the red rose whispers.

I place a finger on my lips. No one needs to know the truth—I'm exhausted. Everything hurts.

"And we can help," the yellow tulip says.

"How?" I ask.

"By healing you," the rose says.

"You don't have to do that."

"Of course, we do," a chorus of flowers sings.

"Your father created us," a white rose says. "And you rebirthed us. We are indebted to you for removing the darkness from us. This is just the circle of life."

"Thank you," I say. "I wish I could stay longer."

"You must go, princess," the flowers say. "The King of Spades eagerly awaits you."

"Let's heal her and her companions," the red rose says. They all begin to sing:

"Refresh their mind
And take away the pain
Like an empty bottle takes the rain
And heal, heal, heal, heal."

My body goes limp, but not in a bad way. All my muscles are loosening and unknotting. After a few panting breaths, I feel a little better, and the bruises on my arms have disappeared. Though I'm still very tired, it's not to the extent I was before.

"Are you well, princess?" they ask.

"Better," I smile.

"Let's get you on your journey," the rose says. "Flowers?"

"Lift off," they say.

The flowers begin to curl and rise up and on top of each other, forming a tight coil. They lift us all up in the process and everything gets smaller and smaller. On the far edge of the platform, the flowers plunge back toward the ground at a steep, straight incline, their texture soft and smooth. They've created a flower slide!

"Don't be afraid," the flowers usher me. "It's fun."

Everett gets onto the slide. "Me, first." He jumps down the slide, squealing in glee the whole time.

Riddel rushes in after him and shouts, "I love Wonderland!"

Ace and Cheshire stare at the slide apprehensively.

Cheshire steps forward at the start of the slide and stares at it. "I don't like the look of this."

"Scaredy cat," one the smaller daisies says.

"How original," Cheshire responds and glances back at the slide. "I'm not afraid..."

I push Cheshire down, and he's gone with a yelp.

"I needed him to stop yapping."

Despite my attempt at humor, Ace's fearful glance has not faded.

"Seriously, you're scared of this and not of the nauseous transport method you use?" I ask.

"I'm not scared." Ace crosses his arms. "I just don't like slides. I'll walk."

"No, you won't," I say. "This is a much faster method, and we need to get to the Spade Kingdom by nightfall because I'm not sharing a bed with Everett and Cheshire again. Everett shoved his food in my face at least ten times and

Cheshire disappearing and reappearing on my head is not nice."

"I know what Everett is like," he says. "You try sleeping in a bed with him and his brothers and sisters. One of them sucked on my earlobe, another slept under my chin which stopped all movement and almost all breathing, and another tried to shove a carrot up my nose."

"Why a carrot?" I ask.

"Turns out Blanc likes to snuggle a carrot as he's sleeping."

I stifle a laugh. "Then this should be easy. You're going down that slide."

"No." He pulls a face.

"You've slept with all those rabbits, that slide is nothing compared to them."

Ace winces.

"Fine, you can ride with me," I say, and grab his hand.

It's sweaty—I ignore how disgusting it feels.

"I'll go in after you," he says.

"No, you won't," I say and usher him over to the slide, removing my hand from his.

He looks down at it. "It's so long."

"Faster for the journey," the flowers say.

"I hate slides," he hisses.

"I'll hold your hand," I say sarcastically.

He closes his eyes. "Okay, okay, when I was younger my sister pushed me down a waterslide and I got badly hurt."

He lifts up his sleeve and twists his arm to show me the underside and the long, thin white scar.

"Nice," I say. "My dad lost his eye."

Ace shakes his head. "No, I'm not going down it."

"Cheshire went down."

"Only because you pushed him."

The flowers around me laugh.

"I won't let you get hurt," I say. "You can sit on my lap."

"That's just degrading."

I wink at the flowers. They giggle back.

Flowers surround Ace and I make him sit down in the slide. I come up behind him and place my legs on the outside of his. "I promise you won't get hurt."

"I think I should—" Ace struggles.

I push forward and we're off.

My stomach drops as we hurtle downward, the wind whipping across my face and gaining speed every second. The clouds whizz by as the ground approaches at high velocity. Feeling a rush of exhilaration, I open my mouth to whoop with joy. The colors of the flowers are remarkable.

We land with a thump on solid ground. Cheshire, Everett and Riddel are waiting for us.

Everett and Riddel are grinning from ear to ear.

"That was fun," Everett says.

I push Ace forward and scoop myself to my feet, dusting myself off.

Cheshire gives me the evil eye. "That was horrific. I almost lost four out of my nine lives from it."

I ignore Cheshire and help Ace up. "See? That wasn't too bad."

"I guess," he says, holding his stomach. "Still, I don't want to do it again."

Chapter Twenty-Seven

ometimes I can't help but wonder if Everett actually knows where we're going. The plucky little rabbit trots along with such confidence. I'm sort of envious of him because he's so young. I never had that kind of confidence at such a young age.

We follow the rocky path up then down then up, around, and down again. It feels like we are going in circles, and yet with every new turn, the landscape continues to change. The flowers' healing abilities have helped but they can only take me so far. I used too much magic back there. The aches in my body continue to moan out to me, letting me know they want rest.

I can't indulge them—I need to get to the Spade Kingdom first. Then I can rest for a bit.

"Hey, princess." Riddel holds back and walks with me. "I know I didn't give a great a first impression."

"It's okay," I yawn. "And call me Lucina."

Riddel fiddles with her fingers. "I've been looking forward to meeting you. You see, I want you and I to be the bestest of friends."

"Right?" I say with a heavy breath.

"Just like my father and my uncle, the March Hare. They were the greatest of friends."

"What about August?" Ace says from ahead.

"I'm allowed to have more than one best friend, Ace." Riddel waves her hands frantically at him.

"I doubt August will like that," Ace says.

"Who is August?" I ask with another yawn.

"He's my Uncle March's son. We grew up together. It was always my brother Rhyme, August, Daniel, Edith and me."

"Edith?" My tone is harsher than I'd intended, but I swallow my twinge of guilt. Ace told me she's fine, but it still bothers me.

"Yeah, she's nice, but she can be so moody sometimes." Riddel rolls her eyes. "Suppose I can't blame her, what with what happened."

I want to ask Riddel more about Edith but I'm finding it too hard to concentrate. I focus my gaze on Cheshire ahead.

Cheshire sits on Ace's shoulder, purring. I think he's asleep. I'm envious because I'm struggling to keep my eyes open. They keep closing and my head gets fuzzier.

"Princess," Riddel grabs me and my head leans on her shoulder for support.

"Lucina," I tell her.

"I knew it." Ace rushes over. "You overexerted yourself again! You're so stubborn."

"Takes that after her mother," Cheshire says, now awake and appearing on Riddel's shoulder.

"Is there any way she can rest in the bag as we walk?" Riddel asks, pushing strands of my hair back from my face. "She can't go on like this."

"We can't stop," Everett chimes in. "We've lost too much time already today."

"You know the bag has to be stationary when living things are in there. I'll carry her," Ace says and crouches on the ground before me.

Riddel helps me get on his back and pushes my hair out of my face.

"Sorry," I mumble into Ace's ear.

"No, you're not," he teases. "You want one my chocolate bars."

I would retort, but my head flops over onto his shoulder. I can smell Ace's hair; it smells of jasmine and honeysuckle. Being carried by him again feels strangely comforting, like a security blanket.

"You're really bad." Ace's voice comes off soft. "Get some rest."

I'm so tired, I can't argue. My eyes close.

"*Lucina,*" Wonder calls out. "Wake up."

My heavy eyelids struggle to open.

"*You have a message coming.*"

"What?" I mumble, stirring on Ace's back.

The clouds are beginning to break, and the sun is low on the horizon. The path has opened out onto a drying meadow surrounded by swirling sandstone outcroppings.

"*Get up!*" Wonder shouts.

The ground begins to tremble under our feet. Ace's hold on me grows firmer and I wrap my arms around him tighter. Riddel grabs Everett from the floor and has her teapot out, ready to defend.

"*It's okay. Listen to the ground.*"

"It's okay," I repeat what Wonder said. "I need to get down and listen to the ground."

Ace helps me down and I place my ear as close to the earth as I can. There are so many voices.

"*We have to get to the princess.*"

"*We have to tell her.*"

This way, I tell them.

The vibrations get stronger and Ace won't let go of me, he holds me tight. The vibrations stop in front of me. I jolt back when a few peony flowers pop out.

"Lucina," they cry out in their childish voices.

I brush my hands softly across the peonies. "Are you okay?"

"The rose queen," they say. "She spoke to the ground, trying to find out what is going on in the region. She heard some dire news through the grapevine."

"What is it?" I ask, still conscious that Ace is holding me by the waist.

"The Pack have taken hold of the Cross Shore Village; it's about thirty minutes away. They have taken all the villagers hostage and plan to burn them all tonight. They have already killed some of them."

"No!" I cry out. I can't deal with death, not now.

I almost collapse, but Ace holds me up. My poor citizens of Wonderland.

"It's a trap," Cheshire says. "You can't go."

"I have to," I snap.

"Alice is using those villagers to get to you," Cheshire says. "You must see that."

"Of course, I do!" I shout. "But I won't stand back and watch my fellow Wonderlanders die."

"You are so incredibly stupid. You don't have any energy—"

Ace speaks up for me and continues to hold me. "She has to go. She'll never forgive herself if she doesn't."

How did he know what I was thinking?

Cheshire rolls his head. "Fine. But, Lucina, you must embrace the darkness."

"What's this darkness you talk about?" Riddel walks over, almost tripping over a rock.

"Isn't darkness bad?" Everett adds, jumping down from Riddel's arms.

"No," the peonies answer Everett. "Sometimes the greatest flowers bloom at night. Take, for example, datura, moonflowers, blazing stars, catchflies, night blooming jasmine and dragon fruit. Some of these flowers have such a strong, sweet scent that it attracts pollinators, and we need them to survive and grow."

Cheshire curls his tail. "Who knew that flowers had brains?"

"They're helping you," I tell him. "You don't need to insult them."

The peonies ignore him and smile at me as I stroke them, saying, "Night-time flowers help spread magic and Spade magic is strongest at night."

"It's why it's always night in the Spade Kingdom," Cheshire goes on.

"I need sunshine," Everett says.

"Same here," Riddel chirps in.

"Your Heart magic is great for healing or for finding things," Cheshire says, "but it won't help in battle. Not yet, anyway."

"She's plenty good on her own in battle," Riddel says. "I heard about what happened with the Behemoth."

I can't help but smile. "Thanks, Riddel."

Riddel gives me a thumbs up.

"It doesn't matter, she's completely drained and even if she calls for the Heart Sword, she can't fight." Cheshire points out the obvious. "If she uses her Spade magic, she won't be drained."

Ace lets go of me and I instantly feel cold. He gazes off into the distance.

"But it's already getting dark," Everett says, his voice thick with concern.

"He's right," I say, my fingers clawing at the rocky terrain. "We'd be cutting it close."

Cheshire facepalms. "You need to have a plan going into this. And you need to use Spade magic. It is your best chance. Spade magic is more offensive."

"We could distract them," the peonies tell me.

"No." I shake my head. "I will not put you in danger."

"But we want to help," the peonies tell me.

"Embrace the darkness," Cheshire tells me.

"No!" I shout at him.

Everyone is staring at me.

"Why are you so reluctant?" he hisses.

"Because I don't want to be reliant on magic." I huff out a breath. "My dad always taught me not to use it and look at me now. I should have listened."

"But it saved us," the peonies say.

"And I don't regret that," I say quickly and glance over to the others. "I don't regret using it in the cases I've used it, but in battle it should just be me—the warrior my dad created."

Cheshire snorts at me. "The Knave's not your father."

"Shut up," I snap.

Ace stands in front of me. "She doesn't have time to learn Spade Magic. She already tried."

"She can do it, if she tries harder," Cheshire shouts.

"We're not going to risk it," Ace says. "And she doesn't need to do this. She has Riddel, Everett and me."

"And us," the peonies blurt out.

"Oh yes, a jumping rabbit, teapot girl, some tiny flowers and the boy who sucks the life of the king." Cheshire rolls his eyes. "What a fabulous team you have there."

I sigh. "He's right."

"What, we're not good enough?" Riddel says.

"That's not it," I say. "It's Ace using my father's magic. I'm not comfortable with it."

"What else are we supposed to do?" Riddel says.

"I will fight," I say. "I can do it. This is what I've done

my whole life. I can distract the Pack while the rest of you get the villagers to safety."

"Your father wants me to use his magic," Ace says, his eyes flashing blue. "And I will do what I must to protect you."

"I understand that, and I will accept you using magic—" I start.

"Good," he interrupts.

"—but to teleport the villagers to safety only. They are my priority and now they are my father's, too."

He scowls at my words. "I can't teleport unless I've been to that place. And now, I've been cut off from the Pack and I can't teleport to places they've been. You know that, I've told you before."

"Then we'll buy you some time to scout the area," I say.

"This is ridiculous," Cheshire's face turns red. "I'm not going to watch you all get captured or worse—die. This is a complete waste of my time. If you listen to me, everything will be fine."

"But you've been wrong, Cheshire. You thought I couldn't find Everett and Ace in the woods," I say.

"But that is only because I don't understand Heart magic. I never have." Cheshire's face grows redder.

"Then believe in me."

"I guess I have no choice," Cheshire says with his slitted eyes. "But, Lucina, you must know that we can't save every life."

I give him a nod but, on the inside, I tell myself otherwise. I will save them all.

Chapter Twenty-Eight

The plan is woefully far-fetched and I'm under equipped for it. No sword or lance, I've just been given a whole load of throwing knives and a dagger. My pleas for a real weapon haven't been heard, and I really wish I could call on the Heart Sword. Still haven't managed to figure that out yet or Spade magic.

I'd even happily accept an axe, though it's more my dad's weapon. It's heavy and better suited for people with bigger builds, but I'd still be able to cause damage.

"Is there a stick anywhere?" I ask. "I can do a lot of damage with that."

"No!" Everyone shouts at me in unison.

"Just stick to the plan," Everett says.

I suppose I'm lucky I have the knives. Everyone goes back to strategizing as my gaze fixates on the riverside village. I pet the peonies; they feel like velvet, it's soothing. They curl and nuzzle into my touch and it's the only thing keeping me calm.

What's happening to all those poor residents is my fault. The Pack is after me and using innocents to get to me. Their cruelty—spurred by Alice—only riles me up.

According to the peonies and Cheshire, card soldiers line the front entrance, eight in total, standing in a horizontal line to block traffic. Card archers and spearman are in high towers and in the upper windows of people's homes.

There are four members of the Pack in the village and there is at least one Pack member and a garrison of soldiers at the other three entrances of the village. There is also one Pack member, the strongest member, Two, in the center of the village. We may be outnumbered and outweaponed but we have Ace and Riddel. Even Everett is good. I don't want Ace using his magic, but I know that's what the king would want—to save Wonderland's citizens.

The Pack are trained, well rested, battle-hardened soldiers. I hate to think of them as soldiers given they're not people, but even I have to admit they're skilled. In truth, I don't know if we can beat them.

From observing the Pack back at the castle, they move like predators, fast and strong and they're aligned with a certain element of magic. In the fight with the Behemoth, they weren't at their best, just toying around with the beast Alice sent to create fear for the Diamond Kingdom. It's taken hindsight, but I realize that now.

"We can help," the peonies say, probably noticing the worry on my face.

"No, you stay back."

The heads downturn. I already have enough weight on my shoulders; I can't protect anyone, not in the state I'm in. My eyes aren't drooping anymore but the aches and pains are still there. The worst thing is, I'm the best fighter among them and I can't do anything.

I think of the Heart Sword, wishing I could summon it. Then again, I don't think I could hold the sword for too long.

The sun has long gone as I stare at the lit-up riverside village. The houses there are tightly crammed together unlike in mine, where they're all spaced out.

"Okay, we're ready," Ace says.

Everyone nods in agreement, even the dormouse in Riddel's teacup. The dormouse is essential to our plan.

This plan worries me, and I silently ask my heart to help us. It gives me a soft thump-thump in reply.

Ace gives the signal, and we spread out.

Riddel and Everett go together, taking the south entrance. Ace will scout the area then use magic to appear inside and take care of the villagers. It'll be up to Hazel, the dormouse, to distract the front guards.

That leaves me and Cheshire to back up the dormouse from afar using my throwing knives and dynamite. I will avoid the dynamite as much as I can; the last thing I want is casualties.

Cheshire teleports us to our hideout in the reeds, close to the river. It's a perfect spot to observe and not be seen.

Hazel takes her position. It's the first time I've seen this little creature on the move out of the teapot. She worries me, being always so sleepy, but Riddel assured me she'll be fine.

Hazel stands in front of the card guards; they haven't noticed her. Maybe we should have used her as a sleuth instead.

"Hello," the dormouse squeaks at them. Still, nothing.

I give Cheshire a dubious look.

"I would eat her," Cheshire says. "If I knew she wouldn't kill me."

I pinch the bridge of my nose; I don't see anything frightening about her.

Hazel waves her tiny hands frantically, and still nothing happens.

Maybe these guards are simply useless.

Hazel curses. She uses words my dad uses—very bad words. Strangely, I can take it from my dad but from that tiny creature, it's unnatural.

Finally, the curse words seem to gain their attention. The card guards point their spears at her. Hazel doesn't flinch and curtseys.

"What are you doing here?" One the guards says in a gruff voice.

"I'm a storyteller," Hazel squeaks. "Just popping into town for some business. I'm sure someone will pay me a pretty penny for a story."

"No one is allowed in here, I'm afraid," says another guard.

"Oh." She releases the deepest and longest sigh I've

ever heard, then slowly raises her head. "Perhaps you would like to hear a story?"

"No," says the first guard.

"Yes, please," says the second. "I miss listening to stories."

"Yeah, it's just a story," adds a third.

"We are meant to be on guard," the first guard reminds them.

"Oh, please. One story is not going to distract us," the third guard scoffs.

The card guards argue, till finally one of them hands a coin over to Hazel. It's almost as big as her, but that doesn't stop her from shoving it into her tiny coat. It disappears into it like it never existed.

My reservations about this plan grow.

"Gather around, soldiers," the dormouse begins. "For I have a tale that will have you questioning your very minds."

"Cheshire," I mutter. "This plan is getting more ridiculous by the second."

"That's why it's good," he whispers.

"Once upon a time there were three little sisters," Hazel begins with a yawn, "and their names were Elsie, Lacie, and Tillie; and they lived at the bottom of a well of treacle..."

"What is it yapping on about it?" The night's breeze causes me to shiver.

"Shh," Cheshire says. "I really like this story."

Hazel continues her ridiculous tale and my stomach slumps. I can't even watch anymore.

"*Watch.*"

I reluctantly watch and it becomes apparent that the

soldiers' eyes are growing heavy and they are yawning. How strange...

One of the soldiers begins to slump against the wall while the other falls down to their knees. One lies his head on the ground. Slowly but surely, they all fall asleep. None of them is questioning the others' movements.

"What are you all doing?" A Pack member arrives on the scene and yells.

That Pack member wasn't supposed to be there. I start to move, but Cheshire places a hand on my shoulder, pushing me down.

"Trust her," he says.

The soldiers do not react to the Pack member's voice, they're lost in a deep slumber. The newcomer steps into the archway, its faceless head scanning the area. It doesn't notice Hazel, who's tucked herself under one of the soldiers.

"Get up," it instructs the soldiers, stomping on one of them. He doesn't move.

Without even looking at the Pack member's expression, I know what it's about to do and I ready a knife.

"*Not yet.*"

But what about Hazel?

Hazel sneaks closer, maneuvering around the soldiers. She's surprisingly stealthy, and fast. She goes into her pocket and a small bomb appears in her hand. I ready my knife. That bomb is not going to do anything to the soldier. Cheshire still holds me down by pressing on my shoulder. My head is full of thoughts and worries but my heart remains still.

"We have an issue," the Pack member calls behind.

Hazel heaves the bomb over her head. It rolls in front of the Pack member's foot, tiny in comparison to its size. My fingers stroke the knife as the Pack member stares at the bomb. It lifts his foot to stamp on it.

There's a white flash and a boom. An explosion rocks the ground. Fire engulfs the entrance. Its roaring blaze is soon replaced by shouts from the guards and the screams of the civilians.

My breath hitches and I rise from the reeds to get a better view. The Pack member's body is broken. It's slumped on the floor, missing its legs.

I blink a few times. How could such a small bomb create such havoc?

"Cover the dormouse!" Cheshire cries.

The garrison soldiers stream out of the barracks in response to the commotion. Archers begin their assault. Almost by instinct, I throw the knives. One goes into a guard's shoulder, pinning him to the tower nearby.

Knives continue to flick out of my hands; some hit targets, but most don't. Cheshire disappears and reappears, bringing me back the used knives.

Alarm bells ring. Riddel, Everett and Ace have begun their assault on the city watch.

Hazel continues to throw bombs out of her coat. One hits the tower and there's an earth-shattering rumble. The ground crumbles and the right tower falls, soldiers screaming within it.

Hazel continues to evade everyone. She runs like lightning, up the walls, flipping and twisting her tiny body.

She's constantly throwing out deadly ammunition.

That teaches me for underestimating her size.

The fire illuminates the village and, thankfully, the grass hasn't been lit. I don't want the people getting trapped in there—the villagers need to get out, and fast. Worry becomes a lump in my throat.

The night air becomes a cacophony of shouting, pounding boots and ringing steel. Black fumes go up into the sky. I recognize the explosive noise of Riddel's tea pot, and I catch a glimpse of Everett jumping around. It looks as if he's flying.

"I need to get in there," I tell Cheshire who reappears.

"No, you need to stay safe," he says. "You don't have the energy."

"But their lives—" I begin.

"I hate this, Lucina, but I know if you go, the whole of Wonderland goes," Cheshire says, passing me my knives. "A few lives over all the lives of Wonderland are a small price to pay. Besides, I told you what we're doing is reducing collateral damage. We can't save everyone."

Cheshire is blunt and I struggle with his words. Though it makes sense logically, death hurts me—even the soldiers'. It's not their fault. Alice is forcing them. I saw that back at the Heart Castle. They have good in them. They even helped me find the crown.

I refuse to stand back and do nothing. The Knave, Dad, whoever he is, taught me to fight for a reason. I believe he was preparing me for this moment.

"So, do I just stand back, and watch Wonderlanders die?"

"Lucina, you're saving so many lives. But you can't save them all."

"But their lives wouldn't be in jeopardy if it weren't for me."

Cheshire does not say anything.

"Fight!" Even Wonder tells me to fight, but I have no energy.

The purple pansies shoot up out of the ground. "We heard you."

"As did we."

Flowers sprout around me in the soaked soil. Dandelions, daisies, lilies, carnations, orchids, tulips, sunflowers, dahlias, marigolds and the red rose surround me.

"Oh, no," Cheshire snivels.

"We will give you as much as energy as you need to fight, Princess," the red rose tells me. "It won't be much, but you can do something."

"Thank you." I gasp, not sure what else I can say, so I caress their petals with my hands.

"But our main job is to protect you," the red rose says. "You're the Heart of Wonderland."

Cheshire snorts. "At least we're in agreement about something."

The flowers form a circle around me and start to sing. Air breathes into my lungs. My vision swirls and the colors sharpen around me; the muscles in my body repair and I awaken.

"Stay safe," the red rose says and turns to the other flower and nods.

The soil parts in front of me and a pocket watch

emerges from the ground with green leaves around it. I pick it up.

"Use this to track the time," the red rose says. "I'm estimating you have twenty minutes of energy. It will ring two minutes before you lose the last of it. You must retreat before then."

Staring down at the pocket watch, I'm reminded of Finn, and my throat twinges. No more deaths.

"I understand." I place the watch in my pocket and rush to the entrance.

Fire burns bright; the civilians can't get out and I can't get in. Hazel continues to do the most damage.

I dash around the side and come face-to-face with the wall of the West Gate. It's so high and tall that nothing could jump it.

"You're so stubborn," Cheshire appears on my shoulder. The wall disappears and I appear within the village in a blink. It seems my body is getting used to teleporting.

"Cheshire..."

"You never ask for help," he says. "But I have to help you and stop you from getting killed. Without me, we both know you'd be dead."

Two card guards appear, pointing and shouting. I can't hear anything, but they lunge for me. I roll between them, slamming my foot into one's leg and whirling my fist around to land on the other's tailbone.

One of the soldiers cries out and falls to the ground, but the first one recovers, lunging toward me. I duck in time. Another soldier comes and grabs my arm; I twist it. No one expects you to twist your shoulder, and by doing so it brings me closer to the guard. I use my other free arm to elbow him in the face.

I turn around, facing another soldier. He darts toward me with a spear. I duck and do a spin kick, forcing the soldier to the ground. Getting up as fast as I can, I kick him down and take his spear.

Nobody would give me a weapon, so I have to take one.

"Lucina, watch out!" Cheshire cries out.

Out of the periphery of my vision, I catch a soldier, spin and whack him with the spear, being extra careful not to stab him accidentally with the spear's head. The soldiers are my citizens, too. They have lives outside of this and I want to do my best not to hurt them. They don't know they're still under Alice's influence, but I can try to save them as much as possible.

More soldiers flank over to me and I do a pretty good job of handling them. Though I have to give some credit to Cheshire. He's whizzing around, sinking his claws—that might as well be knives—into anyone who comes near me. All my attention is on the attackers I'm facing, and I can't stop Cheshire from killing.

There will always be casualties in war, my dad says. *If you can't handle bloodshed, then don't bother getting on the battlefield.*

He's right, but the pangs of their deaths still sting my heart.

I rush to the middle of the village, evading soldiers until I can see the center, where a big pyre is set up. Ace appears and reappears, transporting villagers to safety. At the same time, he's fighting off the Two of Hearts. He flashes in and out, throwing cards, creating barriers, and shooting out magic. It's unbelievable. He's almost got every villager. Thankfully, he's transporting them in bulk.

Meanwhile, Riddel and Everett are dealing with two Pack members. Everett is jumping around with a rope, creating trip areas and making it harder for the Pack members to fight.

I'm watching all this, taking a brief moment to let it all sink in. I'd thought the plan was stupid, but now... I think we can do this.

The blast of a cannon shakes me to the core.

How did they get cannons here?

More soldiers come in, followed by more blasts. I follow the cannons to their source and note they are firing up at the sky, toward Everett.

"Everett!" My voice doesn't carry weight in all this sound.

The cannon ball flies out and my heart stops. I have to save him. Cheshire appears and takes hold of Everett. He pushes Everett away from the cannon ball. The cannon ball explodes and there's a huge blast. Both Cheshire and Everett go flying in different directions.

"Hazel!" Riddel shouts as she throws saucers at the guards.

Hazel rushes over to her with tiny little teapot guns in her hands, blasting anything in sight. I might have to get that dormouse to teach me some moves.

"Go check on Everett and Cheshire," Riddel says, evading one Pack member's sword with her teapot.

Another one runs up behind her. I throw my spear at him and it goes through him like butter. Soldiers, I won't kill. But Pack members? No point in letting Alice's ugly magic keep distorting Wonderland with their existence.

Riddel mouths me a quick thanks. Her teapot snout grows and becomes a sword. Her newly formed weapon clashes with the remaining Pack member's sword. "Go help Ace, I've got this."

Ace is throwing cards at Two. They don't scathe the thing at all. Two's not like the other Pack members. I've seen what Ace's cards can do, burning and cutting off limbs. But Two is made of something else.

Ace summons magic while teleporting over and over. Fire, ice, wind and water; nothing works. Two sends blasts of fire at Ace, who manages to dodge them.

I continue to fight guards whilst trying to keep an eye on Ace. The shimmer of his magic dulls, and his teleporting skills slow down.

He's running low on magic.

Tension coils my muscles, and I start looking around for something to use as a weapon or at least for something to throw. If only Cheshire were here to give me knives...

I really hope Cheshire and Everett are okay.

Two is good. It cuts through Ace's attacks with astonishing speed, using its short sword in one hand, and a dagger in the other. Its fighting style is beautiful, almost like a dance.

I rush over to the pyre.

"Danger! Left. Tilt."

I tilt my head as Wonder guides me, and an arrow rushes

past my cheek. It's the Pack member from before, the one with the spear still embedded into its torso. It comes running toward me, raining down arrows around me.

I roll around the musty floor, grabbing anything I can and throwing it toward the Pack member.

It's evading well. I grab some wood from a broken tower and repurpose it as a shield. An ugly one, but it will do. Arrows continue to rain down and I hold my shield up to avoid them; some of them catch in the wood.

I rush to the Pack member and smack it with my shield. I keep thinking about the time, I need to be fast. It falls back but kicks me down in the process. Punches and kicks are thrown around. I've learned to take far worse hits.

We end up rolling around the ground fighting, and I manage to get on top of it. I smack its face with my fists. It's like hitting a tree. My fists bleed, but I won't stop. Its face spins around.

"Lucina!" I hear a deadly cry.

I twist my head until my eyes land on them—Two has its foot over Ace's chest.

My heart screams in a way I've never known, and my breath comes out in short bursts. I can only stare at the scene unraveling. Time stops and everything else blurs into the background. All I want is Ace.

"Let him go," Two says in a cold, monotonous voice.

Chapter Twenty-Nine

A ce is slumped against the floor, his spine curled in agony. Two holds up his head, grasping Ace's hair.

I hold in a scream of frustration. Ace told me to be careful, when he should've been, too! He can't continue to use my father's powers like this.

"Give yourself up, Lucina," Two says.

Ace squirms under his hold. "Don't."

My heart hammers against my chest. I read the fear in Ace's expression, but I'm helpless to do anything. All I know is nothing can happen to him. My heart squeezes at the mere thought of it.

I shove the Pack member I have back, and it slumps

onto the ground. I hold my hands up. They're soaked in my own blood and I slowly walk forward.

"Don't, Lucina!" Riddel shouts, still fighting off another Pack member.

"Tell your companions to stop fighting," Two says.

"On one condition," I cry out. "You let everyone in this village and my companions go, and I will follow you back to Alice."

"Lucina, don't give up."

What else can I do? I place my hand on my chest. My magic is sporadic and inoffensive. If I did use Heart magic, it'd drain me of the precious time the flowers gave me.

If only I could use my Spade magic...

I should have practiced more. I just never had the time. I've been so focused on my Heart side, but I should have spent more on my Spade. *"Embrace the darkness,"* as Cheshire tells me. He also said Spade magic is more powerful at night.

I scan the area searching for something, anything—there's a water pump behind Two.

Maybe that could work?

"I accept your conditions," Two says.

"Let Ace go," I shout.

Cheshire told me to think logically for Spade magic to work. Water's a clear liquid that has no color, taste, or smell. It can be hot or cold, it's used for drinking and washing. The water pump itself has a spout, a bucket hook, a handle—the end of it is decorated with a pear. It's made from cast iron.

"It's okay," Ace shouts. "My life isn't worth anything."

He has no idea what an understatement that is. Everyone's life is precious, and to me Ace is special because he's... I can't think about it now. Ace is precious like water because it's the source of all life.

There's a rustic sound and the pipes start to sing a chorus. The bricks around the well crumble and the soil sinks. The water doesn't flow, but spits jets of water in chaotic bursts. A pipe flies out and whacks Two onto the ground. In so doing, Ace is released and lands with a heavy thud.

Ace's face is covered in mud and streaks of blood. My heart contracts and twists with pain and anger all at once.

Two struggles to get up as the water gushes all over it. It eventually gets up. Its face snaps toward me and a cruel smile twists it. Shivers travel up my back.

Two charges toward me, drawing its sword out.

Weapon, I need a weapon.

"Lucina!" Daisies sprout in front of me, pushing up a metal spear. I take the weapon.

Two runs toward me and strikes quickly; I block the attack. Two pulls back and circles me.

It has no idea who it's dealing with. I glide across and my spear and its sword clash. It swipes at me with great aggression and I defend, pushing back with equal power.

The air is filled with the hiss and singing of our metal weapons. Two grunts, giving itself away, but I'm ready for it, parrying all its moves. I catch a flash of silver as Two swings the sword high and brings it down on me. Its frustrations start to surface as it growls. I flip backward and kick its arms. It staggers back.

"Come on, Two," one of the soldiers shouts from the sidelines. "She's nothing but a girl."

Two regains its footing and gasps, wiping the sweat on its forehead with its arm. I dart forward and bring my spear down where I suspect its hand would be. I'm met with the trembling clash of metal.

I spin away and jump back, causing it to leap out of way. Before it can get away, I sweep my legs underneath it, knocking back its feet. Two shudders back, briefly regaining its composure. It swings its sword down and metal screeches as our weapons meet. I use my legs to slide up, like a reverse split. He tries to kick but I counter it with my own leg, knocking it back with its sword. It momentarily loses grip of the weapon, but regains it at the last second.

Two lets out a growl of fury as it charges toward me, its sweat dripping to the ground. I'm surprised these mannequins sweat. I didn't think trees do. The first Pack member I met certainly didn't sweat.

I run toward Two, jump in the air and flip over it. The point of my spear touches the small of its neck, the only part exposed in its uniform.

"It's over," I say.

The blare of a small alarm clock jars me.

Oh, no, the timer!

Two ducks to the ground. This one likes to play dirty. Its legs buck out like a horse with his back legs. I sidestep out of the way. Its attacks become more aggressive and quicker, each one countered with ease. Its sword clashes with my weapon, but I parry and block every move. My body gives into the dance of the fight.

Problem is, I don't have much time. I have to win *now*.

The weapons clang together in an ear-splitting roar. I

seize the opportunity as I watch the sweat drip off its wooden face and throw all the weight behind my spear.

All of a sudden, the world starts to blur, and I can't focus. *No, the flowers' energy burst has run out!*

Two's weight pushes me back, it becomes too overwhelming and my spear is forced upward and backward, out of my hands, and into the sky. I fall over and hit the ground with a thud.

Two moves forward and I try to scramble away. It rushes and kicks me in the gut. Pain slams through me and I scream.

Two squats over me and punches me in the mouth; my blood flows freely.

I have no more strength left. All the fight in me is gone.

Two grabs my ponytail and pulls my head up and then slams it into the ground. It repeats the action twice, my face smashing the firm sandy ground harder the second time.

"Well done, Two." That plummy voice, I know it. "I knew I could count on you."

I lift my head and wipe the blood dripping into my eyes.

It's Alice, dressed in a light and fluid gold dress consisting of delicate lace, chiffon and silk tulle. On her head lay several gold chains. No crown.

My fingers instantly go to my headband. It's still there.

I'm forced back onto the ground by Two's foot. My unmoving gaze is on Alice as she walks toward me with a sword.

"You're such a stupid girl," Alice mocks me. "Your father was right to hide you, but he did a terrible job, as always."

"Don't mock my father!"

Anger coils though me; it feels like my whole body is on fire. I can't let this happen. I *won't* let this happen.

Wonderland must be saved. I will not let everyone down, not again. Not like I let down my parents.

Cold wind brushes against my warm cheeks. A clattering sound like wooden wind chimes springs into my ears.

"Get off her," Ace says.

Two's weight comes off me and then it's clashing with Ace.

"Kill that boy!" Alice shouts out. Soldiers flank her. "Then get that girl, but don't kill her."

Ace. I need to save him. I need to save everyone. My vision blurs.

Lightning flashes over the sky, the wind howls and something inside of me rises. I can taste lemon—no, lemon *tarts*—on my tongue. My body begins to course with a tingling, now familiar, warmth.

The only thing that stays in focus is Ace. His blue eyes are filled with concern. His hand is reaching out for me, his mouth moving to words I cannot hear.

Two smacks him. I try to reach for Ace, but my vision is impaired. A boom reverberates in the ground.

I must save everyone.

Conviction spreads through my body. I will save these citizens, I will save Riddel, Everett and Cheshire. I will save Ace. I will undo all the hate; I will save Wonderland.

Light flashes. The trees creak nearby, and the dust whips up into the air. There, in front of me, is a column of violently twisting air rotating. A bolt of purple lighting appears, and the tornado disappears.

The world becomes deathly silent and the moon comes out, spreading its light. Light catches my eye and I find a sword lodged into the ground, tip first. It has a gold cross guard with a heart embedded in it.

"The Heart Sword," Cheshire says. He appears next to me with Everett and Hazel. "Cover her!"

Hazel fires her guns and Everett delves into his bag, pulling out grenades. What is that child doing with grenades? And why am I even surprised anymore?

"*Lucina.*"

The sword calls to me and I stretch out. I roll onto my front and push myself forward.

My fingers slip over the blade. A crack of thunder explodes into my ears. Streaks of black lightening falls out of the sky, surrounding the area, and us with it. The atmosphere turns from dark blue to purple and dramatic winds rise, causing my hair to fly out in front of me.

A loud sound, almost like a loud railroad train, follows. A mass of dense matter flows in front of me and the others, black liquid dripping from it. It forms a spherical black gate with twinkles of light. It twirls like honey around a spinning spoon.

"What's that?" I cry out.

"A portal," Hazel says.

"Get in, everyone!" Cheshire shouts.

"But the civilians—" I struggle to breathe.

A cannon blast echoes.

"We've saved most of them," Everett says. Black dust coats his skin. He tries to pick me up. Bless the little thing, I'm too big for him.

"Get her!" Alice shrieks, her lips stretched out in hate. Her blue eyes are full of venom as she stares at me.

"Get in, Everett!" Riddel shouts. "Ace and I've got her."

I roll onto my back. Riddel grabs both my arms and pulls me up. She wraps her arm around my shoulder and helps me forward, toward the portal.

"Ace!" I cry out and turn back to see Alice with her hand out, glowing with magic.

"He's right behind us," Riddel says.

"What are you all doing?" Alice shouts.

The soldiers are all grabbing their heads, on their knees on the ground. What's going on?

Wind gushes at us as we come closer to the portal and step through. It's like going through the tree to get to the Misty Village. It feels like nothing, and then we're on the other side of the portal.

I push away from Riddel and turn around.

Where's Ace? I can't breathe.

Ace hasn't come yet and my heart pounds in my ears. I need him. I can't do this without him. Every single moment without him makes my heart ache with a sudden and fierce pain. My hearts hammers in my chest and I feel sick.

It should be me, not him. My eyes begin to water and as I try to hold the tears back, my head starts to throb.

I can hear the sound of the battle. It feels like forever as I hold my breath.

Finally, Ace staggers through, the Heart Sword in his hand. The portal closes.

"Ace!" I cry out.

"You forgot this."

He plants the sword into the ground and walks over to me, giving me a piercing stare for what feels like an eternity. Ace then lets out a soft breath and dips his head forward as his body collides with mine.

His arms tighten around me and I can feel his mouth by my ear. "Don't do that again." He buries his head in my hair.

"I'm okay." I squeeze him tighter.

"That's not the point." His grip loosens and he cups my face in his warm soft hands. "You don't understand how important—"

"Where are we?" Everett jumps onto my shoulder, breaking the moment. "Are you okay, Lucina?"

"Not really," I say, pain throbbing throughout my whole body. I look around.

The buildings are like nothing I've ever seen. They're brick structures, elevated slightly off the ground, with tiled roofs folded in a triangular shape. The paths are aligned with trees; pink and white flowers blossom in their branches. The sky is dark, and the largest crescent moon ever hangs above us. It's made of crystals and spreads light in a dotted formation.

"Where in the Underland are we?" I ask.

Cheshire appears on Riddel's shoulder and grins. "The Spade Kingdom."

What trials await Lucina in the Spade Kingdom? And will she and Ace finally find their way to each other? Or will Alice's machinations keep them apart...forever?

Grab your pre-order of book 2 today!

Don't forget to sign up for my newsletter and get your exclusive drawings of Lucina, Ace, Cheshire, Everett and Riddel! Plus, you'll get to read exclusive excerpts and receive news of my newest releases before anyone else.

Sign up here today!

Acknowledgments

The book has been in my head for years and I almost gave it up if it hadn't been for all the wonderful people in my life.

Firstly, I have to thank my parents and my brother for their unbridled faith in me, even when I didn't believe in myself. Thank you for pushing me to chase my dream. A special thanks to my mom for taking me to the library as a child every week and encouraging my love for books.

A massive thanks needs to go to these three incredible women: Kristina Adams for her honesty, wisdom, advice, and faith. Ellie Betts, for being a constant source of positivity and support, and Silvia Lopez for fixing me and my plot problems. I'm lucky to call you guys my friends.

I want to send a particularly gigantic thank you to my editor, Alexa Whitewolf at Luna Imprints Author Services. Thank you for making my book so pretty. I couldn't have done it without you. You've taught me so much.

Huge gratitude to RAIT Visual Works for creating the exclusive drawings of my characters. I have fallen in love with Ace. Also, a massive thank you to Alisha Moore for creating my gorgeous cover.

About the Author

E.V. Rivers was born in Wonderland or likes to pretend she was. Crown of Hearts is her debut novel and the first book in the Hearts of Wonderland series. She writes Young Adult Fantasy and Science Fiction books. And specializes in creating worlds that her and her readers can escape to. She has an MA in English and an MA in Creative Writing.

Visit E. V. Rivers online at www.evrivers.com

Printed in Great Britain
by Amazon